Praise for *The S...*

"*The Suffering* is a horror lover's drea... and desiccated corpses. I cringed. I grimaced. You won't soon forget this exorcist and his vengeful water ghost."

—Kendare Blake, author of
Anna Dressed in Blood

"Rin Chupeco deftly combines ancient mysticism with contemporary dilemmas that teens face, immersing readers in horrors both supernatural and man-made. *The Suffering* is a chilling swim through the murky waters of morality."

—Carly Anne West, author of *The Bargaining* and *The Murmurings*

Praise for *The Girl from the Well*

★"Chupeco makes a powerful debut with this unsettling ghost story."
—*Publishers Weekly*, starred review

"[A] Stephen King–like horror story… A chilling, bloody ghost story that resonates."

—*Kirkus Reviews*

THE
SUFFERING

RIN CHUPECO

This is for lovers of ghost stories everywhere—

there is nothing behind you. I'm almost sure of it.

Published by Sourcebooks Fire, an imprint of Sourcebooks, Inc.
P.O. Box 4410, Naperville, Illinois 60567-4410
(630) 961-3900
Fax: (630) 961-2168
www.sourcebooks.com

Library of Congress Cataloging-in-Publication Data

Chupeco, Rin.
  The suffering / Rin Chupeco.
    pages cm
  Sequel to: The girl from the well.
  Summary: "When an old friend disappears in Aokigahara, Japan's infamous 'suicide forest,' Tark and the ghostly Okiku must resolve their differences and return to find her. In a strange village inside Aokigahara, old ghosts and an ancient evil lie waiting"-- Provided by publisher.
  (13 : alk. paper) [1. Ghosts--Fiction. 2. Good and evil--Fiction. 3. Horror stories.] I. Title.
PZ7.C4594Su 2015
[Fic]--dc23
                                    2015009885

Printed and bound in the United States of America.
VP 10 9 8 7 6 5 4 3 2 1

CHAPTER ONE

TAG

I'm no hero, believe me. I've never rescued babies from burning buildings. I've never volunteered to save humpback whales or the rain forest. I've never been to protest rallies, fed the hungry in Africa, or righted any of the eighty thousand things that are wrong with the world these days. Heroism isn't a trait commonly found in teenage boys.

Stupidity though? We've got that in spades.

Stupidity is why I'm huddled behind a large sofa bed, underneath a heavy blanket, drenched in my own sweat despite the AC humming in what is otherwise silence. The television is tuned to the least scary show I could find: a *Jersey Shore* rerun—horrifying in its own way, but not in the way that matters, which is the most important thing. I stare at the TV screen—and not because I'm eagerly awaiting Snooki's next freak-out. I watch the screen because I want to know when it's coming to find me.

Earlier this evening, I'd taken a raggedy-looking doll—its cotton stuffing already scooped out—and replaced it with uncooked rice and a few fingernail clippings. And I'd sewed it up with red thread. When you've done this as many times as I have, sewing becomes as good a weapon as any. Then I waited for three a.m. to roll around before filling the tub with water and dropping the doll in the bath.

"Dumbelina, you're *it*."

The name was not my idea, but it was what I had to work with. Using the same name that Sondheim and his girlfriend used in the ritual they started and never finished—that's how it knows you're singling it out. Just to ensure there were no misunderstandings, I said "You're it" two more times.

The doll, like most dolls, said nothing. It gazed up at me from beneath the water, a drowned, ball-jointed Ophelia with synthetic brown hair and plastic eyes in a yellow broadcloth dress made in some sweatshop in China. The doll was common enough, the kind that could have been a knockoff of a knockoff.

The air changes. Then that invisible spider crawls up my spine, tickling the hairs behind my neck. I have come to know this spider these last couple of years. It whispers there's something else in the room, breathing with you, watching you, grinning at you.

I *hate* that damn spider.

For one moment, the doll's stringy brown hair glitters a shiny black under the fluorescent lights. For one moment, the doll's glassy gaze takes on the faintest tinge of malicious self-awareness. For one moment, that *thing*'s head breaks through the water's surface and *looks* at me.

I switch off the lights. I back out of the bathroom and close the door. I hide.

It sounds pretty idiotic, playing hide-and-seek with a doll. It's not. It's part of the rules I gotta play by.

The first rule is this: I have to finish the game. No matter what happens.

I've taken a mouthful of salt water at this point, and I begin counting in my head. *One thousand and one, one thousand and two, one thousand and three, one thousand and four…*

On the TV screen, an orange-skinned, heavily built Italian guy with gravity-defying hair is arguing with another orange-skinned, heavily built Italian guy with gravity-defying hair.

…one thousand and five, one thousand and six, one thousand and seven…

I briefly wonder where Ki is. She's often been quick to turn up when I've done other harebrained rituals like this one. At the moment, she's nowhere to be seen, which worries me. It's not like she's got something else to do.

I'm no hero, but I do have a superpower. Except my superpower tends to wander off when she's bored.

…one thousand and eight, one thousand and nine…

The noise of the television fizzles out. Then the sound returns, but it's warped, like an inexperienced DJ is spinning on a broken turntable and he has the song stuck on repeat. The voices drop several octaves until they're rough and scratchy and incomprehensible. *Jersey Shore* switches to static.

Immediately, my gaze swings back toward the bathroom door, which is standing wide open.

I'm pretty sure I closed it.

Something is moving around the room. I'm hoping it's Okiku, but I doubt it.

It sounds like something is dragging itself across the floor. Like it isn't quite sure how to use its legs properly yet.

I risk another glance over the sofa bed.

Wet tracks lead away from the bathroom, water stains seeping into the carpet. The television screen is blank, though the disturbing noises continue.

And then I see the doll lying facedown in a puddle of water several feet from where I am.

I retreat back into my blanket fortress to retrieve a plastic cup half-filled with the same saltwater mix that is in my mouth. I also pick up a small paring knife. Then I emerge from my hiding place, peering nervously up over the sofa again…

…and I come face-to-face with the doll, which is perched atop it. It has a small, peculiar, black gash across its face, which on a person would have been a mouth.

The doll in the bathtub didn't have a mouth.

It lunges.

I duck.

It sails over my head and crashes into a painting behind me. I have enough presence of mind not to swallow the salt water or spit it out. I don't waste precious seconds looking behind me—I make for the closet, my backup hiding place in case anything went wrong, which it almost always did.

I slip in and slide the door shut behind me, wriggling in among the clothes and shoes, trying to make as little sound as I can. You don't need to find the most complicated hiding spot when a ghost is hunting you. The instant you trap them inside a vessel, like a doll's body, their perception of the world becomes limited.

I wait for several long seconds. Everything's quiet, but I'm not buying it. If you move when they're there to see, they'll find you. They'll find you *fast*.

Through the small slits of light coming in through the slatted closet door, I make out a movement. Then I catch a glimpse of yellow as something small and decidedly doll-shaped shuffles into view.

It's crawling on its hands and knees.

Its every movement sounds like crunching bone.

It's searching for me.

I hold my breath and wait until it twitches away.

The second rule of the game: it gets to look for me first. Then it's my turn. We swap roles every few minutes until someone succeeds. First one to stab three times doesn't get to die.

Time's up.

I count another ten seconds, because starting my turn late is better than starting it too early, while *it's* still on the hunt. Then I step out, curbing the desire to take the coward's route and hide 'til morning. Or better yet, to race out of the apartment screaming like a little kid.

The doll lies flat on its back, its midnight-black eyes boring through the ceiling. It isn't moving.

5

I run toward it, knife raised and ready, because the rules say I have two minutes, but experience says these bastards cheat. When it comes to dealing with ghosts, the general consensus is to hit first and hit hard, because chances are you'll be dead before you can get off a second attempt.

I strike. My knife finds its mark, plunging into the doll's chest. I spit the salt water that's in my mouth onto the doll, soaking its cotton dress. "I win!" I sputter and then rip the knife free so I can stab it again.

The television chooses that moment to flicker back on. Momentarily distracted, I glance at the screen. The two guys are still arguing. When I look back down, the doll is nowhere to be seen.

Crap.

Trying not to panic, I search the room as quickly and as thoroughly as I can. I check under the couch, the bed, even take another quick look inside the bathroom. Nothing.

A drop of water landing on the carpet in front of me is the only warning I get. I have just enough time to look up as the doll bears down on me from the ceiling. Its mouth is too big for its face with rows of jagged-looking teeth and its eyes a terrifying window of hate. The two thoughts that immediately come to mind are *uh-oh* and *damn it*.

Ever had a possessed doll slam itself into your face at Mach 2 speed? It's like getting hit by a carnivorous chicken. I crash to the floor, the doll still clinging to me, jaws snapping at my cheek. I grab it by the scruff of its neck as I cry out in pain. I force it away, putting myself out of reach of those canines. What I don't expect is for the doll's neck to extend several inches from its body, still gunning for skin.

"SON OF A—"

I hurl the doll across the room. It hits the wall and flops onto the floor.

Something's wrong. After that first stab, it shouldn't be able to move, much less attack me like it's rabid. And the last thing I want is to get bitten.

The third and final rule of the game is this: *don't* lose. I'm not entirely sure what would happen if I did, but I don't want to find out. I've tagged it once and been tagged once. Not good odds.

A loud, ripping sound screams through the doll, which twists and writhes on the floor.

Its dress bunches up, something shifting underneath the cloth. I can see the red threads unraveling, stitch by painstaking stitch. I leap forward, burying the knife once more into that writhing mass. The doll falls limp.

"I win!"

But when I raise my hand again to deliver the third and final blow, the doll's body tears open. A hand bursts from the center of its chest to grab at my wrist. The hand is followed by a yellowed arm and shoulder. Another hand forces its way out, and then *another*, and *then* several more.

Finally, a head leers out of the tattered doll's remains. A horribly disfigured face sits atop a form that isn't so much an actual body as it is a confusing protrusion of arms.

It wails—a mewling, yowling sound—and reaches for me again.

I've never punched a woman before—dead or alive—but this feels like the time to be misogynistic. The creature reels back, loosening its hold, and I scramble backward. It crawls toward me again, and I kick it right in the jaw. I need another stab with the knife to end the ritual, but I'm not entirely sure how to keep it still long enough to do so without getting my own limbs chewed off.

Then something falls from the ceiling, and the creature is pinned underneath two pale hands, which would be slim and lovely if they didn't look like they've been decomposing underground for the last few centuries.

"Okiku!" I gasp.

There are similarities between my Okiku and the many-armed woman, in that they are both (a) dead, and (b) bloodthirsty when they've got a target in mind.

From behind her curtain of hair, Okiku looks almost quizzical. Her hands are steel vises, fueled by three hundred years of old grudges and tempered by her surprising fondness for me. Nothing the other creature attempts could dislodge her.

"Thanks." I pant, taking aim and driving the knife one final time into the point where the seven-armed woman's neck is joined to the rest of her, and then I brace myself.

"I win!"

The most horrible earsplitting wail I've ever heard rends the air, and the ghoul *explodes*.

I hit the ground, covering the back of my head with my hands, more from the force of the impact than from instinct. The wailing peters out, and I take that as a sign to lift myself up and assess the carnage.

The blast has shattered a small art-nouveau lamp, a Waterford vase, and the drooping clump of chrysanthemums that had been cowering inside it. A thick cloud of dust settles onto the floor and over the furniture, but all that's left of the creature is the ruined doll. Its black eyes are as creepy as ever, but at least its slit-mouth is gone.

I've read about *hoso-de* before. Generally, these benign spirits, characterized by multiple arms, are found in most Japanese households. Why it was so angry and what it was doing in the good old U.S. of A., I have no idea. Perhaps there's a foreign neighbor in this apartment block. People always bring their ghosts with them, holding on to them like faded photographs.

Okiku, naturally, sits in the center of the whole mess, impassioned as always, with broken remnants of the fight strewn around her like a dirty halo.

"I hope Sondheim's not expecting me to pay for this," I mutter, standing and trying to shake the sawdust from my hair. My spirit companion says nothing. Okiku never says much, never gives any indication of what she's thinking. I'm almost used to that by now. I ramble enough for both of us.

Okiku drifts over to me and places a finger against my cheek where the *hoso-de* scored a bite, the way Okiku always does when she wants to know if I'm all right. Which is rather nice of her. Up close, her face is the stuff of nightmares, an amalgamation of what it's like to be alive and dead all at once.

I'm almost used to that too.

"Never been better." I grin, trying to hide my shaking knees.

This was not the first attempt at exorcising ghosts for either one of us. Over the last year, I've gone against faceless women, disfigured spirits, and grotesque revenants. Some people have dangerous hobbies, like skydiving and driving in monster truck rallies and glacier surfing. Me? I cast my soul into the churning waters of potential damnation and wait for a bite. And Okiku's been doing this for *three hundred frigging years*?

Just to err on the safe side, I pour the rest of the salt water onto the doll's remains and sweep them into a large garbage bag. Okiku watches me but doesn't help. From the books Kagura lent me, I know the *hoso-de* are creatures of wood. Spirits of water, like Okiku, can't touch their vessels without having their own strength sapped. Fortunately, the fight didn't last long enough to weaken her.

I turn off the TV, then paw through the blankets to find my cell phone and punch in a few numbers. "It's done," I say as soon as Sondheim answers.

I don't have to wait long. Andy Sondheim plays wide receiver for Pembrooke High's football team and is so far up the social ladder from me that it's like trying to scale Mount Everest. With him is his perky cheerleader girlfriend, Trish Seyfried, though she's not quite so perky at the moment. Sondheim likes to boast about having his own place, even though his parents pay the rent. They're away on enough business trips that I suppose it's almost true.

He and Trish are fully dressed now. I'd assumed they'd just gotten back from some party and were making out before they'd called. Both are still white-faced and trembling, which I'll admit I enjoy, because when he's not in fear for his life, Sondheim's usually a jerk.

Okiku ignores them. She's been counting tiles on the floor, black hair flapping behind her like a bird's wing. Neither Sondheim nor Trish sees her. Most usually don't.

"It's gone," I tell them wearily, not bothering with the details.

"Damn, Halloway," the jock says, looking around his apartment. "How about doing it without trashing the place?"

I suppose a show of gratitude was too much to expect. "I got the job done, all right? That's more than you were able to do." I lift the garbage bag. "Wanna burn it?"

Sondheim takes a step back, eyeing the sack like it ate his grandmother. "Uh, no way, man. I'm not touching that."

Figures.

"You're sure it's not going to come back?" Trish speaks up uncertainly. "I mean, really sure?"

"Positive."

"My mom's vase." Sondheim moans. "And the painting's got a hole in it!"

"It's only a Manet reproduction," I say. "And kitsch is in nowadays." The side effect of being a spoiled rich kid is that I know how much things cost.

The jock glares. Okiku stops by the vase's corpse and begins counting the broken pieces.

"I should never have listened to you," Sondheim snaps, turning on his girlfriend. "Why the hell did you want to play some stupid ghost game anyway?"

"Beth and Lisa played it," the cheerleader whines, tugging at a strand of golden hair. "Nothing happened to *them*."

"That's because you didn't follow the rules." I speak up, not feeling particularly sympathetic. One-man tag is a ritual that has no real purpose other than to mess with nearby spirits. Invite one into a doll's body, fool around with it for an hour to prove your manliness, then—hopefully—send it back to where it came from without repercussion. It's supposed to be a test of courage.

"You didn't use salt water, you didn't bother cleansing the place with incense beforehand, and worst of all, *you didn't finish the game*. You might have gotten away with that if you'd been in a public place, but by summoning a spirit here, you might as well have drawn a large exclamation point over your house."

Both stare blankly at me. "How the hell could we finish the game after seeing that…that *thing* stand up?" Sondheim demands.

"Beth and Lisa said the doll just lay there when they tried it," Trish chimes in.

Inwardly, I groan. About the only smart thing they did tonight was call me for help, though being woken up at two in the morning by people who never give me the time of day isn't something I enjoy. I don't even know how they got my number.

"Yeah, well, if you're not prepared to see things go bump in the night, then don't go playing with dolls in the first place."

I heft the garbage bag over my shoulder, knowing this will be the first and only time I score one over on Andrew Sondheim. "And one last thing, not that I'd recommend there be a next time—but at least pick a better name than 'Dumbelina.' You don't want to anger the creature before the game even starts. You might not wanna take it seriously, but believe me: it takes you very, very seriously. Now if you'll excuse me, I've got a doll to burn and classes in the morning."

I walk out, Okiku trailing after me. I can hear bits of an argument starting up again after the door closes behind me. The two of them will probably tell everyone what happened here tonight, stirring up new rumors to cement my status as a freak, but I don't really care. Trish has a fondness for hyperbole, so it's not like anyone in school will believe her.

It's 4:30 a.m. and I'm tired—but glad I only live a few blocks away. I bike back to my house and let myself in, not bothering to be quiet about it. Dad's away on business and won't be home 'til late afternoon, so I've got plenty of time.

I burn the doll in a metal trash bin I found in a junkyard several months ago. Most days it sits half hidden behind some bushes in the garden. Dad probably doesn't even know it's there. I've used it about thirty-five times.

It's a quick and easy bonfire. I empty the contents of the garbage bag into the can, making sure I don't leave anything out, then strike a match.

The doll burns easily enough. Its beady black eyes watch me until its face disappears into the flames and smoke. Soon, nothing will remain of it but black soot and angry memories.

When there is nothing left of the doll, Okiku smiles. She always does.

It's not that I *have* to do these exorcisms. I'm not responding to some higher calling that insists I don a cape, cowl, and tight spandex to rid my city of crime. I'm not about righting wrongs. All these creatures I've been trapping and killing during the last several months—there's no real purpose to it. I tell Sondheim not to meddle in things he has no understanding of, but I'm just as guilty. I mess around with spirits, test the boundaries of my fears, see how far I can step over the line without falling over.

Besides, Okiku delights in the hunt. She ended life as a victim and started death as an avenger. She doesn't kill for any higher purpose. She doesn't need a reason to take someone's life. She does it because she can. And I get that. I've been a victim for most of my life. She changed that.

I tell myself I'm doing this—ridding the world of these things that go bump in the night—because I want to. I tell myself I'm doing this because I'm not going to spend the rest of my life as prey.

I tell myself it's an adrenaline rush.

And, admittedly, that's where the stupidity comes in.

Okiku senses where my mind is wandering, and curiosity crosses her dead, mottled face.

"I'm all right. Let's finish this."

She smiles again.

Together, we stand and watch the night burn.

CHAPTER TWO

GIRLS

I used to forget it was Okiku and not the masked woman of my childhood in the room with me. I used to wake up screaming with nightmares. The only times I've ever seen Okiku look helpless are when I buck out of bed covered in sweat and crying. She'll wrap her withered arms around me; she's not used to comforting anyone, but she tries all the same.

Then a *miko* of Chinsei shrine, Kagura, offered to teach me the rituals, teach me how to exorcise the demons in my head and the demons around me. "To protect you," she said. Everything I know about containing spirits, I learned from the former priestess.

The first exorcism I performed on my own was nine months ago in Japan. The ghost had appeared to be a kindly old lady, asking for something sweet to drink. When I produced the doll and apologized, she was no longer kindly. Or old. Or, after an unexpected transformation, a woman.

Kagura scolded me, said she wasn't teaching me these traditions so I could go out and be proactive without supervision. If she'd had her way, it would have been at least two more years before I could execute these rituals on my own.

I pointed out the need for constant practice and that Okiku was there to make sure I got out with my skin intact. It took a lot of convincing—and stretching the truth about how frequently I use these talents and on what—though Kagura has never stopped worrying. Between her and my cousin, Callie, I've got all the mothering I could ever need.

After I caught my first spirit, I slept like a baby for the first time in months. Most mornings arrive easy like that now.

This morning, I wake sputtering out tangles of hair. Sometimes I suspect that Okiku's dark locks have their own sentience. They slip beneath my pillow and burrow into my blankets. A chosen few wrap around my arm like a protective cocoon.

All the while, Okiku never moves. She's curled up on the ceiling, near the headboard, and her hollow eyes stare straight ahead without blinking. To call what she does "sleep" is like calling couch surfing an extreme sport.

You'd think that waking up every day to see what most people would consider a dead body would have driven me crazy a long time ago. But dead bodies don't smell of incense and eucalyptus. Okiku's scent dances into my bedsheets and lingers on my skin.

I roll out of bed, tired but too keyed up to sleep, the adrenaline still somersaulting in my bloodstream. I hop into the shower. Okiku is a considerate roommate, quick to leave me to my own company the instant she thinks I'm getting naked. It's a good compromise, because she's the only reason I bother with clothes when I'm in my room.

By the time I'm out, she's awake, hair tamed and thrown forward over one gaunt shoulder. A book is open in her lap. Words fascinate her, and this month, she's all about Murakami Haruki novels. She looks up from the page, staring mournfully out the window. I recognize the look on her face. It's why she's been so distracted. Okiku enjoys catching spirits and chasing after dolls, but that's not the reason she's here.

"Another one?"

She nods and points a finger out the window, as if the perp she's after is just around the corner.

Okiku has never been wrong when it comes to tracking down murderers. I could almost pity the guy. Almost. "That's five in three months. You're on fire, Ki."

"I see no conflagrations." Okiku's sense of humor died centuries ago with her physical body.

"How about we find him tonight? That sound good?" I know better than to put myself between Okiku and her target when she's marked the hunt. Drag things out for too long, and she gets ornery. The faster she can get her hands on whatever asshole she has in her sights, the better it is for everyone involved. Except for the person in question, of course. It's Friday, so I figure I can sleep in during the weekend to make up for these two nights of vice.

She perks up at my suggestion—and I mean, really perks up. For a heartbeat, the putrefied spirit standing by my windowsill fades, and a beautiful brown-eyed girl in a simple kimono looks back at me.

It takes a tremendous amount of concentration for Okiku to will herself into the form of the teenager she used to be. It's easier for her to keep old habits and the horrifying face she's worn longer than she was alive. But when the moods suit her, she makes the effort. And every time she does, I can't stop my breath from hitching in my throat. The sunlight leaches away the remains of the revenant I know and adore to reveal the girl beneath the ghost.

"Thank you." Even her voice sounds different—no longer the coarseness of sandpaper, but light and clear. She smiles at me one last time before allowing her features to be reclaimed by the night. Pale death and decay steal back her face.

I leave her to her own thoughts and head down to breakfast. Mrs. Lippert is the closest thing we have to a housekeeper. She comes in mornings and does a bit of cleaning. More importantly, she's a fantastic cook. As I slide into my seat, she lays down a breakfast fit for a king—or a hungry seventeen-year-old boy: sizzling bacon, ham-and-cheese omelet, freshly squeezed orange juice, oven-baked bread, and her special homemade jam. My stomach rumbles its approval.

"All set for spring vacation?" she inquires as I dig into the bacon.

"Yup," I say, mouth full. Despite constantly switching schools and states, this is my senior year, and the one thing I'm looking forward to is graduation.

"How are your grades doing?"

"4.0 GPA, last I checked."

"And your SAT scores? They came back yesterday, right?"

"Yup, 1570." Mrs. Lippert beams at me from across the table. Mom died a couple of years ago, and with a dad away for weeks at a time, I'm not bashful about taking whatever praise I can get.

I return to my room to retrieve my bag, but not before taking a quick detour. In the back of my closet, I dig out a small plastic container, pick out two random dolls, and stuff them in my backpack along with my emergency sewing kit and tape recording of Shinto prayers. You never know.

"I'm ready, Ki. Let's—"

She steps *into* me…

She runs along the river.

Lights twinkle before her, bobbing up and down along the stream, beckoning her to follow. It is not supposed to be a joyous occasion, but her laughter carries in the air. She runs, stopping only when she hears her mother's voice call out behind her, telling her to slow down.

One of the lights comes to a stop on the riverbed, sputtering, struggling against the reeds. She pauses beside the water's edge, crouching down to study it more closely.

It is a chochin, *a lantern, the paper so delicate that clumsy hands would tear at its surface. There is a short inscription on one side, where someone has written down their prayers and secret wishes, a common practice among the villagers before these* chochin *were surrendered to the river.*

I wish for happiness, *it reads.*

So do I, *she thinks.* I, too, wish to be happy, forever and ever and…

A careful push sends the little lantern on its way to join its brethren sailing several meters ahead. She watches it for a while, long enough to ensure there are no other obstacles in its way.

I wish for happiness.

She waves at the chochin. In a way, it's also her chochin now. She begins to run again—

"—go." The vision clears as my brain slams back into my body. Almost immediately, the exhaustion from my poor night's sleep drains away, and I feel sharper, more alert. More complete.

I can feel Okiku humming, even as I leave the house.

***

I may not pass for popular, but I'm still not the statue to everyone's pigeon. I don't think most people in school know what to think of me, much less to which end of the high school spectrum I belong.

Take, for instance, the BMW Z4 I park in the school lot. Dad bought the Bimmer for my sixteenth birthday and for passing my driver's test. You'd think the car would put me in with the cool kids, because it's practically considered unpatriotic to ridicule anyone with a nice car at Pembrooke High.

But it doesn't. The reason lies mostly with Okiku, though I can't blame her for being protective of me. I've talked with her numerous times about curbing her enthusiasm for mayhem, but I'm not sure how much of it she's taken to heart. After a mirror inexplicably splintered, slicing through the arm of a quarterback who was about to deck me, and when a water fountain exploded on some jocks who'd had problems with my Asianness, people stopped trying to bully me.

Rumors spread about strange events at my previous schools, that my mom had been locked up in a mental asylum and died under unusual circumstances, not to mention claims by the rare, insightful few who could glimpse Okiku around me when her guard was down. Nobody really believes what those kids say anyway, but the general consensus is that something's not quite right about me. They're scared of me and would rather not have anything to do with the creepy Japanese-American outsider.

Except, as I discovered, when they need an exorcist.

I'm hoping my adventures from last night will go unnoticed, because I don't see Sondheim as the type to admit I had to defend his virtue from a possessed doll. By the time lunch rolls around and not a whimper is heard, I start to relax.

I use my phone to check email in between bites of my sandwich. The first is from Kagura, and I smile as I read.

Some people have funny stories about how they met their friends. "Funny" is not the word I would use for our introduction. When I first met Kagura in Japan a couple of years ago, she was one of many shrine maidens who used an elaborate doll ritual to exorcise a demon that'd possessed me for ten years.

Kagura and her aunt run an inn near Mount Fuji now, but she still travels to the Chinsei shrine to keep things in order there.

Callie and I visit her every year. When someone saves your life, it's a hard bond to break.

> Hello Tarquin,
>
> I hope it is not too early for me to congratulate you on your upcoming graduation. Brown University is an excellent choice—though if you ever change your mind and come to Todai, I would be more than happy to assist you with the enrollment process. Your parents are both alumni, which should work in your favor.
>
> Saya is doing very well. She works at the Adachi Museum of Art now and has become a keen gardener. I told her you and Callie will be visiting during your Easter break, and she has happily booked a room at Kamameshi as well.

Saya was one of the other shrine maidens from where Kagura served. No matter how many times they assure me otherwise, I still feel guilty, knowing I was responsible for their unexpected change in careers.

> The crew of American ghost hunters I mentioned before have finally arrived. They had initially asked me to provide them with the necessary research about Mount Fuji, but now they also want me to assist them in their filming at the Aokigahara forest. They are investigating the legends of the Aitou village, said to have existed inside Aokigahara during older times, though no evidence of it remains today.
>
> Garrick Adams, one of the ghost hunters, says I was

recommended to them because my father studied records of this village in detail and was the expert in the matter. The ghost hunters would like access to all the research and findings I kept when he passed away. Adams-san also believes that as a former miko, I would be of great help dispelling any ghosts they may encounter along the way.

Still, despite their credentials, I have my doubts. I understand their interest, but Aokigahara is not a place to meddle.

They will be leaving a few weeks before you arrive, so it is a shame you and Callie will not be given the chance to meet them. They seem to be quite popular in the United States.

I've heard of them. Garrick Adams and Stephen Riley are spirit investigators and the hosts of *Ghost Haunts*, a paranormal reality television show that's had some good buzz as of late. Adams and Riley are known for their wildly unorthodox attempts to taunt ghosts into maiming or possessing them—whatever helps their ratings, I guess. I try to imagine them with the ever-cautious Kagura and nearly choke on my sandwich.

I'm afraid Brown's for me, I type back, but I like the idea of postgraduate studies at Todai. Dad wants me studying in America for the time being. It might be good to actually know what it feels like to stay in one place for four years.

Ghost Haunts is a big show on cable here. But watching guys flail around with a camera doesn't sound like very convincing

television to me. No harm in showing them around the place, I'd
say, and it'll be great to see you on TV! Any chance you can get me
some autographs?

I pause, searching for a font that would best convey my sarcasm,
then give up. It would probably be lost on the *miko* anyway.

Send our love to Saya-san. Looking forward to seeing you guys
in a few weeks!

My email sent, I thumb through the rest of my inbox and grin
when I see another new message. This one is from Callie.

"I hope that smile's for me, Halloway."

I glance up to see Trish Seyfried standing by my table, but she
isn't who spoke.

I don't discriminate against cheerleaders. There's bound to be *at
least* a couple of intelligent, sassy girls for every giggly group of brainless
Trish Seyfrieds. And Kendele Baker fits that profile. She volunteered to
be my lab partner two semesters ago, and it took a few classes for me
to realize she wasn't afraid of me like her friends are. That makes me
nervous—especially when she insisted I tutor her in Spanish. Beautiful
green-eyed brunettes don't usually want much to do with me, but at
least I now understand who Trish got my number from.

"I just want to thank you again," Trish says, moving to sit across
the table from me while Kendele takes the empty seat on my right.
"For saving Andy and me from the zombie."

Zombie? "Zombie?"

"Well, it was kind of like a zombie, wasn't it? If I told everyone it was just a doll, it would sound kind of silly."

I groan.

"Trish is joking, right?" Kendele asks. "I mean, you don't exorcise zombies—you lop off their heads."

"It wasn't a zombie," I say. "It was a seven-armed Japanese woman."

Kendele breaks into laughter. Nobody ever believes me.

She changes the subject, much to my relief. "Hey, there's that new movie coming out, *A Walk in the Rain*. Ever heard of it?"

"Not really. I'm not into chick flicks."

"It's playing tonight at the mall," Kendele persists, smiling at me. "What do you think?"

"Uh, that's great," I lie, because the title alone sounds like I'd rather have my teeth drilled. "You and Trish ought to go, if you really want to catch it."

Kendele's mouth falls open and Trish has a giggling fit. I don't understand girls at all.

"Actually, I have a better idea," Trish pipes up before Kendele can say anything else. "Keren McNeil's having a party later tonight. It's that big house over on Buckle Street. Wanna come? As, you know, a thank-you for everything. Like a reward for helping Andy and me."

I think Trish and I have very different definitions of what constitutes a "reward."

Kendele shoots her a warning glance. "I don't think Tark's interested in going to a party full of jocks, Trish."

"Why not? I'm sure he is."

I clear my throat. "That sounds really, um, cool. But I've already got other plans." That was true enough at least.

Trish shrugs. "Bummer. Well, if you have time, feel free to stop by. Kendele and I will be there, and I'm sure the guys won't mind."

Kendele's still frowning at me when she and Trish get up to leave. Once they're gone, I relax. I've never really gotten the hang of talking to girls, and Kendele's acting especially odd today.

I turn back to my phone and Callie's email. My cousin's a junior at Boston University, but we visit each other during the longer holiday breaks. Callie's not a big fan of Okiku, though Okiku has been nothing but nice to her. Some prejudices are hard to break.

Hey, Tark!

I'm going to keep this short and sweet. I have a date with Trevor in five minutes, but I wanted to dash this off to you first.

I pause to roll my eyes. Trevor Goodman is Callie's new boyfriend.

It's official. In addition to our Japan trip, I'll see you and Uncle Doug for your graduation. After all, I'm pretty sure finishing high school wouldn't be the same without me there to celebrate!

I'm so proud of you. I know Uncle Doug agrees, and I know Aunt Yoko would too. You've grown into such a good person. You've always been more like a brother to me than a cousin. An annoying little brother, but hey—no one's perfect!

Okay, wrapping up now before I get too mushy. How are things with Okiku? All that night creeping is bad for your health. Can't you guys figure out a way for Okiku to go out on her own so you can stay at home and be safe? (I know I've asked this a billion times before, but I'm thinking there has got to be a better way.)

See you in a couple of weeks! Japan!!!

I swallow another grin. From the way she talks, you'd think Callie had never been to Japan before, despite us making a yearly trip together.

I finish the rest of my sandwich with little interruption and move to stand. My chair scrapes back and bumps into someone behind me.

"Hey!"

Great. Of all the chairs in all the cafeterias in all the Washington, DC, private schools, golden boy McNeil is standing behind mine.

I turn. The star quarterback frowns at me, his teammates surrounding him. I accidentally jostled his tray when I stood, and water's spilled over his sandwich.

"Sorry," I say and take a step to leave, but one of his flunkies, Matheson, blocks my path.

"That's all you gonna say, Halloway?"

Inwardly, I sigh. Bullies have avoided me since that water fountain incident, but that doesn't mean some people aren't itching to try again.

"Accidents happen." I try to edge away from the boys, but a sharp prod on my shoulder forces me back.

"Looks like someone owes McNeil a sandwich, freak."

I dig into my pocket and hand McNeil a ten-dollar bill—partly because it was my fault, but mostly because I'm not in the mood for a confrontation. The jock looks taken aback by my easy acquiescence, but I should have known better than to expect McNeil's goons to be satisfied. Fact is, Matheson looks insulted, like he was the one I'd bumped into.

"Hey, you scrawny little Chink—"

He reaches over to grab the collar of my shirt.

There's a sizzling, searing noise from overhead, and that's all the heads-up I get before the fluorescent lights above us explode. I leap out of the way, and McNeil and his friends jump back as a cascade of sparks spill down between us. The light fixture spins crazily to one side, but the wires are still intact, which keeps it from crashing to the floor.

The cafeteria is silent. Everyone stares at the broken lights, then back at us.

"Like I said…"—I wave the ten-dollar bill at McNeil, trying to act as if I'm not fazed despite nearly jumping out of my skin—"accident. Here."

McNeil recovers. "Don't sweat it, Halloway. It's just a sandwich. Let's go, guys."

Matheson scowls at me and strides off after him, the rest of their friends close behind.

I look up to the ceiling again, and Okiku is there, staring after the boys. Her shoulders hunch forward. Her hands form claws against the cement. She's rattling, as if she's about to go on the attack, and she's—

hunger hungry kill peel off their skin

cut it thin take heads and limbs

little dark little dark kill

Uh-oh…

"Ki!"

She jerks away and disappears, leaving me alone with a roomful of strangers. I take a deep breath and slowly let it out, slowly becoming aware that people are still looking at me. The whispers are starting.

"Show's over, folks," I mutter, stuffing the money back in my pocket and catching sight of Trish and Kendele loitering by the doors. Trish looks both fascinated and terrified. Kendele is a little harder to decipher. She watches me, a strange look on her face.

With as much dignity as I can muster, I stride out of the cafeteria to the restroom. I check to make sure there's no one else around before sagging against one of the stall doors.

"Okiku."

She appears, settles on the ceiling, and looks everywhere but at me.

"Ki, what was that all about?"

"It is nothing."

"Like hell it was," I say. "You were about ready to flay those guys alive."

"I do not like them."

"No one in their right mind likes them—which says a lot about the students here, since they do. Are you feeling antsy about tonight?"

A pause, and she nods. I have a feeling she isn't telling me everything, but I let that pass. "Don't worry about it, all right? I know you're impatient, but let's not freak out any more people than necessary. Can you hold off 'til then?"

She nods again, this time with more determination.

"Good." Still, I can't shake my unease as we leave the restroom. Okiku's never kept secrets from me before, but I'll have to pry them out of her after tonight's work when she'll be more at ease.

It's going to be a long night.

CHAPTER THREE

HUNTERS

I can tell by the smell of food as I walk through the door that Dad's been home for at least an hour. As a lauded connoisseur of takeout in the greater DC area, I've learned to interpret my father's moods by the food he brings home for dinner. Lo Wan's means he's brought his work home with him and shouldn't be bothered for the rest of the night. Thai Mam means he plans to relax for the evening, maybe watch a game or two.

Kouzina takeout, from the Greek place he knows I like, means he wants to sit down and have one of those father-and-son talks with me, which never deviate beyond asking how school is going and expressing mild disappointment at the dearth of extracurricular activities making up my social calendar. Japanese food from the Sushi-ya takes this a step further, with the conversation at the table revolving around musical lessons and sports camps he suggests I sign up for, though I've always found a million and one reasons why these were bad ideas.

This time, it's different. There is a faint scent of burned pasta and my eyes widen. Dad's attempting to *cook*, which could have no possible happy ending without the fire department on standby.

I drop my backpack on the couch and race to the kitchen, where Dad is juggling an assortment of prechopped herbs sealed in tiny, expensive containers, the kind specifically marketed for those who have no idea how to work a stove but would like to give it a try. He'd changed out of his business suit into a polo shirt and pants that could only be described as part jeans and part sweats.

Dad can speak four languages and wring out millions of dollars in settlement clauses with no more than a PowerPoint presentation, but put him in front of anything that involves preparing food and it's like a kitten attempting to power a lawn mower. The most horrifying words that could ever come out of my father's mouth in the kitchen are "What does this knob do?" and "I'm sure that was supposed to happen."

The pasta is more than done. The gas flame underneath is turned to its highest setting. There's barely enough water in the pot but enough leftover foam that Macbeth's witches would dance around it. I switch off the burner, and Dad pauses in his herbal acrobatics to glance over his shoulder at me. "You're home late."

"You killed the pasta," I reply. "I'm calling 911."

"Are you sure? I put it on maybe twenty, twenty-five minutes ago."

"*Twenty-five minutes?*" I peer into the pot, at the mushy mash of noodles that are more Al Capone than al dente, and sigh. "Dad, the package says ten."

"Really? I thought it would take longer. Let me go make the pesto and then I can—"

"Out of the kitchen," I command, poking him in the shoulder. I've had a couple of growth spurts lately. Dad's still taller, a couple of inches short of six feet. I've been slowly but surely making up the difference.

He retreats, not without some relief, though he makes a play at reluctance. "You sure? I could help—"

"You can help by setting the table. Not everything in the house has been insured yet." My cooking is nothing to write home about, but at least it is edible.

With Dad safely out of the way, I dump the noodles in the trash and start a fresh batch, pouring the premade pesto sauce he brought home into another pan. Inside, I'm worried. The last time Dad tried to cook, it was right before he told me we were moving to Applegate to be closer to my mother. I didn't react well.

Once both sauce and pasta are done, I carry them to the table.

"Smells a lot better than anything I might have made," Dad admits, inhaling deeply. Unmoved by human appetite and good food, Okiku counts the floor tiles again, like the number might have changed since yesterday. Okiku has been with me for two years, but she can always find something to count.

"Well, spill it out," I say as we take our seats.

"Spill what?"

"All this." I gesture at the pasta. "We're not going to move again, are we? Can't we at least wait 'til I graduate? I'll have to move for college anyway, so it won't matter as much."

"Tark, what are you talking about?"

"Every time you try to poison me with your cooking—"

Dad snorts.

"—it's always before springing some surprise on me. Surprises I don't usually like. So what gives?"

Dad raises his hands. "Can't a father want to cook and spend time with his son?"

"Nope," I say, and Dad's grin fades a little, spotting the agitation I'm trying to hide.

"Tarquin"—he places both elbows on the table and leans forward—"I promise you there's no other motive. I've just gotten back from a grueling work trip negotiating with a few hard-nosed *and* hardheaded businessmen from Beijing, and the only thing I've got in my head right now is enjoying the little time I can spend with you this weekend before I do the same thing all over again on Monday. I know that the last few years have been a little…difficult, but I'm glad we've gotten to the point in our relationship where we can actually talk."

That is true. Three years ago, Dad and I had been nothing more than housemates, sharing the same rooms but little else. I start to relax. "Really?"

"Really. Although I'm not sure I like the insinuation that my horrible cooking always precedes horrible news."

"My theory was that after surviving whatever you set out for me to eat, any other news would be easier to stomach."

We burst into laughter. Okiku looks up from counting, startled by the sudden noise, then loses interest after seeing we mean nothing by it.

The pasta winds up being pretty tasty. Dad can pick out good food, just not make it. "Wanna watch the game later?" he asks as we're clearing the table.

I hesitate. "Sorry, Dad. I kinda have plans. That okay?"

"Oh? Going out with friends of yours?"

"Yeah, I guess you can say that."

I hate, *hate* lying to him, even if I think I've got good reason to, but I don't have much choice. I feel bad, knowing he'd been looking forward to hanging out with me, but Dad looks pleased. He's been after me to be more social, to go to parties and pep rallies like a normal teenager, and I can tell he considers this a definite improvement over spending Friday night holed up in my room. I don't want to frighten him with the truth.

"In that case, don't let your old-fogy dad stop you. Where are you going?"

Trish's invitation to the jocks' party is the first thing I can think of. "Um, there's a party not too far from here. Over on Buckle Street."

"All right, as long as you're home by…ten-ish?"

"One a.m.?" I counter.

"Eleven."

"Midnight."

"Deal."

It's my turn to make an offer. "I don't have anything planned for Saturday…"

"Ah, that reminds me. A business partner gave me two tickets for the game at the Verizon tomorrow night. Wizards versus Cavaliers." He smiles at the look on my face. "I take it you're interested."

"You're the best, Dad!" I jump up to give him a quick, fierce hug before taking the dishes back to the kitchen. My enthusiasm fades though, as I contemplate the night ahead.

Fifteen minutes later, Dad is settled in front of the television and I'm off, Okiku trailing after me in eager anticipation. Dad's usually away, so when Okiku gets her urges, I rarely have to sneak out while he's in the house. As it is, I make sure he's focused on the college basketball game before making my escape. I'm pretty sure he'd wonder at my need to bring a heavy backpack to a party, or why there are gloves, a lower face mask, and a dark hoodie inside, if he deigned to check.

I hop into my Bimmer and pull out of the driveway, keeping my breathing even, which I've found is the best way to keep calm.

It's hard to explain what I feel when I go hunting with Okiku. On one hand, I'm constantly tormented by the idea that I might get caught, that the police might one day piece together all these unexplained crimes and find enough evidence to attribute them to me. On the other hand, I thrive on the danger. The idea that I am helping put the scum of the earth back where they belong—which, ideally, is six feet under—is an unnatural high that I both hate and enjoy.

It's a nice night, so I've got the top down, and Okiku all but stands up in her seat, hair streaming in the wind as I tear through the silent streets that lead into busier intersections. Okiku's finger moves toward the east and I comply, steering the car in that direction. I could never explain how Okiku can pinpoint where these people are, but she's always been right. We've been indirectly responsible for closing some cold cases in the last several months, and I'm sure that if the Washington PD believed in either ghosts or vigilantism they'd be sending us gift baskets by the dozen.

She points north as I drive past a few more streets. Our destination is almost always an apartment complex or a cheap hotel a few miles from the interstate. Every now and then, it's a private residence, nestled among other identical houses in the suburbs. It's horrifying that perps like these live among us. But Okiku leads me past the rows of houses and into the commercial district of town. When she signals for a halt, I'm almost sure she's joking.

"A Five Guys? Ki, why are we at a Five Guys?"

She shrugs. I suppose cold-blooded killers have to eat too, so I park and we venture inside. There's a big crowd, and in my case, this is an advantage. The less obtrusive I can be, the better.

I sidle into an empty seat, the smell of fries percolating the air. I scan the throng of people, ready to tell her that she must have made a mistake—until I see him.

I don't have Okiku's second sight. I need to be within visual range of the person to make the connection, but that first recognition never fails to curdle my gut.

What I hate about most of these perps is how *normal* they look. Like they have the right to sit at any Five Guys in any town in any country in the world and be served a bacon cheeseburger and a side order of fries like everyone else. I hate that no one else around them can see them for the putrid waste of flesh they really are.

Mr. "Normal" here has red hair and brown eyes. He's wearing a faded Rolling Stones shirt and jeans. He's eating his burger like the only thing he's ever murdered in his life was a cow.

The rotting corpses of the three girls crawling over his back beg to differ.

It always hurts to look at them. You can tell how long they've been shackled to their killers by their condition, and these poor girls have been prisoners for a long, long time. Their eyes have sunk almost below their sockets, and their hair's matted and stringy, revealing bits of crumbling skull. Their bones show through parts of their skin, which sags at the elbows and shoulders. I've seen other, more decomposed dead children, but I avert my eyes anyway. I can't look at them without seeing my own damage. Not too long ago, that could have very easily been me.

What hurts even worse is the living, breathing girl across the table from him. She's blond and rosy-cheeked, nibbling at her fry. A possible victim? It churns my stomach, and I wish I hadn't eaten dinner before we headed out.

Okiku is quiet, but her eyes are intent on the murderer. I can feel the shadows she keeps inside her snaking out. They reach hungrily for the man but are kept in check by the noise of people and the threat of discovery.

I've felt those shadows myself. I've woken up in the middle

of the night enough times, pale and sweating—and bawling my
eyes out, I'm not ashamed to admit—because the strange malice
festering inside Okiku occasionally finds its way into me, the

festering, festering,

make them break

them take them

shadows' voices curling into my mind. When there's a delay
in Okiku's special brand of justice, it's harder to contain the
darkness inside her, and she knows it. Her desire to catch these
cutthroats quickly is as much a way to stop my own terrors as it
is to quell hers.

I could stay home while she's out on these nightly haunts, but
that's not an option. We've tried. Okiku hadn't been gone five
minutes when I was confronted by a wayward ghost. I'd trapped it
in a doll by the skin of my teeth, never more grateful to Kagura for
her lessons. Okiku had returned not long after, sensing something
was amiss.

Whenever Okiku strays too far, other *things* start moving in
to claim me as their territory. They want a body to take over. To
many spirits, Kagura says, I am prime real estate, easier to inhabit
because of my previous possession. But as long as Okiku is around
to defend her territory, they leave me alone. When she's more than
half a mile away, the rules no longer apply.

I'm relieved when the man gets up half an hour later. The girl
skips forward to hold his hand, much to my own horror. I follow
them out into the parking lot, arriving at my car just as they climb

into a white Buick. Okiku and I tail them as they pull out into the street.

By the time they stop, I am a riot of nerves, wanting this over and done with. All throughout the ride, I worry about the girl, who has no idea what's about to happen. To minimize any evidence I might leave behind, Okiku often forges into these places alone while I wait nervously in the car a block away, hands primed on the wheel like any self-respecting getaway driver.

Once he's dead, the deed done, I can go home and climb into bed and console myself that one less bastard is preying on the world tonight. Sometimes I even feel good about it.

I note the room both the man and the little girl disappear into—Room 5. Then I drive to find a place to park.

"Go get him, Ki."

Okiku's been gathering herself up to spring, stiff and taut as a silver-slicked bow. She is gone before I finish speaking.

I take a deep breath, hunker down in my car, and squeeze my eyes shut. I fiddle with my leather gloves, hoping it won't take long.

It doesn't.

Within minutes, I hear him in my head—a high-pitched cry that echoes into the night air. I pan the area, half expecting someone to come and investigate the source of the sound, although I know no one else hears.

And then the visions start, and I cease caring about much else.

sweet dark the dark calls kill him dying on a bed kill him watching always watching

fear he runs screaming feast on him take the
eyes
sunken beautiful staring eyes
crying
girl
rip him rip him bleeding
bleed

I grit my teeth, trying to drown out the sounds in my head, the final images I see: Okiku standing over the bloodied corpse, its face already starting to bloat. I've seen most of Okiku's victims, but you never get used to it.

I wait tersely for several more moments, until I sense Okiku emerging from the motel, passing through the door to Room 5 as if it was never there. I feel her moving to where I sit, and that's my cue to get out of the car.

She carries three glowing orbs of light against her chest, and her expression is one of contentment, despite her sadness.

My relief is immediate. Three orbs means the three sad ghosts I'd seen are no longer forced to spend a lifetime on their killer's back. It means that somewhere inside that motel room, the little girl is safe.

Okiku stands in the middle of the small parking lot, stalling before she has to release the lights into the sky, as she has done countless times before. When she finally opens her arms to welcome the night, I can see the wistfulness on her face. These children will escape into the heavens, though she will not. I know I'm part of the reason Okiku stays, to stave off spirits who wouldn't be as kind to me as she has been—but I suspect there's something more to it than what she tells me.

To watch these glowing children, taking on the semblance of bright fireflies and winging their way up, is one of the most profound things that I will ever know. Whatever they might find on the other side, I hope and believe it'll be better than the brief lives they led here. In those moments shortly after they take their place among the stars, I feel a sense of peace, a peace I know Okiku shares.

That feeling dissipates as reality sets back in.

I don my face mask and pull up my hoodie. Okiku looks curious when I turn back in the direction of the motel.

"I need to make sure the girl's okay, Ki."

Okiku understands the concept of crime prevention now. I was her first successful experiment. But the last thing a little girl wants after potentially debilitating trauma is to be confronted by a terrifying specter telling her everything's going to be all right.

I probably shouldn't have tried to make sure she was all right. If the door to the room had still been locked, I would have considered being selfish, but unfortunately, it opens at a touch.

The little girl is on her knees, crying before the desiccated corpse.

I swallow the bile that threatens to inch past my throat and move toward the child. She looks up at me, her beautiful blue eyes tear-stained and red from weeping.

"Daddy's not moving," she cries.

I don't know what to say to her.

But I do what I can. I carry her away from her dead father, and she clings to my neck like I was not responsible. I keep my mask on but stay longer than I should—long enough to see her tucked into the bed of that small room and to watch her cry herself to sleep. Long enough to lie to her, to tell her he's in a better place.

I call 911 from a nearby phone booth, keeping my voice a whisper as I relay details to the operator. I tell her I heard screams coming from one of the motel rooms but was too scared to check it out. I never remove my gloves, never put my hoodie down, and wipe the phone clean just to be certain. I make sure to leave no traces of myself behind.

I don't wait for the police or the ambulance to arrive.

Instead, I drive until I find another parking lot—at a Costco—and stop the car so I can hold my head in my hands, with only the occasional sounds of vehicles passing by to break through the guilt I feel.

Sometimes I forget that assholes have children too.

"Tarquin?" I hear Okiku ask, the worry echoing in her rattling whisper. She understands that this can take a lot out of me, some days worse than others, but it's not like either of us has any choice in the matter. She says my name again, and her voice changes.

"Tarquin." I feel her hand on my hair. Then both her hands reach down to gently cup my face, and I look up to find her studying me. She's adopted human guise again, and while her hands are cold to the touch, her eyes are warm. When she hugs me, it's awkward because Okiku never really learned how.

It's not like we both have any other options.

"I'm fine now," I say after a minute, squeezing her hand. "Let's get home."

But she shakes her head. "No."

"No?"

She turns to me, and I realize with dismay that the

take their eyes their limbs their heads

gouge out the pretties gouge

slither slither tiny festers hate

malice isn't completely gone from either of us. Ki's gotten hold of another scent, and the voices aren't letting go until that's over and done with too.

I check the time—9:30 p.m. Early enough for one more hunt. I don't want to spend another night with crazy in my head if I can help it.

"Where to?"

CHAPTER FOUR

THE PARTY

"I can't believe you actually made it!" Trish Seyfried squeals as I walk in.

I can't believe it either. Pulling up beside the McNeil residence felt even more incredulous than stopping by Five Guys, but Okiku doesn't waver in that regard.

"You've got to be kidding me, Ki."

It's a rhetorical question, but she shakes her head.

"McNeil's? There's a killer at McNeil's? If you wanted to go to the party, you didn't need to go through this roundabout way to—"

filthy necks kill strangle him take him

take the eyes

Ah, hell.

"Fine, fine," I grumble, still half convinced this is all a mistake. If there was a killer studying at Pembrooke High, I know I would have spotted him long before this. "At least let me check it out before we do anything."

The implication that someone I know from school might be a

murderer isn't lost on me. For once, I'm letting morbid curiosity take the reins. Something tells me I'm not going to like it, but I want to confront whoever it is before I sic Okiku on him.

There's a reason I don't go to these parties, and I'm already regretting setting foot in the place. Though the host is one of the few popular kids who's never gone out of his way to bully me, Keren McNeil's a wide receiver beloved for his ability to catch sixty-yard passes as if there aren't a dozen defenders on his tail. He's nice enough for a jock, except he hangs around with big-headed athletes like Matheson who talk smack about smack and treat the rest of us common mortals like dirty jockstraps. A lot of girls find these guys attractive, which is why I don't understand a lot of girls.

I flash Trish a weak smile and catch sight of Kendele sitting on a couch with her back toward me, Hank Armstrong's burly arm around her shoulders. The smile twists into a grimace. "Yeah, well, thanks for inviting me."

Trish may be the only person pleased to see me. A few of the jocks eye me with derisive smirks. Some cheerleaders do the same, watching me like I'm a frog on its way to a dissection. Trish, as always, is oblivious. She grabs my hand and leads me into the kitchen, babbling a mile a minute as she does.

"Come on, let's get you something cold to drink. I know you're not used to these kinds of parties, so I thought I'd show you around. You've never been to, um, McNeil's place before, right? His parents are away for weeks at a time, so this is where we usually hang. They've got a wide-screen TV and an Olympic-sized swimming pool. The only downer here is that the neighbors are sorta dicks. Every time we turn the stereo up, they start complaining. McNeil's dad knows the police commissioner, so it's okay if they threaten to call the cops, but the interruption's kinda annoying, you know?"

I didn't know, but I don't care. As Trish talks, my eyes wander over the rest of the crowd. The usual suspects are there, talking and laughing. Maybe it's the image of the little girl kneeling beside her father's corpse that's still swirling in my head, but I just want to lash out at someone.

"Are you good friends with McNeil?" I ask.

Trish pauses, a sudden edge in her voice. "I—no. Not really. It's not like I know McNeil well or anything. I'm just here 'cause the other cheerleaders are."

"What's he doing here?"

Sondheim isn't happy to see me. He's scowling because Trish is still clinging to my hand.

"I invited him." Trish sounds defensive. "He helped us out last night. Don't you think we owe him?"

Neither of them notices Okiku stepping out from me and heading off to explore the rest of the house. The McNeils are filthy rich, and this looks more like a mansion, with expensive-looking leather sofas and a home entertainment system that puts Dad's to shame. Not many breakables in the room, I note—guess McNeil knows his friends better than to leave them lying around. The smell of beer is strong, and I can already see a few couples making out.

"Fine, whatever. Look, it's Keren's house, and he gets to invite the people he wants to invite—no offense, pal. He won't like outsiders barging in, and just 'cause you think we owe—"

quiet little lingering sweet blood

drink up drink up drown

find him—

I interrupt Sondheim; it's getting harder to smile without looking demented. "You don't mind if I just hang around? I'm sure McNeil won't mind one more person. Trish is right, you know. It's an honor to get invited to these things."

Sondheim hesitates. "Yeah. Um, I guess. Hey, babe, how about grabbing us a couple of beers?"

Trish blows her boyfriend a kiss and saunters off. A few of the jocks and their girlfriends are watching a college basketball game on a forty-inch wide-screen in the next room, hollering insults. The rest are sprawled on chairs and couches, laughing. McNeil looks up and raises an eyebrow when we approach, his tone curious.

"Who invited him?"

"Trish," Sondheim says. "He did her a favor for some class, and she wanted to thank him."

"I know a better way she could thank him," a guy named Krajnik calls out, and the group howls. Sondheim flushes. I suspect that even among the football superstars, he still ranks on the lower totem pole of jocks.

I look around, half expecting to see someone wander by with incorporeal kids climbing up his back, but no such luck. I can see Matheson's with the group, still glaring at me, obviously not having forgiven me for lunch. I rack my brain, trying to come up with things to say.

"So. Hanging around and drinking beer while watching the game. Is that all you guys do at these parties?"

The grin freezes on McNeil's face. "Yeah. Why not?"

"Always thought you got wild at parties. I was pretty sure you guys had more balls than the one you pass around on the field."

The laughter is louder now. McNeil chuckles. "Brought a smart-ass with you this time, Andy." But no one complains when we both find empty chairs to sit.

"Wish you'd brought some more girls instead, Sondheim."

"McNeil, you're the one with the pool of groupies to choose from," someone else counters.

There's not much talk after that; whatever conversation there is gets swallowed by the cheers and hoots directed at the television screen, where a rival college team is getting its ass whooped by their opponents. I take the opportunity to scan the room, hoping to catch a glimpse of a corpse hanging off someone's back, because the sooner I spot the killer, the sooner Okiku can do what she needs to do and the sooner I can get out of here. My eyes wander back to Kendele, and more than once, I have to force the scowl off my face at seeing she's still talking to Armstrong.

"Hey, McNeil," one of the guys says in between half-innings. "You still going out with that girl? That redhead with the pigtails?"

"Not anymore. You have any idea what I need to do to—" McNeil stops, sneaks a look at me, and then grins. "Go ahead,

Garcia, but I'm not holding my breath that she'll say yes to an ugly mug like you."

More guffaws all around. Trish reappears to hand Sondheim his beer, then hesitates when she sees the others.

"Where's mine?" McNeil reaches for the beer she was about to hand to me. She startles and drops it. I'm not much on booze anyway, so I retrieve it and toss the can to him, a little confused as I watch the now-pale cheerleader hurry away, and as Sondheim gets up from his chair to follow, I cast another quick glance around but don't see anything out of the ordinary. Are there more people upstairs? Tendrils of voices still

sweet death claw and tear

rip him up

stroke through the edges of my mind, which means Okiku hasn't found him either.

"What's up with your eyes by the way?" one of the girls asks me. "I've always meant to ask."

"What do you mean?"

"Why are they blue? Aren't you, like, Chinese?"

"Japanese."

"Isn't that almost the same thing?"

"He's only half Asian, Danielle," a voice behind me responds. Kendele is standing with her hands on her hips, looking none too pleased to see me. Hank Armstrong is nowhere in sight. "I wanna borrow Halloway for a minute."

"Ten minutes in and you're already a stud, Halloway," McNeil drawls. "See what good company does for you?" The guys crack up, and I shrug—good-humoredly, I hope—before standing to follow Kendele to an unoccupied sofa in the least populated part of the room.

"What are you doing here?" she hisses, flouncing down onto the cushion.

"Trish invited me." I don't know why I sound so defensive, but I do. "You were there."

"I know that, but why did you come?"

"Why not?" I cast a pointed glance around the room. "You think I'm not up to the male standards?"

Kendele turns red. "That's not what I mean and you know it."

"Then what *do* you mean?"

"You aren't them."

"No shit, Sherlock."

"No, I mean you aren't *them*. You're not an asshole. I saw your face just now. Whatever they were talking about, you obviously didn't like it. There are other wannabes out there who'd like to be part of this even if it means they have to be jerks, but I know you're not one of them. So why are you here?"

"Why are *you* here?"

"Because most of the cheerleaders are dating the jocks! And they're cheerleaders I happen to be friends with, and friends stick with friends even when they outvote you on where you want to spend your Friday night! Nadia thinks the cheerleaders need to hang out more often anyway, so we can work better together on the field or whatever. And you still haven't answered my question!"

"Maybe I *want* to be an ass." She looks really upset at that, which puzzles me. "Being your lab partner slash tutor for a couple of semesters doesn't make you the expert on who I am."

"If I thought you were an asshole, I wouldn't have asked you to be my lab partner in the first place, you idiot. Trish didn't ask you here to the party because she wanted to thank you for whatever you did for her and Sondheim. She was only using that as an excuse. She thought she was doing me a favor."

I blink. "I don't get it."

"For a smart person, you're pretty dumb, aren't you? I didn't want you to come here, but I *did* want you to ask me out," Kendele huffs. With any other girl, it wouldn't have sounded so feminine. "Honestly, you must be the most oblivious boy I've ever met. I flirted with you, I picked you for my lab partner, and you barely give me a second glance in class. I invite you to a movie earlier today and you blow me off. I was waiting for you to take the hint, but…"

"You were asking me out?" Kendele Baker wants to ask me out? I'm aware of my mouth hanging open, and it takes a good minute to weld it back shut. "Why?"

Kendele giggles. "Why? I don't know. You're different from all the other guys. I know that sounds so clichéd, but you really are." She leans toward me. "I mean, other than being such a hopeless, insensitive, inconsiderate…"

We're inches apart, and she smells good, a mix of perfume and mint. I rally one last time. "What about Armstrong?"

"He wishes he could, but I'm not interested. I turned him down earlier because *I'm* not oblivious." She shifts closer. "Was I wrong?" she whispers. "You don't like me at all? You've never thought about it?"

I wish I could say I wanted to reject her advances. Or that she isn't right.

I'm not aware she's already on me until I feel her kissing me. Her lips are soft against my mouth—and sweet. She's obviously done this before. I haven't. I'm nervous it might show.

My hands settle behind her back—more from a lack of anywhere else to put them than anything else—while she presses against my chest and lets out a little sigh.

"Was this your first kiss?" she teases when we both come up for air.

That is such a typical Kendele question. And it's typical Kendele challenge, which I can't resist. I shut her up by kissing her again, quick and hard, relying on instinct. She's breathing hard when we end it, her thin veneer of coyness giving way.

"The answer is yes." My voice is a rough parody of how I usually sound, and I nearly lose my ability to speak completely at her next suggestion.

"Would you like this to be the first of many things we can do tonight?"

"You slumming in Chinatown now, Kendele?" someone catcalls from across the room.

THE SUFFERING

"I'm Japanese," I mumble.

"Shut up," Kendele says, for both me and the heckler's benefit, and kisses me again.

Then the lights go out.

I sit up, dislodging Kendele in my surprise. Yelps and startled laughter drift across the room, along with a few curses as people stumble in the dark. I look out the nearest window. From the streetlights and the glow from the other residences, McNeil's seems to be the only house affected.

"Fuse must have blown," McNeil's voice growls from somewhere. "Damn contractors."

"What's happening?" Kendele asks. I start to shake my head before remembering she can't see me. I hunt through my pockets, fishing out a penlight I always keep with me in case of emergency.

"I don't know." I flip on the light. Someone has found a couple more flashlights, and several people are using their cell phones for light, splaying the beams across the room. "Looks like it—"

A heavy thump sounds from upstairs, and a few people cry out. Nervous chuckling resumes but is silenced when the screams start up again, this time in fear.

Flashlights are trained on the staircase, when two people in states of undress come running down. Fletch Graham and someone I assume is his girlfriend clutch blankets and, in Graham's case, a strategically placed pillow. The girl is still screeching her lungs out.

"There's somebody upstairs!" she wails.

"What the hell are you talking about?" Saunders snaps.

55

Graham's face is pale in the beams of the flashlights. "There was something in the room, man. The lights went out, then there was someone crawling and groaning on the ceiling. Scared the shit out of me…!"

I don't need to wait for the rest of their explanations. I pull gently away from Kendele. "Wait here," I tell her and then brush past the shivering couple to run upstairs.

It's easy enough to track which room the couple bolted out of. Graham's pants trailing into the hallway where he dropped them are practically an arrow.

"Okiku," I hiss as I step in. "I know you can hear me. What was that about?"

She doesn't respond. My impatience mounts, but I can do very little about it because McNeil and some of the other guys appear behind me, scanning the room for signs of an intruder. I step to one side and let them search, knowing they'll find nothing.

"Doesn't look like there's anyone here," McNeil finally says in disgust. "What a wuss."

The tension in the air disappears. The other boys depart, laughing with each other, eager to roast their teammate for his cowardice.

"He better pay for my sheets too," McNeil mutters, still irritated, scooping up the offending covers and dumping them back onto the bed.

As he does, I see Okiku, standing stock-still on the ceiling, staring at McNeil with that look. I can feel her tense, can feel the darkness spiraling out of her, and the *hunger*

hungry want kill
kill him pleasures kill
take him sweet blood is sweet hunger kill kill KILL
KILL KILLKILLKILLKILLKILLKILLKILLKILLKILL

closing in around us, around the jock.

She gurgles.

"No!" I jump between her and the boy before Okiku can spring, and by the time McNeil turns back to me, she's gone.

"What's wrong with you?"

I grab the first thing I can reach—an antique picture frame from a dresser. "You nearly knocked it over," I tell him. He's nowhere near the frame, but in the dark, it would be hard for him to tell for sure. "Don't want to scare everyone downstairs."

The boy laughs. "Yeah, good point. You're all right, Halloway." He claps me on the back and grins."

He hurt them.

"What?"

Okiku's standing beside me before McNeil can take another step out of the room, and her face is terrifying to behold.

He *hurt them.*

"You say something, Halloway?" The jock turns around just as Okiku steps back into me.

It's true: Okiku can access every thought in my head. But she respects my privacy enough not to. The same holds true for me and her thoughts, but I avoid them. Her memories might drive me permanently insane.

Okiku's also strong enough to discern the thoughts of most ordinary people, to draw out their memories with just one glance. It's how she knows things.

There are many good reasons why she doesn't share them with me.

This is one of those rare times where she removes that filter between us—

drunken little bitch froth

mine hate spewing lust sweat

mine

you deserve it filth

rage ask for it

ask for it whore

filth filth filth FILTH FILTH FILTH

The blurry tangle of booze and skin is almost too much for me to handle. Okiku mercifully shields her thoughts from mine, and the relief is instant. When I come to, I'm lying on the floor and don't even recall falling over.

I can make out McNeil's shadow looming over me, and I shove his hand away, angry, when he tries to help me stand.

"Jesus, Halloway. What's wrong with you?"

"Did you rape them?"

"Huh?"

"Marjorie Summers. Abby Thorpe. Isabella Santiago." I saw them all in my brief exchange with Okiku, the things she'd seen McNeil do to them. Winning their trust, plying them with alcohol, taking advantage of their drunkenness. Taunting them to find anyone who'd believed them, secure in the knowledge that no one would.

There's a sick little psychopath lying underneath that golden boy image of his, and for all my experience with serial killers, even I had the wool pulled over my eyes. I now understand Okiku's hatred every time McNeil wanders into her vicinity, and part of the hate now festers inside me. I want to scrub my eyes from the inside out.

And the expression on those girls' faces. I've seen that same look on all the ghosts Okiku saved.

"Trish Seyfried. She's next, isn't she?"

McNeil hasn't gone as far as he had with the others, but he's been harassing her. Cornering her in the girls' bathroom. Shoving his hand up her skirt when Sondheim's not around. Telling her it's her fault for dressing provocatively. He's no longer taking the time to win her over like he had the previous girls, which tells me his violence is escalating quickly. From what I've seen of his mind, I can no longer doubt his intent.

The way Trish jumped from McNeil's touch when he reached for the beer, her obvious unease when he's around…she's frightened.

There's only one reason why Okiku would single him out.

Even in the darkness I can make out his smile. His voice is almost patronizing, convinced he can persuade me to believe otherwise. "Who's been telling you those lies? One of those girls? They can't prove anything. The way they dress all the time, it's like they're asking for it anyw—"

My fist connects with his nose, muffling the rest of his words, but I hadn't taken into account that he is made of granite. I step back, flexing my hand, quite happy to risk a little more pain if I can throw another hit. For his part, McNeil looks more shocked than hurt.

Why do I hunt down these assholes? Because I was born three hundred years too late to get revenge on the man who'd killed Okiku.

Because like hell I'm angry.

"I know what you've done to them," I snarl. "If I have to make it my life's work, I will find all the evidence I need to see that you serve time for every girl you've hurt and thrown away. Count on it."

The couple hadn't bothered to draw back the curtains. From what little light comes in from outside, I see the smile freeze on McNeil's face. His mouth curls into a cruel snarl.

You never really know how much of a mask someone wears until they peel it off.

Strip off the good looks and the confidence, and underneath that layer of skin there's a monster lurking inside Keren McNeil, one he hides from everyone else.

A six-foot-tall, one-hundred-ninety-pound quarterback versus a lean Japanese kid barely pushing one forty-five? Not much of a contest and not something I'd considered when I threw the first punch. McNeil's swing catches me right in the stomach, and I'm on the ground before I know what's going on. I dimly hear yelling, but I'm having trouble hearing, as if sounds are coming out of second-rate speakers with a cheap bass. Pain blooms along my sides, and I realize in between the spurts of hurt that McNeil is kicking me, so I put my hands out to block him.

McNeil is roaring at me too, but my mind doesn't process the words. I don't need to hear them to know what he's shouting.

And then the onslaught stops.

I crack open an eye to find McNeil staring over me. He's no longer angry. Quite the opposite; he looks like he's about to wet his pants. His eyes bug out of his head, his mouth open in stark terror at something no one can see but him.

And me.

Okiku shuffles toward him in her full diabolical glory. Her hair hangs low, and she is making soft, gurgling sounds at the base of her throat. This is her death rattle—the last sound she made before she died and the last sound her prey hears before they do.

"No, Okiku," I croak out, but she doesn't listen. When she gets worked up like this, she never does. I try to get up again, but my ribs protest my movement and I double over, trying to will more air into my lungs.

And then I can feel Kendele there, hugging me tightly. "You're an idiot," I hear her whisper hoarsely.

McNeil had fled. Okiku is nowhere to be seen, and I'm worried about what she might do if left to her own devices. I'm in no condition to go after her, and my hope is to get out of here, at a farther distance from McNeil than she can stray from our bond.

"Can you get up?"

"Barely." There's a crowd of people who've gathered at some

point during my ass-kicking, though no one but Kendele bothers to help. With her support, I get back on my feet and reject her worried offers to bring me to a nearby hospital.

"I'll be all right. I don't think anything's broken, and I, ha, still have all my teeth."

"Don't you dare treat this like a joke!" Kendele looks on the verge of crying.

"Sorry. I have to get out of here, Kendele."

"What do you mean? We need to get you medical—"

"I have to get out of here!" I'm trying hard not to panic. "McNeil's life depends on me getting the hell out of here as fast as possible. The farther away I am, the better. It's important, Kendele."

She relents at the distress in my voice. "Fine. But I'm going with you then. This party's outlived its fun anyway."

McNeil's blows turn out to be less painful when I'm standing, and I'm able to totter down the stairs with little assistance and make it to my car without any other interference. Once Kendele slides into position beside me, I gun the engine, taking one last look back at the dark house. There's still no sign of McNeil.

What worries me is that there's no sign of Okiku either.

CHAPTER FIVE

THE DATE

"I'm not going home," Kendele says the instant the car is out of the McNeils' driveway. "And I want you to see a doctor."

"You're not my mother, Kendele." I feel like a herd of cows has been stampeding the flamenco somewhere between my fourth and fifth ribs, but I keep my driving steady. "And it's not like she had much say for most of my life either."

"Tark, anyone with a brain can see that you're hurt. You have to at least make sure nothing's broken. Are you seeing double? Is there anything you can't move?"

"I'm fine, Kendele. I've been in enough fights to know the difference between getting beat up and getting a pancreas kicked in."

She crosses her arms, assessing me. "I suppose," she concedes, although reluctantly. "So typical of you men not to want any help. What did you do to make McNeil punch you anyway?"

"I punched him."

She stares. "You punched McNeil? Tark, you're crazy! Whatever possessed you to do that?"

"Did Trish ever tell you that McNeil's been harassing her?" We stop at a red light, and I turn to face her. Okiku is still nowhere in sight.

"What do you mean?" The expression on her face tells me all I need to know. "What are you talking about? What did Trish say?"

I set my jaw. "Never mind." If Trish hasn't told her, then it isn't my place to, though it may be too late to close that particular box. "Look, let's just forget about it."

"Easier said than done," Kendele says, but to my surprise, she's quick to change the subject. "Look, whatever it was, I'm sure you had good reason to punch him. If you don't want to tell me right now, that's fine. But I want something in return."

"And what's that?" I ask, suddenly wary.

"I was serious when I said I didn't want to go home just yet. If you're as uninjured as you claim to be, then we should have time to grab something to eat first, right?"

I open my mouth. For the first time in my life, I can't think of anything witty to say, so I close my mouth again. "Are you...asking me out?"

She flashes a triumphant grin. "*Now* you finally get it."

***

I probably wouldn't have chosen a food truck for a first date, but it's late, most of the restaurants of choice are closed or closing, and I didn't want to fall back on someplace trite like Denny's or

Applebee's. Kendele admits that she's never had pho before, so I drive us over to the corner of Twentieth and L Street, where one of my favorite food trucks—easily noticeable by its punk decor—is stationed.

Okiku's absence worries me though. I keep an eye on the rear-view mirror, expecting her to appear at any moment, and my nervousness increases with every minute that goes by.

It's probably nothing. Okiku knows never to stray too far, and the lack of other spirits in the area trying to haunt me seems to imply that she's nearby, even if I can't see her. Besides, if anything happened back at McNeil's, I'm sure Trish would have contacted Kendele about it by now.

"This is amazing," Kendele says and slurps happily at her bowl.

She doesn't seem to mind the informality of it all. Pho Junkies doesn't offer much variety—their menu consists mostly of either Vietnamese noodle soup or rolls—but I've sampled practically everything and it's all good.

Kendele chose a steak pho. Being less discriminatory about what I put in my mouth, I opted for the "all the meats" selection. "I've never eaten at a food truck before," she confesses as I sit beside her on a small ledge along the sidewalk, placing a plate of shrimp rolls between us. "And this is really good. How did you learn about this?"

"You drive around an area enough times, you find out all these hidden culinary gems. Remind me to treat you to a lobster roll at the Red Hook next time."

The instant the words leave my mouth, I feel like kicking myself. It sounds presumptuous to think there would actually *be* a next time. I make up for the lapse by taking a swift slurp at my own bowl, nearly burning my tongue in the process. At least the pain in my ribs is going away. Fortunately, McNeil was too enraged to think about going for my face or my genitals—and just hit the places where the bruises will be easy enough to hide, easy enough to heal.

Kendele only laughs. "Oh really? So you're telling me you like prowling the city late at night, on the hunt for the best food bargains in the city? You don't happen to run a food blog by any chance?"

"Nothing that requires me to actually do work." I'm starting to relax. She's obviously trying to avoid talking about the incident, and I don't want to ruin the ongoing moment between us either.

Some instinct makes me look up from my soup to where several folks are still in line at the truck.

Okiku wanders through the crowd, silently counting the people as she passes. A part of me relaxes upon seeing her; another part freezes up.

I've never gone on a real date since Okiku took up lodgings with me—or, admittedly, at any point before that. I'm not sure how she's going to react to Kendele, but she avoids looking my way, concentrating more on a group of teens clamoring for spring rolls than on us.

"Hello? You still there, Halloway?" It takes me a second to see the hand Kendele is waving in front of my face. "You spaced out there for a second. Am I boring?"

"No!" That comes out higher in pitch than I had intended. "I mean, no. I'm sorry. A lot of things happened today that I wasn't really prepared for."

"Tell me about it." Kendele wriggles closer, nearly dislodging the plate of rolls between us. "But only if you want to."

I'm not used to Kendele being so tactful, and from the way she's fidgeting, I assume she isn't either. I say, "Hypothetically—if you were in a situation where you had to do something kind of illegal, knowing it would help put someone away who deserves it, would you?"

She chews thoughtfully on a bean sprout. "I guess that would depend on what's involved. You mean like killing him? Hypothetically speaking."

I definitely don't want to go into more detail. "Or maybe just illegally detaining him and stuff. It would be a really bad idea to let this person loose."

"How bad of an idea?"

"Kicking-Hitler-out-of-art-school bad. Hypothetically speaking, of course."

"A poorly drawn painting sounds better than a potential holocaust. But what does this have to do with everything that just happened?"

I take a deep breath. "I seriously think McNeil's been taking advantage of girls in school, Kendele."

"Including Trish? Was that why you mentioned her before?"

I was hoping she wouldn't be that perceptive. "Well…yeah. And the thought of him getting away with all of that makes my blood boil."

"Taking advantage of them? How so?"

"I'm thinking sexual assault. Not with Trish yet, but I think she's next. I confronted him about it."

Kendele eyes me through the steam rising from her bowl. "Did he admit to this? Was that why you punched him? Do you have any proof you could show to the authorities?"

I couldn't exactly introduce Okiku into evidence—but I'm glad Kendele's not dismissing my claims out of hand. "It didn't take much to fill in the blanks. But it's not the kind of confession that would hold up in court. I've had enough experience with this sort of thing to know."

"I feel like there's a lot more to this than you're telling me."

I watch Okiku lift her head and close her eyes and spin slowly in a circle, like she does when she's deep in thought.

I opt for the closest thing to the truth that I can tell Kendele.

"There's someone I'm very close to." I clarify again, and Kendele looks at me, surprised. "She's the most selfless person I've ever met, and she's stuck her neck out for me on more than one occasion. She's had a rough life, and assholes like McNeil make her think that she's not worth saving. So no, I don't regret punching him. If anything, I wished I'd punched him harder."

"She must be very important to you."

Okiku opens her eyes, her attention suddenly focused on a small errant firefly clumsily weaving its way through the air above us, mistaking the glare of a streetlight for a potential mate. She reaches an arm up, but the glowing orb escapes her outstretched fingers. It bobs higher, into the trees overhead, and she smiles at its antics. It's an odd expression to see on her pale, withered face. I smile too, despite myself.

"Yeah. She's the most important person in my life right now," I say. "I almost think I would kill for her if I had to. I mean, hypothetically speaking," I add, realizing how much I'm giving away.

Kendele doesn't seem to notice. Her own smile looks a little sad. "Do you love her?"

"Of course. I already said she was important to me."

"That's not what I meant. Are you in love with her?"

"What?" That throws me off guard. I take my eyes away from Okiku to gape at Kendele. I'd never really thought of it like that, and I don't know what to say. Sure, I care for Okiku, and she could be ridiculously pretty when she wants to be. But there's also the matter of her being a three-hundred-year-old ghost, and that's not a quality one usually looks for in the ideal girlfriend. "It's…I don't know. It's a lot more complicated than just that."

Kendele shakes her head. "You either love her or you don't, Halloway. How hard is it to figure out? And people think *women* are difficult to understand." But my answer seems to improve her mood, and she attacks her pho with newfound gusto. My eyes search the crowd again, but Okiku's disappeared.

Kendele expertly steers the subject to lighter matters, and by the time we finish our meal, it's nearly midnight.

She slides back into the passenger seat of my car with a small sigh of satisfaction. "That was nice. You know, I've wanted to ride in this car since the first time I saw it."

"Was that why you volunteered to be my lab partner?" I edge the Bimmer out into the street.

"No, I volunteered because I wanted to see if you kissed as good as you look."

I keep my eyes on the road, but I'm sure the tips of my ears are burning bright enough to create my own headlights. I sense movement behind me and glance in my mirror to see Okiku sitting calmly in the backseat of the car, watching Kendele with peculiar detachment.

Crap. My earlier worries resurface. I've never driven a girl home before—never had another girl ride in my car even—and I'm not sure how Okiku's going to react.

"Trish was all for me just walking up and planting one on you before you could get away, but I wasn't sure you'd appreciate that."

Between Okiku and the current topic of conversation, I'm not sure how I'm going to get home without transforming into a riot of nerves. "Thanks for being considerate," I mumble.

"I am going to talk to Trish about this though. About what you told me. On one hand, I'm mad that she didn't trust me enough to tell me, and on the other, I feel like I'm a bad friend for not figuring it out sooner."

"I probably shouldn't have told you. It wasn't my place to."

"No, I'm glad you did. I'm glad we left the party early. I'm not glad McNeil punched you, obviously. But I might never have known that Trish needed help, and you might still be oblivious." She giggles when I turn red. "We were doing nicely until the power went out. Wasn't that weird by the way? I've been over there several times, and that's never happened before."

I couldn't resist. "With Trish or with someone else?"

She smiles at me. "You're so cute when you're trying not to be jealous. Yes, with Trish. I'm not the type to hook up with random guys at parties—or anywhere else. If you must know, you're the first guy I've thrown myself at, but that's because you're so dense."

"Thanks. I think."

"I'll tell people you made the first move if you want. I've got a reputation to maintain."

"Why do you hang around with those jerks anyway?" I can't keep from asking.

Kendele makes a face. "I guess it's mainly because of Trish—and also because I hang out with the other cheerleaders, and they tend to hang out with the jocks. They're harmless enough from what I've seen of them."

"You know, not many other people would have believed what I said about McNeil. You're a lot more understanding than I thought you would be. Thanks for that."

"I never had you pegged as a liar, Tark. It's one of the things I like about you."

"I'm not exactly the best catch at school." It sounds like I'm trying to fish for compliments, but Kendele could have snagged any other guy in school—and definitely one without my stellar reputation.

She shrugs. "I'm not sure why to be honest. But sometimes, I feel that you actually *like* and even encourage people to say odd things about you. Because it makes it easier for you to push people away. And in your own way, I think you're a bit dangerous."

"Me?" I ask, disbelieving. "Kendele, a jock just almost knocked me out with one punch."

"I think you could have done worse to McNeil if you really wanted to, but you held back. You're not the type of guy to show off, because you don't care what other people think about you. I kinda like that."

I stay silent, a little shaken that she's figured me out so well. We pull up by her house, and she hops out.

"You know all this from being my lab partner?" I ask.

"*And* being tutored by you. Don't forget that. Incidentally," she adds, making her way to my side of the car, "you were supposed to ask me if I was right."

"If you were right about what?"

"About you kissing as good as you look." She bends to peck me on the lips. "Very dense," she says, laughing, before skipping up her driveway and letting herself inside. I stare stupidly after her before remembering that I am not alone in the car. I clear my throat several times before I find my voice again.

"Okiku?" She stares at me with the strangest expression, looking almost perplexed. I pat the passenger seat and she complies, drifting over, and I drive back to the intersection.

I'm not entirely sure how to explain Kendele to her—I don't even know how to explain Kendele to myself—but Okiku doesn't express any interest, so I decide to let it pass for now. In fact, she's the one who takes the initiative and starts talking after we stop at a red light.

"He is one of them."

"What?" That throws me off for a bit. I figured she wanted to tackle the Kendele issue first.

"The boy with the brown hair. The boy with the dead eyes. He is one of *them*."

"Wait. Being a serial rapist is one thing, but you can't tell me that McNeil is planning to kill—"

"One of *them*." She makes the statement the way a judge would pass a death sentence.

"Okiku, there's no way McNeil has ever killed anyone. People would know. I would have seen him covered in those—"

"He has not. But he will."

"What makes you so sure?"

"I know. He feels like the others."

Sometimes Okiku's ambiguity can be irritating. "Okiku, if he hasn't killed anyone, you can't just go and do whatever you want with him. There are rules."

"Not my rules."

"Look—I know he's done some terrible things. But we agreed to go after the people the law can't touch, remember? Believe me, I want McNeil to pay too. But we can't do it your way. We have to go through the law first."

"Not my rules."

"I forbid you to do this, all right? You can't—" I break off. Okiku is looking at me with real anger sparking out of her dark eyes, and the occupants of the car next to us are looking at me, puzzled at why I am conducting an impassioned argument with my car seat. "We'll talk later," I finally add as the light turns green.

We don't talk later. Okiku is silent all the way home and disappears shortly after I enter the house. She's never been angry at me before, but I suppose there's a first time for everything.

I can feel Okiku somewhere above me when I enter my room, invisible but—I suspect—sulking. I call out to her, but she doesn't answer, and I sigh. I feel too exhausted to attempt reconciliation.

Maybe tomorrow when the world doesn't feel like it's steamrolling over my back, I decide, crawling into bed. When that frozen look on Okiku's face, Kendele's kisses, and that little girl crying out for her father finally stop preying on my mind.

***

The irony is that the rest of the weekend passes smoothly.

I go to the game with Dad. We stomp our feet, jump out of our chairs, and holler 'til our voices grow hoarse. Dad doesn't notice anything amiss with me, and I'm glad. I've squirreled away secrets for years, too many for a father to forgive.

I spend the rest of Sunday puttering around the house, mostly in front of my laptop, doing all the homework I've been putting off and telling myself that I won't have to cram like this again until college starts in the fall.

Okiku keeps her silence. I call out to her when Dad isn't around to hear, trying to entice her to listen, but in the end, I'm left baffled by her stillness.

Sunday evening, I receive a call from Kendele. Not entirely sure if she is going to ask me out again, I answer, nervousness hiding underneath a thin veneer of bravado.

"If you're planning on slumming it with me at the food truck, Kendele, I really think that you should—"

Kendele's frantic voice disabuses me of that assumption. "Tark, I'm at McNeil's. Something's happened. I think you better get here as soon as you can."

The jock has been missing since Friday night. Everyone thought he'd stomped off to sulk, but he was supposed to meet his parents at the airport the next day, and they grew frantic when he didn't show up. They couldn't file a missing person report until at least twenty-four hours had passed, so they and some members of the football team had started searching the neighborhood. It was Sondheim who found him inside a small, abandoned shed on an overgrown lot only two blocks from McNeil's house. I learned that most of the jocks hung out there some weekends, smoking where their coaches couldn't see.

Kendele called me fifteen minutes later.

I brush past the crowd that has gathered, brush past Kendele's next round of protests and stand in front of the shed, staring inside.

McNeil is all huddled up, curled in a fetal position with his hands over his head.

His face is bloated to twice its size and rotting, like he'd been held underwater for days.

My stomach clenches, and I suppress the urge to be sick.

His face…

It all comes back to me.

Blood splashed on the bathroom tiles.

I'm taken back two years—to when I was still in Maine and staring at Todd McKinley's head sitting on the sink, his features so twisted that his mother would never have recognized him.

Todd McKinley was the first person the masked woman of my childhood killed in an attempt to free herself from me. Today, I see him clearly, as if it's only been hours since his murder. McKinley's dead face resembles Keren McNeil's, the McNeil without his fake face of joviality or his fake face of anger, but his real face, gray and defiled and foul, his tongue hanging loosely out of his mouth like he's a rabid dog that had to be put down.

The shadow of the masked woman who haunted my nightmares for so many years fades. Now there is Okiku in her place, staring down at her creation with quiet serenity.

CHAPTER SIX

AFTERMATH

Okiku doesn't approach me until Wednesday—after the news crews with their explosive headlines have wrung as much as they can from Pembrooke High and its so-called football heroes. After Keren McNeil's body has been taken away—after reporters have deemed the pictures too disturbing for mainstream media.

After I've been called to the principal's office to give my own statement to the police officers waiting for me there. After witnesses single me out as a potential suspect because of the fight I had with McNeil that Friday night. After Kendele, Trish, and the other football players who'd seen me leave—even the guys at Pho Junkies, observant enough to recognize me from photos—provide me with the alibi the cops ask for, confirming my whereabouts at the time of the murder.

After the police grill me about the similar circumstances of another jock's death at my old high school. After I say, "You don't have to beat around the bush, Officer. I didn't kill McKinley. I didn't kill McNeil either, and at least a dozen people can attest to it. Yeah, Officer, I'm pretty unlucky that way."

After my father arrives at school, demanding to know why I'm being treated like a criminal.

Because I'm not a football jock, Dad, is the right answer. I may not have been smart enough to prevent McNeil's death, but I'm smart enough to keep my mouth shut. The hunt to find McNeil's killer is treated with such fervor that all these people clamoring for justice disgust me more than I can say.

Because nobody would ever believe that he was a scumbag.

He's not who you think he is! I want to tell them, but I know that ship has long since sailed.

Kendele asks me how I'd known McNeil could be in danger that night at the party. The police have turned to other, more promising leads—rival teams, jealous friends, spiteful ex-girlfriends.

I shrug because nobody ever believes me, because Okiku is my secret to keep. "I don't know. I just had a feeling."

"That's a pretty accurate feeling." She was with me during the time McNeil was supposed to have died, so she isn't suspicious. But she's worried.

I don't answer. I expect her to recoil, but she doesn't let go of my hand. "I believe you."

"You do?"

She blushes. "Trish told me everything. You were right. I feel stupid for not seeing it sooner, especially with the way he talked about other girls. I don't think they'll be able to do much about it now that he's dead. Trish doesn't want to say anything, and I don't think the other girls will either. But for what it's worth, I was right about you. I knew there was a reason you went to the party, which was because you suspected Keren. I just…I can't believe someone I know could do something like that."

She didn't quite hit on the right reason I was there, but it was the closest I could afford to tell her. "Everybody knows a killer," I say, "even if they don't know they do."

For the rest of the week, Dad watches me carefully, waiting to see if I'm going to break down the way I did at my last school. He insists on bringing me to a therapist, and I let him, mostly because it makes him feel better.

I'm even cheerful about it. I tell the therapist I'm all right, that I feel bad about McNeil dying, but that I can't feel guilty about something I had no control over. The therapist appears satisfied but suggests future sessions. I tell Dad I'd rather not, that I don't want to spend senior year under a microscope. A lifetime of talking to therapists has taught me the right manners to display, so he believes I'm fine, even when I don't believe that myself.

Because I don't feel bad that McNeil's dead. And that frightens me.

Okiku sits in on the therapy session, and I know she's distressed because she doesn't count anything in the room. She just stands there and stares at me with her pitted eyes, waiting for me to acknowledge her. I don't.

For the next day, I ignore her. She says nothing and waits.

***

"How did you know?" Trish asks me. There are dark circles under her eyes, and she looks tired. "About McNeil being…horrible to me? Not even Andy knows." She's accosted me in the parking lot en route to my car and refuses to leave until she has answers.

"I know the signs. I've seen them before. Don't worry about it."

"Did you curse him?"

"What?" I wasn't expecting this question.

"Like with that doll. I saw his face. I don't think anything human could have done that to his face."

I've underestimated Trish. Of everyone, she's hit the closest to the truth.

She surprises me further by drawing close and dropping a kiss on my cheek. "If it really was you," she says softly, "thank you. I promise I won't ever tell anyone. I owe you that much."

I watch her walk away, my hand pressed nervously against my cheek. I have definitely underestimated Trish.

I haven't been checking my email for the last few days, and by the time I finally work up the energy to do so, it's Friday. The first email I see, the most recent one, is from Saya. For a moment, I am alarmed, wondering if the McNeil news has reached even Japan, but Saya hates technology and thinks the Internet is some kind of worldwide conspiracy. Her letter tells me something even more frightening:

Tarquin-san, it is Saya. I am asking a friend of mine to type this for me.

Kagura once sent me your email and I am thankful I thought to keep it.

Tarquin-san, Kagura-chan's missing.

What?

I find myself on my feet without knowing I'd stood up, the chair overturned behind me. I stare at my screen in shock as the letter goes on:

> She and some Americans went into Aokigahara last Monday, and no one has seen or heard from them since. I am very worried about her. They have been searching for many days now, and police from America have already been alerted. If you know anything about Kagura or this American film crew, please let us know immediately.

Underneath is a small postscript, no doubt added by Saya's friend:

> Please if you can come to help, come quickly. Saya is very frantic.

No. No, no, no.

I scroll though my email and see that Kagura sent me a reply a few days before that I have not read. Heart pounding, I click on the link:

> I suppose it would do no harm to show these hunters around. Aitou village has been lost for so long that it is doubtful we will find it even if we spend weeks searching Aokigahara. As strange as it sounds, the more I look through my father's research,

the more I am intrigued by what I learn. He's been gone for some years, but I almost feel like he is close by, helping me.

I am sending you a photo of the crew—the autographs you asked for are safely with me, but you must come here to get them!

I click on the attachment and wait for the photo to finish loading. I asked for the autograph as a joke more than from any real interest in the crew, but Kagura had taken my request literally.

In the photo, Kagura is standing beside the ghost-hunter crew. There are, I count, seven of them in total, posing for the picture.

At least, I assume this is the crew, because five of their heads are missing.

The only ones with theirs intact are one of the ghost hunters and Kagura herself. They look back at me with distorted faces, nearly unrecognizable and terribly contorted, as if their faces had been rendered in soluble paint and left out in the rain. Only Kagura's *haori* tells me that it's her in the picture.

Other than the lack of heads, nothing is out of place in the photo. Amid the trees, I can make out what is probably a temple, with the curved roofs common in Japan's traditional architecture. Further in the distance, I can see what I think is Mount Fuji. Otherwise, there's only foliage.

I peer closer at the screen, trying to find something, anything, that might give me a clue. "What did you get yourself into, Kagura?" I whisper, acknowledging the hypocrisy of my words. "Where are you? Damn it, couldn't you at least have waited until we got there to protect you like you've always protected us?" I focus my attention on Kagura's face, trying to envision what her expression might have been before something twisted her features.

As I do, something moves behind Kagura.

It opens its eyes and looks at me.

I leap back, nearly tripping over the fallen chair in my haste.

Crap, crap, crap, *crap*.

"It wanders," Okiku says quietly. She is standing beside me with her hands folded in front of her and her head bent.

"What…what is this?"

"A spirit. It is not happy. Something has happened to Kagura."

I swallow. "She's…they're not dead, are they?"

"I do not know. But she lingers close to the spirit world."

"I have to find her." The shadow has retreated behind Kagura. It was a black silhouette with no clear form or shape, but I know instinctively that it's a woman. And that it has Kagura.

And that it wants to play.

I stare hard at the photo for a long time, but the creature does not reappear.

"If Kagura's in trouble… I owe Kagura a *lot*, Ki. I practically ruined her career, forced her to relocate… Obaasan and Amaya died because of me. I need to know what's going on. If this…*thing* has her, then the police won't be much help."

"Are you still angry at me?" Okiku whispers.

I glance back at her. Her face is lowered. I sigh.

"Okiku." I abandon the laptop for the moment to sit on the bed, patting at the empty space beside me. "Come here."

She complies, eyes still downcast. Once she's within reach, I tilt her chin up and make her look back at me. Her expression gives nothing away, but I can feel the unease rolling inside her. For all her bloodthirsty antipathy, Okiku is just a girl who never really got the chance to be one.

"When we're angry at each other, we have to sit down and talk it over. If we don't, our hurt will stay between us and cause us pain when we least expect it. It's normal to sometimes be angry at me, in the same way it is normal for me to sometimes be angry at you. But that doesn't mean I hate you or anything close to it. Do you understand?"

She doesn't say anything, but her eyes tell me she does.

"Good. Now we're going to talk like I promised we would. I'll start first, all right?" I take a deep breath. "I was angry at you because you killed that boy after I asked you not to. It's...it's not right. You can't punish someone for something he hasn't done yet."

"He hurt many girls."

"That isn't enough to kill him. Jailed for as long as possible? Yes. But not killed."

"I cannot prevent his crimes if I let him live. His desires twist the longer he remains unpunished. He will kill next time."

"You know the rules, Okiku. You can't kill him for *thinking* about committing a murder. I mean, had you noticed anything odd about him before?"

"The girls opened something inside him. Violence excited him after that. He would do it again, and he would be worse each time."

"People think about murdering people all the time, and they never do."

"He wished to kill you."

I stop. "Me?"

"I saw it, after you hit him. He would kill you, even with witnesses. Had he been stopped that night, he would have found you alone someday and beaten you until you could no longer move. I saw this in his head. I refused to wait for him to act on his urges." Okiku closes her eyes. "I am sorry that I did not listen. But he was going to kill you."

I am silent for a few minutes. If Okiku says McNeil was going to kill me, then McNeil was going to kill me. Knowing this makes me feel all the more terrible that I haven't been nice to her the last couple of days.

"Okiku, I'm sorry. But you still need to tell me before you act—even when someone wants to kick my ass. I feel bad enough about this whole mess—"

"But you do not feel bad he is dead."

"That's not the point! It doesn't matter whether I feel bad about it or not. It isn't right! That's why we only do this to murderers that the legal system can't touch. If you're going to run around killing people you just don't like, then what makes you any different from—"

I blurt out the words before thinking my way through them, and immediately I clamp my mouth shut. But the problem with a being having access to my thoughts is that Okiku is quick to pick up on what I don't say. Her eyes narrow.

"I am nothing like *her*."

"I didn't mean to insinuate that you—"

"*I am nothing like her*." She rises from the bed. Before I can stop her, she disappears into the wall, leaving me half rising from my seat, hand reaching out to where she was moments before.

I groan. *You've done it this time, Halloway.*

My laptop chooses this moment to sing, announcing an incoming video call. My relief fades when I realize who is on the other end.

"What the hell is going on over there?" Callie's face fills the screen, and I wince. I shouldn't have been surprised. My cousin knows how Okiku's victims look afterward. "Tark! Is this Okiku's doing? Is Okiku there? Whatever possessed you to make such a public—"

"Before you bust my ass about it, Callie, this was all an accident." I lower my voice, hastily plugging in my earphones before she becomes too vocal. "He was attacking me, and Okiku…took some steps, okay?"

"'Took some steps' is an understatement. Tell me everything," Callie commands. "I want to know what the news hasn't been saying."

It doesn't take long for me to relay the details, and Callie calms down in the interim, her initial fury turning into concern. "Oh, Tark," she says, sighing.

"Don't you 'Oh, Tark' me, Callie. What else could I have done?"

"*Not* punch that boy, for starters. But given the circumstances,

I can't really blame you for that, can I?" She pauses. "How's Uncle Doug holding up?"

"I'm not a suspect or anything, so he's fine. He took me to a shrink again, but that's his answer whenever he thinks something's wrong with me." I take a deep breath. "Callie, would you think less of me if I said I don't feel bad at all?"

"What do you mean?"

"I don't care that the guy's dead. Even if I'm to blame for it. Do you think I've been doing this so long that I'm starting to be numb to stuff like this?"

"What you really mean to say is, if Okiku's starting to rub off on you, right?"

I nod. Callie always did know me well.

"I may be suspicious of her, but Okiku did save your life—and mine. I can't ever repay her for that, so the least I can do is try to understand her. It's your arrangement that I don't like. If she didn't need to drag you along with her each time she went out hunting, I'd be more supportive. I think you and Okiku need to sit down and have a real heart-to-heart."

I snort. "Maybe you should be my shrink. But there's another problem, Callie."

"Another one? Are you trying to set some kind of world record?"

"Kagura's missing."

Silence on her end. Callie stares at me from the screen, chewing on her lower lip as she processes the announcement.

"She and some people from that *Ghost Haunts* show were

investigating some village near Mount Fuji, and nobody can find them. I want to help search for her. There's something in those forests, and I know Okiku and I can figure out what it is."

"Tark, you've barely squeaked out of trouble. Now you're proposing we go look for a strange village that may or may not exist? At a place we've never been to?"

"What can I do?" I demand. "I can't just sit here and pretend everything's fine. I'm not telling Dad. He'd stop me from going. I know you're looking forward to our hot springs trip, so I understand if you don't want to get involved."

"Don't be ridiculous. Of course I want to help find Kagura, brat. But—are you sure? Uncle Doug doesn't mind us leaving so soon after everything that's happened?"

"Actually, Dad thinks you're a treasure. Why do you think he always asks you to tag along on these trips? He still feels guilty about what happened in Mutsu." Callie was severely injured two years ago in Aomori from an unexpected earthquake at the shrine we were visiting. At least, that is what we told my father.

"We don't know if we can help Kagura from Japan any more than if you stayed in Washington and me in Boston." Callie knows and is less eager about my habit of acquiring dolls than Kagura was. "But you're going to do it anyway no matter what, right?"

"I owe Kagura my life, Callie."

She sighs. "I know. And I owe her mine. I want to help too."

"Are you grumpy because you're leaving your boyfriend for

a few days? I don't think Dad's going to pay for Trevor to come along by the way. You'd have to smuggle him in your suitcase."

Callie sticks her tongue out at me. When we finally log off, I lean back against my chair, resuming my study of Kagura's strange photo. "Time to return the favor, Kagura-chan," I tell it.

I reach out one last time to Okiku, but she senses me and shies away, retreating. I sigh and decide not to push it, and I head to bed.

I'm not sure at what point during the night Okiku comes back, but I wake to find her sitting beside me, watching me with a worried look on her face. It's an expression I've never seen her wear before.

"Okiku," I whisper. This time, she does not move away. My hand finds hers and envelops it tightly.

Her features are softer now. The gash of her mouth is tempered, the skin of her eyes no longer taut. I squeeze her hand and offer her my apology: "Hey. Wanna go to the creek?"

***

We're not supposed to be at Rock Creek Park at this time of night. The area is closed to visitors until dawn, and I'd get my ass kicked if I was found loitering. I suspect it's Okiku's influence that's always ensured I never get caught.

We camp out at our favorite spot—a small clearing with a stream that eventually leads into the Potomac River some miles out. It's deep enough in the thicket that we're not visible to roving rangers but not so dense that I'd get lost without my incorporeal companion. I bring a couple of sandwiches in case Ki's hungry, though she never is.

We never come here for the picnics anyway. We come here for the fireflies.

You don't usually get large swarms of them in DC, but there's something about Okiku that they love and that brings them out in droves. They never show until we're settled in, and then they come creeping out in ones and twos—and then soon enough, there are small clouds made up of fireflies.

I have never seen anything Okiku enjoys more than being the center of these fireflies' attention. They wind through her hair, braiding into her dark tresses until she's wearing a crown of stars on her brow. When there's no one on our list to catch, this is what curbs the whispers in her head, and I'm only too happy to accommodate her.

She's always so beautiful this way.

As always, we don't need to talk. We sit and watch the fireflies flutter around Okiku, and once again my hands find hers.

She's still hurting, I can tell. We aren't quite okay yet.

But the thing about me and Okiku is that I know we will be.

CHAPTER SEVEN

CLUES

"This cannot possibly end well," Callie says.

I respond by dangling the Kewpie doll in her direction. Kagura was quick to explain to me how the *ningyō* dolls often used in the *miko*'s rituals are more a matter of aesthetics and formal tradition rather than of necessity. Any doll will do as long as it's got all its body parts intact.

"You scared of this little thing?" Two years ago, my level of freak-out would have surpassed Callie's. "I thought you girls loved playing with dolls."

"Not dolls with evil spirits trapped inside." Callie swallows. She arrived in Washington, DC, the day before, and we'll be leaving for Japan tomorrow. "This cannot possibly end well," she says again.

"Shush."

Dad is working late, so we're going out for burgers—right after a quick detour to the nearby cemetery. Callie keeps fidgeting because she's not used to the smell and the graves, but I've done this before. "It won't be long now. She always comes like clockwork."

Several minutes roll by, and she appears soon enough. A little old lady materializes out of thin air, hobbling down the road. I wait for her to stop beside a grave several feet from where we're hiding. She looks down at the tombstone with a peculiar expression on her face, which I've learned from experience is just the calm before the storm.

"I don't see anything," Callie whispers. She hasn't seen anything for years, but she still insists on coming along on each hunt I make while she's visiting, as if her presence can deter horrible things from happening.

"Shush." Normally, I would leave incorporeal elderly ladies alone, choosing to target the spirits that have real malice in them. But this one is different.

Sure enough, the earsplitting howls start as the old woman begins venting her anger at the tomb's occupant. I cover my ears and groan. Her unearthly screams are the reason I found her in the first place.

"Tark? What's wrong?"

"*Shush*." I creep out and play the file I'd recorded on my cell phone. Sonorous, melodic chants fill the air. I can't master all the mantras Kagura and the other *mikos* have learned since their novitiate days, but I've found playing a recording of the hymns they sing works just as well. It doesn't matter that they're Buddhist chants and the old lady's clearly an angry, white American. Kagura says it's the energy that flows through the song that makes all the difference.

The old woman turns her bulging black eyes to me and shrieks. The chants wrap around her transparent form, making her immobile and helpless. I raise the Kewpie doll, and like a magnet, she is pulled toward it, heaping endless insults at me even as she struggles against the unseen tow. I reel back from the recoil as the doll sucks her in—

She was hiding underneath her kitchen table, clutching her baby tightly to her chest, as gunfire sounded through the clearing outside. She closed her eyes, mouthing wordless prayers as the toddler squirmed and screamed, the sound lost amid the roaring of cannons. Bits of wood and ash rained down from the ceiling. The whole house shuddered and still she prayed—hoping her baby would survive this battle, this war, *hoping she would survive. Anger at both the Union and the Confederation alike—*

—staggering, but Callie's hands on my shoulders help me regain my balance.

"I felt some kind of wind," she murmurs as I stop the recording. "Did it…?"

I show her the doll. Its eyes are now a rolling, endless black. I take out my knife and waste no time plunging it into the doll's small body, ending the ritual.

"Fantastic. Can we burn it now?"

"Nope."

"Why not?"

"She's over a hundred years dead. Civil War era probably, given most of the inhabitants in this graveyard. She called me a little coot."

"Did you do that Vulcan-Jedi mind-meld trick with her too?"

"First of all, I do the Vulcan-Jedi mind-meld trick with everything I trap. Secondly, you do realize Vulcans and Jedi come from two completely different movies, right?" I stuff the doll into my backpack. When we return, I'll add it to the growing pile of other similarly possessed dolls that are in my suitcase along with my clothes, toiletries, and books. The first time I made the trip to Japan with compromised dolls in tow, I actually worried if customs inspected visitors' baggage for sentience. They didn't. "Any spirit that's been around more than a hundred years is harder to get rid of, so they'll have to be burned at Obon."

Burning the dolls traditionally takes place during the Nagashi-bina Festival in early March, but few places in Japan practice this anymore, so the Obon festival works just as well. Because it takes place in July, when I'm not around, Kagura usually performs the task in my place. Just thinking about her sends another stab of worry through me.

"And how many of these hundred-year-olds do you have at the moment?"

"Eleven." There's a decided dearth of exorcists in the United States today, so ghosts have been accumulating over the years. "I've been saving this one for your arrival."

"Well, thank you *so* much. Can we leave now? That angel statue's been looking at me weird."

I spend the walk back to the car pointing out other statues that are looking at her weird, much to her irritation.

As I drive, I tell Callie about the old ghosts I'd caught this year:

the redheaded little girl I found crying by the Lincoln Memorial, the no-faced woman wandering near a small Asian grocery, an old man haunting an abandoned house three blocks down. She doesn't say much until we're seated at Denny's and halfway through our orders of country-fried steak and shrimp.

"I've been doing a lot of research about this Aokigahara Forest." Callie eyes me, nibbling at her fingernail. "Tark, it's known in Japan as a popular place for people to commit suicide. But there isn't any information about a village inside it. Are you sure about this?"

"You've been asking me that ever since you've arrived, Callie. Trust me on this one. How about a more mundane question, like 'How's school?' or 'Why are you getting more handsome every time I see you?'"

"Never." Callie slurps at a milk shake. "But I *will* ask how school's been. The police still there?"

I lower my fork and scowl at my plate. "Not much. A couple of boys are still under investigation for the murder, but I don't think the things McNeil's done will ever see the light of day. I don't think any of the girls are going to file a lawsuit against his family, especially because he's the local hero."

"How have you and Okiku been? Normally, I'd need a crowbar or a crucifix or something to keep you two apart, but I've barely seen her since I arrived."

Okiku is the only ghost Callie can see nowadays. She isn't sure why this is, but I'm assuming their shared personal ordeals may have something to do with it.

"She's still around." I can feel her inside the kitchen, counting orders and burgers.

"What about that heart-to-heart I suggested?"

"I already tried. She didn't take things too well."

"Oh?"

"It was kind of my fault."

Callie rolls her eyes. "I'm shocked. I really am. How do you get into an argument with a ghost exactly?"

"I compared her to someone else."

"A girlfriend?"

"Of course not!" But Callie catches me reddening.

"Oh ho! So there's a girl involved!" She claps her hands in glee. "Who is she? Is she cute? When do I get to meet her? *Do* I get to meet her while I'm here?"

"Kendele's not my girlfriend, and you're not meeting anyone because break's started, so there's no way you get to embarrass me in front of people."

"Ooh, so her name's *Kendele*. Did she make Okiku jealous?"

"Do you even know how ridiculous that sounds? Okiku's my…" I trail off, trying to figure out what Okiku is to me. I've never really thought about that. It's always just been something I've taken for granted. She's got her bloodlust and her unending need for vengeance—but I also know her as the young girl by the window, watching the daylight each morning. "It's complicated," I finally say, echoing what I'd told Kendele. "She's special."

"You didn't tell your girlfriend about Okiku, did you?"

"Absolutely not! And she's not my girlfriend!"

"Then what's wrong with Okiku?"

"I might have inadvertently compared her to *that* woman without meaning to."

This shuts Callie up for a minute. Finally, she exhales noisily. "Well, if you'd compared me to her, I'd be pretty pissed off too."

"Thanks," I say.

"Just trying to make you feel better."

"You're not very good at it."

Callie's smile fades. "Maybe I'm just trying to make myself feel better. I'm worried about Kagura too, Tark. I hope she's okay."

"Yeah," I say, and we fall silent for a few moments, thinking about the shrine maiden and about all we owe her for the debts we may never be able to repay. "I hope so too."

***

I meet with Kendele only once before leaving. She's hanging around the lawn the next morning, waiting for me.

"Are you stalking me now?" I ask, glancing back warily at the house to make sure Callie isn't watching.

She smirks. "You wish. I was running errands, and this is my route. And now that you're here, I wanted to see if you were okay after everything that happened last week."

"You didn't need to—but thanks."

"Wanna hang out?"

"I have a plane to catch later."

"Oh." She looks disappointed. "Where are you going?"

"Visiting friends in Japan with my cousin. It's kind of a thing we do every year."

"Maybe next time then," Kendele says, smiling at me before walking away. I watch her leave, still not sure about her motivations. I've never had any close friends, definitely no girlfriends, but she's making me rethink everything I've missed out on, making me wonder what else I may have missed.

Kendele pauses at the end of the block and turns. "This is the part where you're supposed to run after me," she calls back. "Ask me for a rain check."

"Huh?"

"Ask me for a rain check, dummy."

"Uh…how about a rain check?"

"I'll hold you to that." She laughs and turns away again. "So dense." She says that loudly, in case I couldn't hear.

I head back to the house and find Okiku studying me from the window of my room. She gives me a small smile and disappears.

***

Callie and I meet Saya at the Shizuoka Airport after a brief layover at Shanghai. It's always disorienting to see her and Kagura out of their shrine-maiden outfits. Saya wears a thick blouse and a long skirt, which exudes a much different aura than Saya in a red *hakama* and her white *haori*.

"You've gotten so tall, Tark-chan!" she exclaims, cupping my face with both her hands. "And Callie, even more beautiful now! I wish we could have met again under better circumstances."

"You are looking lovelier than ever, Saya-san," I tease. Japanese people tend to be very reserved, even with friends, but Saya surprises me by hugging me tightly, then latches on to an equally startled Callie.

She fills us in on more details as her Toyota Prius chugs through the green landscape to the small inn that Kagura runs with her elderly aunt. "She's been missing for nearly a week," Saya informs us, fingers drumming worriedly against the wheel. "Kagura's aunt, Fujiko-san, is nearly wild with anxiety. Many international news crews have arrived at Mount Fuji, and the local police are not used to this attention. The American crew that came here to film is more popular than we thought."

This is true enough. News about the inexplicable disappearances of Adams and the *Ghost Haunts* team have been coming through mainstream American media, though Kagura was never mentioned by name.

"We're going to find her, Saya-san," Callie says fiercely. "We're not leaving Japan until we do."

Saya smiles at us in the rearview mirror, though the worry continues to crease her brow. "I hope so. It is too late to join the rescue efforts at Aokigahara today, so I propose that we go to the Kamameshi Ryokan and leave for Mount Fuji in the morning. I believe Kagura's aunt would like to speak with you two first anyway."

I nod. She'd know best what's going on.

The Kamameshi Ryokan is a quaint inn offering some of Honshu's fabled hot springs. Kagura's aunt, Fujiko Kaji, is waiting for us by the entrance, looking much older than her sixty-five years. Still, the smile she bestows on us is warm and genuine.

"We are so happy to have you both here again, Tarquin-san, Callie-san," she says. "Kagura has been looking forward to your visit for weeks." The corners of her mouth turn down at the reminder that her niece is missing. The *Ghost Haunts* crew also stayed at the inn, and I know she's blaming herself for their disappearance as well.

"We're here to help as much as we can, Auntie," I tell her in my best Japanese. My proficiency has improved over the years, and with the possible exception of my somewhat atrocious accent, I can passably converse in the language. "Tomorrow morning, we intend to go to Mount Fuji and volunteer."

"Then you must rest well tonight," Auntie insists. Ever the perfect hostess, she continues, "I know you both insist on paying for your stay each time you visit, but it is my turn to insist that you do not. Your help is payment enough."

We are shown into our rooms. As in most traditional inns, there is very little furniture in mine, except for a small dresser and a comfortable-looking futon. Some sumi-e paintings are dashed across the wall. A sliding door is all that separates the room from a large hot spring simmering outside, its steam snaking through the cold, brisk air like an ascending dragon.

Auntie bows as I step into the room. "I hope you and Tarquin-san will feel comfortable here, Okiku-chan."

Auntie has never seen Okiku, though Kagura has told her about my ghost's presence. I don't know how much Auntie knew about Kagura's previous duties as a *miko* serving at Chinsei, but she never seems bothered by Okiku's presence, addressing her just like she was another one of the inn's guests.

"If you need anything else, do not hesitate to ring the bell—or ask Tarquin-san to do so for you—and call for me."

After Auntie leaves, I change hurriedly into a blue *yukata* decorated with small, white irises and look around for Okiku. The sliding door has been pulled back slightly to allow a little steam from the spring to drift into the room, and she is sitting beside it, her now-human face almost contemplative. She's never voiced it aloud, but I suspect Okiku enjoys these trips. Hot springs were something of a luxury back in the older days, I've read, and servants would never have been able to afford such visits.

"It is good here," she says, staring out over the dark water and watching the small ripples.

"Very," I agree and then hesitate. "Are you still angry with me, Ki?"

She pauses, mulling over the question carefully before turning to me with a small smile on her pink bow mouth. "It is of no consequence," she says before turning back to ponder the rising steam and the darkening night.

***

Auntie was a well-known chef in Osaka before moving to the Yamanashi Prefecture to run the inn, and dinner is a testament to her skill. Her specialty lies in the *kaiseki-ryōri*, with each dish carefully selected to complement both the menu and the season and then artistically prepared.

The first course is baby carp simmered in a ginger sauce with salmon roe, black beans in a sweet dressing, and shrimp rolled in kelp. It's followed by large prawns in fried dumpling strips and rolled omelets with pieces of ginkgo nuts for garnish. I am pretty proud of Callie and me. Not once do we attack the food and swallow everything whole like the hungry barbarians we know foreigners like us can be.

By the time the next course arrives—simmered vegetables with slices of tofu and a rice ball steeped in a thick daikon soup base—we've come to the conclusion that Auntie does not want to talk about Kagura while we eat. All it takes is one look from me, and my cousin understands that I'm not willing to talk to Auntie or Saya about the whole McNeil thing either. Instead, we chat about the new improvements to the hot spring baths, Saya's work at the museum, and Callie's studies in Boston.

All the while, more food arrives—sweet, red mochi rice that

arrives in its own round ceramic bowl, miso soup with an unexpected hint of pumpkin, grilled strips of squid in special vinegar, and raw salmon so fresh I can almost taste its heartbeat. We are effusive in our praises, and a quick, appreciative smile dances across Auntie's face at our enthusiasm.

"There is something I would like to show all three of you," she says after dinner. We follow her out of the dining room, down the narrow corridor, and into a small room that I immediately realize is Kagura's. Japanese rooms are supposed to be sparse to the point of austerity, but books line nearly every wall. Still others are relegated to neat piles in one corner because the shelves can no longer accommodate more.

Most of the books are about Japanese history and ancient philosophies, and many appear to be treatises on Buddhism and Taoism. Kagura has been helping her aunt run the Kamameshi Ryokan for the last two years, but Kagura has also always been the complete epitome of a shrine maiden.

"Kagura has always been a bright girl, so I do not always understand the things she is involved in," Auntie confesses. "But the night before she disappeared, before she was to show the American crew around Aokigahara, I saw her looking through there." She points to a small trunk tucked away in another corner of the room. "I have not touched her room since, but I think you three may have a better understanding of what might have happened."

"Did Kagura say anything to you before she left?" Callie asks as I kneel before the trunk.

"She was worried. She said there was a reason her father had not been successful with his research. Kagura's father is my brother-in-law, Kazuhiko Kino," Auntie explains. "He was a noted historian who specialized in folklore and local legends in the Honshu area. The legend of the Aitou village was his particular specialty. He'd been obsessed with the stories ever since he was a boy. Many historians do not believe the village exists, citing a lack of proof, but Kazu always believed. He even claimed to have been to Aitou, but he never gave details. Whatever secrets he kept, he was always adamant that the village exists. I do not think any of his colleagues believed him though."

"That's odd. If Aitou village was his pet project and everyone knew it was, why wouldn't he want to talk about the specifics?" I lift the lid of the trunk. It is filled with several old notebooks and smaller, intricately designed wooden boxes.

"Kazu had always been an odd man," Auntie says. "He placed great importance on his work. In the months leading to his disappearance, he had uncovered something he said was vital to his studies and swore he finally understood the village's curse. He pursued this research without thought to anything else, ignoring even my sister and Kagura."

"I'm sorry," I say. "Did you just say he disappeared?"

"Ten years ago in Aokigahara. I always thought one of the reasons Kagura decided to come with me here was to be closer to the place her father had devoted his life to researching."

"Kagura never told us about this," Callie remarks.

But Saya nods. "It is not something Kagura liked to talk about. She attempted to find her father shortly after we arrived by using the research he left behind, but she was never successful. She had come to terms with her father's death—until this film crew came."

"Oh," Callie says, her voice softening. She's uncovered a small bundle of photos, taken in the style of twenty or so years ago. She holds one up. It's a picture of a girl grinning at us with her hair done up in pigtails. A solemn-looking man carries her on his shoulders. It's obvious they're related. They both have the same high cheekbones, the same upturned nose.

Upon closer examination, I notice the man is wearing something around his neck: an odd-shaped stone tied by a thin cord.

"Kagura with her father," Auntie murmurs.

This is the only photo in the pile of Kagura taken at that age. The rest focus on the man. Kazuhiko Kino never seems to smile. In most of the photographs, he's older. He stoops and has traded in the dark of his hair for gray-white. Lines and crow's-feet are more evident on his face. Only one photo shows him as a young boy, clad in an uncomfortable-looking *yukata*, and he's still just as somber. Even here, he's wearing the strange necklace.

"He wears a *magatama*," Saya tells us, following our gaze. "He seems to have worn it all his life. But what does he need protection from, I wonder?"

Magatama were jewels made from precious stones, each shaped like a comma or half of a yin-yang symbol. They were especially important in Japan, honored as sacred. Many shrines had their own versions that were considered religious objects.

"I think you should keep these," Callie tells Auntie, depositing the photographs gently into her hands after we've looked through them. The latter nods, her eyes misting over. To dispel some of the awkwardness, I draw out the first of the notebooks and open it, trying to be as gentle as I can. "They're in Japanese," I report, disappointed.

"Kagura translated several of those she considered important for the Americans' benefit. I believe she left most of them behind."

It takes a few more minutes to find the notes in question, scribbled in the *miko*'s neat, even handwriting.

Aitou was said to have been built in the early 1900s, sometime after the rise of the Meiji government. Accounts regarding this village were sparse, for Aitou was considered a mysterious and troubling place even then. What is known is that the leader of Aitou was one Hiroshi Mikage, once a noted *onmyōji* in the court of Emperor Taishō before he fell out of favor for some unknown transgression. It has been speculated that the sorcerer was caught dabbling in forbidden magic.

Mikage fled with a handful of followers and was said to have changed his identity to avoid the notoriety, as the name "Mikage" had become associated with evil and dishonor. No one knew where he went after that, and most believed he had succumbed to his own vices or that the demons he summoned had claimed his soul at last. But his contemporaries at court suspected he was harder to kill than that.

Only a few years later, there was talk of a mysterious village within the forests of Aokigahara. The village leader was said to have discovered a gateway to hell and tamed it with a complex ritual. A few exorcists from court tried to investigate these rumors, suspecting it was Mikage's doing—it were not more than five years since his exile—but none of them were seen after entering Aokigahara, which only added more fuel to the fires.

The woods of Aokigahara bolster this mystery. No map has ever been made of the winding forests, and even those armed with the best compasses and equipment have lost their way.

Over the years, Aokigahara has become infamous as a place for suicides, and I believe that somewhere within that thick expanse, the Aitou village and its leader somehow encourage these dark deaths.

"I believe Kagura-chan lent another book to one of the Americans," Auntie says. "A diary, I recall. It might still be in his room."

"This is weird." Callie, who was also rummaging through the trunk, holds up another notebook. "This one doesn't seem to have anything written in it."

She is right. It looks just as old and faded as the rest, but its yellowed pages are unadorned, while the others had been filled with spidery Japanese writing.

"Well," I grunt, struggling to lift a heavy tome from the bottom of the trunk, "this one looks like it's got too much stuff written in it. Let's trade."

"Nuh-uh." Callie flips through several pages of the smaller book and then blinks. "Wait. There's something here." She turns the page toward us, showing us a few lines of text.

Her voice shaking, Saya translates:

To live forever, one must use the gate.
To live forever, eight must be sacrificed.
To close the gate, seven must suffer.
To rule the gate, the eighth must be willing.

The *miko* is trembling as she lays the book down and points at a drawing on one page.

"This symbol is that of a torii—a traditional Japanese gate that marks the entrance to sacred places. But it is different."

Callie and I stare at each other.

"What do you mean by 'different'?" my cousin asks.

Saya's lips tremble. "Here, it is drawn upside down. It is a hell's gate."

CHAPTER EIGHT

THE DIARY

I take most of Kagura's handwritten notes back to the room with me. Auntie protested, fearing that I would not be able to get a good night's sleep if I dwelt too much on them, but I insisted. There must be some kind of clue in these pages, something to help me find Kagura or at least know what to expect when we head out to Aokigahara tomorrow.

Curiosity may have killed the cat, but the proclivity for it continues long after one becomes a ghost. I can sense Okiku's interest as I stumble back into the room with an armload of reading and some tea Auntie prepared for me.

Okiku thumbs through the books while I settle in. There doesn't seem to be much chronology or organization to the research. One moment, Kagura could be writing about traditional paper dolls and their relevance to the local culture, and in the next, she would start on arranged marriages with little segue. If this was the research her father left behind, I wonder just how sound Kazuhiko's mind was to begin with.

Still, though no common themes string these notes together, there is a lot of information on every subject he tackled. I learn that traditional paper dolls were more common in rural villages than in the bustling metropolis because they were cheaper to produce.

Bridal dolls were used to represent young girls during special wedding ceremonies, Kagura wrote, *though the practice was rare. They are, however, always used for ritual weddings in the village of Aitou. None of the villagers, not even the parents of the bride and groom, are present to witness these ceremonies, except for the kannushi and his assistant priests.*

I lean forward, fascinated to learn more about Aitou, but I get my hopes up too soon. I turn page after page without any other mention of the village and instead come across a large section devoted to the preparation and herbal use of belladonna.

I skim through most of it, losing interest after reading long passages of medical terminology and obscure scientific terms. Immediately following that is a treatise on raising silkworms, which is even more tedious.

I'm about to give up when I find a note from Kagura addressed to one of the American ghost hunters.

I apologize for the lack of cohesion in these pages, but my father seemed to believe these details were important to his research. I have all his notes, but I can find no trace of the sources he used for his descriptions of Aitou. There is no corroboration from other records, which I also find odd.

There are other documents that have been passed on to me, such as the red parchment, which ought to have information more to your liking. I do not know where my father found this parchment, but it is not in his handwriting, and it is much older than the others appear to be.

Two other books should be of some use. The Book of Unnatural Changes is a daunting read, so I have translated the passages that my father singled out. I remember him being quite excited when he first brought this book home. He found it in an old temple that was about to be torn down. He said the book helped him solve the supposed "curse of Aitou," though he never elaborated. I wish I had asked him for more information then.

I have translated those passages to the best of my ability, but a few words are lost in the translation.

The second book is a girl's diary. It was his most prized possession.

I am still quite adamant that you and your crew carry a few of the wooden spikes I have given you. The stakes were carved from the fallen branches of a tree at the Chinsei shrine that we consider sacred. Should we encounter anything untoward in our search for Aitou, they should offer some protection, as should the ofudas.

Kagura had schooled me in the ways of the *ofuda*. It's a long strip of cloth made of dry hemp that's covered in writing, usually an invocation to a deity or a shrine's protection—in our case, the

Chinsei shrine, the most powerful one I know. *Ofudas* are often used to keep ghosts away, which is why I've never had much reason to use them. For one thing, Okiku would complain.

But a red parchment? I check the rest of the pages, but none of these transcriptions seem to come from that document.

Okiku floats in the air above me, content to browse rather than single out any document in particular. I halfheartedly poke my way through *The Book of Unnatural Changes*, but it gives me a headache, so I turn back to Kagura's notes instead. I'm relieved that she has been very succinct in her summaries. Most of the transcribed passages stem from a chapter called "On the Methods of Conducting Obscure Ceremonies" and make up no more than a couple of pages.

Eight is a number of infinite potential; therefore, it follows that the use of eight rituals in succession both invokes the highest chance of success and wields the greatest power. Eight rituals are needed for a hell's gate. Eight rituals necessitate eight sacrifices. Only seven are required to close the gate, but eight are needed to rule.

Each ritual pacifies the hell's gate and prevents its power from being unleashed until the seventh ritual can be performed, closing the gate. But to rule the gate, an eighth and final ritual must be performed while the gate remains potent. This can be minutes or up to three years after the seventh ritual.

All must perform the rituals according to the balance of elements available. If the fire element is strong within the area, you must strengthen the ritual with water. If wood is dominant, then one must temper the ritual with metal.

Okiku is of water. I remember her battling the masked woman in black and shudder. The demon had been a creature of fire, and what I saw of that fight had not been pretty. Water trumped fire, but the demon was strong, and killing it took a lot out of Okiku.

To rule the gate, it is important that the last sacrifice must be willing.

But to close the gate, all seven sacrifices must suffer to slake hell's hunger.

The one to succeed shall know power. He shall rule demons and win victories; his enemies on the battlefield shall lie in the millions. He can challenge even the might of Enma Daiō, the King of Hell. All of Japan shall fall at his feet if he wishes it.

How seriously did Kagura treat all this, I wonder. Did she believe in her father's research? Did the *Ghost Haunts* crew? All I've seen them do on their show is huddle inside dark rooms, flail their arms, and scream at nothing, so it's hard to believe how serious they are.

He can also exchange the powers of a hell's gate to resurrect a soul. Within the Hundred Days of Mourning ritual, he can restore that soul to its previous form.

Only the most powerful of onmyōji should perform these rituals. A lesser priest will not survive the gate's fury.

Should any of these rituals fail, then the sacrifices shall be released back into the world of men. Those who face their wrath are doomed.

Should the gate fall, only one hope remains: use the vessels to trap the sacrifices and perform a final ritual in their presence.

There is little else to do then but to accept fate as the gods have decreed.

"Silly of me to think this would make sense," I grumble, glaring at the large book like this is all its fault.

Auntie found the girl's diary that Kagura referred to in Stephen Riley's room, laid on top of his futon. I tackle that next. The diary's been well cared for, despite its age. The pages turn easily, as if it's been read often.

Whoever wrote this was no Anne Frank, but there's something compelling about the way the girl chronicles her life. There's a sadness to the entries that lingers, though the girl is gone.

And fear, I realize, as I read on with Okiku looking over my shoulder. The girl was very much afraid.

Taishō 7th year, August
Father insisted that I wear my karaginu mo today and criti-cized me for the color combinations I had chosen for my sleeves. His obsession with court functions has grown worse over the

years, and I do not understand this idiosyncrasy. Few people visit this village, and it is unlikely the emperor would pay his respects so far from court, as Father seems to expect. He and the others who oversee the ceremonies think the same way.

I pause to google the date on my phone. The Japanese created era names for their calendar when inauspicious events happen or when a new emperor ascends the throne. I learn that the Taishō era covered the years 1912 to 1926, to mark the rise of the liberal movement and the beginnings of democracy in Japan. The seventh year of Taishō meant this was written in 1918.

Taishō 7th year, September

The fireflies have arrived early this year. I can see a few of them in the gardens by my window, flying over the grass and winking at me while the night slowly falls. I cannot help but feel jealous of them. I wish I too could set foot into the gardens and dance among the flowers. But I cannot. I am like a bird in a cage, waiting for a spring that may never come.

Taishō 7th year, October

I dreamed that Yukiko-chan was buried underneath the shrine, that she was alive and dying all at once. Father laughed at me and said that my friend was traveling the world with Makoto-kun and that I will do the same with Tomeo when my turn comes and we are wed.

Taishō 7th year, November

Some of the assistant priests told Tomeo that it is possible to return from the dead. If you are in possession of immense spiritual energy, they say you can bring a soul back from the underworld. Tomeo says the kannushi has been talking a lot about this lately. Father laughed when I asked him, but there was a strange look on his face.

Tomeo asked the priests about my ritual, wanting to be sure everything will turn out well. I told him the kannushi has performed this ritual many times. Everyone in the village knows why it is done.

Father says I have strong ki, like all the chosen—that I attract demons and bad luck into the village. That is why I am to be sent away, so these evil spirits will follow. The ritual will protect me from the worst of these spirits, and my marriage to Tomeo is part of that protection.

Our village has never experienced drought or pestilence or plague, and Father says it is because the ritual is always successful.

I am not afraid. Not if I am with Tomeo.

Still, Father says my presence in the village makes everyone nervous, and I cannot help but feel guilty. Did Yukiko-chan feel the same way before her ritual?

Taishō 7th year, December

Tomeo and I talked about what we would like to do when we leave Aitou. He wants to work as a carpenter. I asked him what he thinks I would be good at, and he said all he wants is for me to be his wife.

I cannot be happier.

Taishō 8th year, January

Do the others in the village still remember me? I have been locked inside this room for nearly three years now. I know that many look down on me because of my eyes, but Father believes I am doubly blessed because of them. He says it was because Mother was a beauty from Akita, of the Ainu tribe. Tomeo tells me I am beautiful. His approval and Father's approval are all that matter to me.

Did Yukiko-chan also worry about being forgotten while she waited for her ritual here? I still remember Yukiko-chan. I remember her kindness. Father says that Yukiko had great spiritual power—she could have been trained as a priestess and would have been quite strong. It was a shame, he says, that the gods chose another purpose for her.

On the day of her ritual I remember Yukiko's parents presenting a kimono before the whole village. It was the most beautiful green kimono with cranes looking out through the bamboo and plums. They gave it to the assistant priests to give to Yukiko-chan. When I think of Yukiko, I like to imagine her wearing it. Father gave me my own kimono to wear for my ritual—white with wisteria blossoms wrapped around cherry trees.

Will everyone remember me when my turn comes?

Taishō 8th year, February

I took something from Father's desk today and gave it to Tomeo. I have heard Father say it is a charm that wards off demons, and with the ceremony drawing closer, I am worried. I cannot shake the fear that something bad is going to happen, that Tomeo might be harmed. I hope the charm will keep him safe.

I am not proud of what I have done, but I would do it again.

Taishō 8th year, March

The ritual is tomorrow, and tonight I must purify my mind and body to purge all the evils inside me. But I am uneasy.

Father was irritated when he visited me this morning. Yukiko's father had come to him and wanted to search for his daughter outside the village. It seems he has been having dreams about her and is convinced that is an omen that something terrible has happened to Yukiko. He would not stop until Father showed him the path she took out of the village. And now there will be a slight delay in my ceremony because of that.

Tomeo came to visit again this afternoon, and he was angry too. He said Father lied about the ritual but that he wants to find proof before confronting him.

I told him Father has been performing the ritual for many years, and each one has been successful, but now I am anxious. Tomeo promised to return, but night has come, and he isn't here. The tea Father gave me is getting cold, so I have set it aside. I will wait for Tomeo. I hope nothing has happened.

The entries all appear to contradict Kazuhiko Kino's assertions that sacrifices were being made as part of some pagan ritual. If this girl was one of the chosen maidens, nothing in the diary indicates anything out of the ordinary. If you consider ritualized marriages "ordinary" anyway.

Just to make sure I've read everything of importance, I steal out of my room and head back to Kagura's. I rummage through her trunk again and am rewarded when I spot a small, rolled-up parchment that is a strange reddish color. The edges look like it was once rescued from a fire. I bring the scroll back to my room, and Okiku sits beside me, peering over my shoulder. I'd been hoping for a drawing or at least something that would transcend my basic understanding of Japanese, but all I see is six lines of undecipherable text.

Kagura was right. This does not resemble Kazuhiko Kino's writing at all. From the faded ink, it doesn't even look like it was written during this century.

"This is pointless," I mutter.

"*The maiden and the boy must be willing.*"

I turn to look at Okiku. Her eyes are trained on the parchment.

"*All girls eight through twelve shall bring their* hanayome ningyō, *each in their likeness. When the door closes, the sun shall die. When it is reborn anew,* she *whose doll is honored shall be chosen, and* she *must be willing.*

"*For three years,* she *must keep with no one but the* boy *for company. And then* she *shall be clothed and bound and honored, and* she *shall become unto fireflies.*"

The quiet stretches on as we both stare at the text, trying to come to grips with what Okiku has just read. This could easily be the incoherent ramblings of a madman who'd imbibed one too many cups of sake. But I have seen many, many girls turn into fireflies, and there's only one unfortunate requirement for them to make that transformation.

"Okiku, what's a *hanayome ningyō*?"

"A bridal doll."

I reach for Kagura's notes and quickly find the passage I'm looking for.

Bridal dolls were used to represent young girls during special wedding ceremonies.

"Okiku, this refers to a sacrifice, doesn't it?" I continue reading from Kagura's notes:

"*To live forever, one must rule the Gate. To rule the Gate, one must be sacrificed. To be sacrificed, one must be willing.*"

I pause. "None of the girls must have known what was about to happen to them. Did these people seriously kill girls in some obscure ritual, expecting to reveal a hell's gate?" I feel awful for the girl who'd written that diary with such high hopes for her future. What had happened to her?

Okiku says nothing, but I know her answer. There's a strange light in her eyes. This ritual is sounding more and more like the

World Cup for serial killers, and she's just itching to intervene. I'm not as enthusiastic about it.

"Tark? You still awake?" Callie peeks in from outside and frowns when she sees the books strewn about. "Tark, you need some rest, remember? Tomorrow's gonna be hectic enough as it is without the jet lag."

"I was just looking through a few things." I can't tell Callie what I've found. She's already worried, and anything more would freak her out. "Doesn't that also apply to you? What are you doing up this late, Callie?"

"I can't sleep," she admits. "My mind's going a mile a minute. I'm concerned about Kagura, and I'm concerned about all this… research. It sounds pretty fantastic to me."

"You would have said the same thing two years ago."

"Ugh. Don't remind me." Callie spots Okiku and gives her a small smile. "I was talking with Auntie after you left. Do you really think Kagura's father could have found a village inside Aokigahara like he claimed?"

"It's hard to believe that no one's seen it before."

"According to Auntie, he claimed to have proof, but it could never be substantiated by another independent source. Apparently, he said he was going to find more evidence—to find someone—but he never returned. That was ten years ago."

"Why didn't Kagura tell us about any of this?"

"Auntie said she never really talked about it, though Kagura had been to Aokigahara several times looking for him."

Callie sighs. "And now she's missing too. Personally, I don't know what to make of it. It's not like anything weird happened before she'd left, right? Auntie says lots of people have lost their way inside Aokigahara. Something about GPS devices and cell phones not working when you're inside. And from what I can tell, it's a pretty big forest. Tark, are you listening?"

Callie's words jog something inside my head. "Sorry, you were saying?"

"Honestly, Tark! I've been prattling on and on, and you haven't listened to anything I've said—hey!"

She scowls at me as I take a picture of her with my phone. The flash makes Callie look pasty white, though it does nothing to hide her full-on glare. I show it to her, chuckling.

"I'm kidding," I say. "I heard every word. And now it's my turn to tell you not to worry. Go and take a dip in the hot spring or something."

She smiles at me. "Yeah. Maybe I will. I need a soak. As long as you promise to stop looking through those old books and get some sleep."

"Cross my heart. Can I ask a favor?"

"What is it?"

"In the event, you know, something happens to me—and I mean that in the most hypothetical sense—you'll do everything in your power to fi—"

Before I can finish, Callie bounds to my side and claps a hand over my mouth. "*Absolutely not*," she says severely. "I absolutely *refuse* to do anything on your behalf, Tarquin Halloway. The last time you said something as half-assed as this, you tried to stab yourself and I spent a week in a hospital. So you'd *better* take care of yourself and not do anything stupid. Because I'm not gonna bail you out again. You hear me?"

I mumble a "yes" through her fingers and hold up my hands in surrender.

"Good. Now I feel like I need a drink."

"Me too?" I ask hopefully.

"Nope."

"Meanie."

"Not my fault you're underage."

"You were too until a couple of months ago."

"I know. Ain't that great?"

"You're getting to be a real alcoholic these days, Callie."

"Shut up."

I keep grinning until she leaves. Then I stare down at the phone in my hand before taking a picture of myself. Okiku watches me as if she already knows the outcome.

The picture flashes on the screen. Maybe I already know the outcome too, because I'm not surprised by what I see.

"Figures."

Taking my own advice, I shed my clothes and step out into the hot spring, the heat of the water and the biting cold of the night warring against my skin.

I find a comfortable spot and sink in to my neck, closing my eyes and breathing deeply because I'm not sure when I'll be back here—if ever. When I open them again, Okiku is lurking by the spring's edge. She turned away when I began shedding clothes, but now she is looking down at the water, and her longing pulls at me.

"Ki, you can come in with me if you want."

"It is not proper."

"If it wasn't proper, it wouldn't be communal. Come on."

For all my bravado, it's my turn to face away and wait, listening for the splash that never comes. By the time I realize ghosts don't make ripples, Okiku is already in the water, still fully clothed. The rising steam fogs my vision, so all I can make out is her mass of hair near the farthest edge of the spring.

"I'm sorry, Ki." I say.

"Why?"

"You saw the photo I took of myself. You know what that means."

"It is never too late for anything."

Another minute passes before I speak again. "You sure you're not mad at me anymore?"

"It is of no consequence."

"You know, that's girl code for you're still mad at me."

She says nothing.

"Okiku, can you do something for me? Can you promise not to kill anyone without at least talking to me first? When you start feeling these urges, I would rather you give me a heads-up so I can look for alternatives. Like, you know, maybe keeping out of the guy's way and not publicly antagonizing him in the first place."

"Do you not trust me?"

It's hard to pick up emotion from her dry monotone, but I can tell she's hurt by my suggestion.

"Okiku, don't be ridiculous. I trust you with my life, and that's kind of the problem. What we did nearly put us in the spotlight, and that's the last thing we want if we don't want to get caught. Well, if we don't want *me* to get caught anyway. You're beyond the scope of legal jurisdiction. Do you understand?"

"Why do you do this?"

"Well, killing someone under the assumption that he might hurt someone in the future…"

"No. Why do you fight for him when you feel nothing for his death?"

Okiku always knows how to get to the heart of the matter.

I dip below the water, blowing bubbles out of my mouth before I resurface. "You're right. I don't feel bad at all, and I feel bad about not feeling bad. But we can't allow our personal feelings to get in the way. We break the law every time we kill one of these murderers. Let's not add killing *future* murderers to the list, because that category doesn't leave a lot of people outside it. It…it keeps us from being *them*, you know?"

"It prevents other innocents' deaths."

I close my eyes. "Even so. I'm sorry, Ki."

This time, she takes a little longer to respond. "I understand."

"Good. Now come here, and let's hug it out."

"No."

"Don't be shy. I can barely see you in all this steam. Oh hey, maybe I'll be the one to go there."

I splash noisily toward her, but by the time I make my way there, she is already out of the spring, shaking her head at me and my peculiar enthusiasm.

"Come on," I cajole, laughing, but she ignores me and drifts back into the room.

Without Okiku around to tease, there isn't much else to do, so after a few minutes, I emerge from the spring, slip into a fresh *yukata*, and crawl onto the futon.

I pick up my phone and stare hard at the photo I took of myself. Okiku curls up on the floor beside me, watching me watching. Nothing crawls out of the picture. Nothing curls around my features like it did in Kagura's photograph. Nothing moves.

CHAPTER NINE

THE VILLAGE

I don't realize the extent of the search party until we arrive at the base of Mount Fuji, near the entrance to Aokigahara. The area is teeming with people, mostly police officers and volunteers. There are also reporters with cameras—many of them foreigners—harassing a few of the cops. I assume the media's on standby in case there are any developments.

A few of them zone in on us, though the animation in their faces dies as we make our way to where a crowd of volunteers waits for instructions.

I shift my feet, unable to hide my unease. I don't like reporters, though I admit past experiences may have colored my judgment. Okiku is less biased than I am. She drifts between a reporter's summation of events and his cameraman, peering inside the lens while the former prattles on. I'm sure anyone in the audience with an inclination toward mediumship is going to get a kick out of *that* broadcast.

I haven't slept much. I woke up in the early hours of the morning and reread the diary and the notes on *The Book of Unnatural Changes* so many times that I'm sure I could quote the book verbatim by now. But I don't feel tired. If anything, something in those pages gnaws at me, but I don't know what exactly or why I feel on edge.

Auntie dropped us off after extracting promises that we keep her informed as soon as we learn anything. Saya, who shouldn't be traipsing about forests at her age anyway, decided to stay behind with Auntie to keep her company.

"I didn't think there would be this many people," Callie admits, looking around.

"Yeah, well, nothing says 'Pull out all the stops and leave no stone unturned' like a cable network breathing down your neck because you've lost their reality TV stars slash meal tickets."

"But that's a good thing, right? I don't think they would have been this proactive if only Kagura was missing."

I remind her that the ghost hunters are the sole reason Kagura is missing, making Callie's case for them null and void.

One of the volunteers in charge signals for attention, silencing Callie's attempt at a comeback. It's probably better that she doesn't know about my distorted photo. I'm not sure what it means myself. I remember the photo Kagura sent, with her face as disfigured as mine and most of her companions missing their heads.

I don't know what the disfigurement means, but I'm almost certain that the lack of heads means that they're dead.

I tug at the backpack I'm wearing. Earlier this morning, I stole into Kagura's room and pilfered supplies. I plan to apologize to

Kagura if—*when*—I find her, but I still feel guilty. I half expected Callie to be suspicious, because she always seems to have a nose for knowing when I'm up to no good. But other people in the group are carrying knapsacks, and so far, she's oblivious.

The volunteers are divided into small groups, each led by at least one person familiar with Aokigahara. Callie doesn't understand as much Japanese as I do, so I relay the instructions to her as our leader drones on.

"Stay on the marked paths. There aren't a lot of them, so always remember to keep to the buddy system and know where your partner is at all times. Don't stray from where you can see your group. If you see anything unusual, call out to others before investigating."

Most of the local residents, we discover, call Aokigahara "Jukai"—literally, the Sea of Trees. Despite the number of tourists that visit each year, most refuse to even set foot inside the forest, believing that spirits and demons lurk in it.

Our leader also warns us about other possible dangers, and we're each handed whistles to wear around our necks in case we need to call for assistance. There's a chance we could get lost, that we could trip and injure ourselves, and—this is what chills me—that we might find dead bodies as we search. Aokigahara isn't called the "suicide forest" for nothing, I suppose.

It's still early morning when our group is given clearance to enter. Aokigahara is a deceptive forest. It has all the hallmarks of a popular tourist destination: narrow but well-maintained hiking trails with a surprising amount of litter, not to mention strips of tape and ribbon wrapped around tree trunks. The leader explains that hikers use them as markers to maintain their bearings. Later on, one of the other volunteers whispers to us that some of the tapes were left by those who came here to kill themselves, in case they decided to change their minds. The revelation horrifies Callie.

A few miles into our hike, anything resembling civilization disappears. Roots crawl across the hard forest floor, and it's easy to trip if you're not constantly looking down. We're outside, but the trees make it feel claustrophobic. They reach hungrily toward the sun, fighting each other for drops of light, and this selfishness grows with the darkness as we move deeper into the woods.

It's quiet. The silence is broken by the scuffling of feet or snapping of dry twigs as we walk. Every so often, volunteers call back and forth to each other, and rescue dogs exploring the same vicinity that we are will bark. But there are no bird calls, no sounds of scampering squirrels. We're told that there is very little wildlife in Jukai. Nothing seems to flourish here but trees.

This deep into the woods, any roads and cleared paths are gone. At times, we're forced to climb to a higher ledge or slide down steep slopes to proceed, and there's always some root or rock hiding to twist an ankle.

And yet—the forest is beautiful. I like myself too much to seriously think about suicide, even during my old bouts of depression, but I can understand why people would choose to die here. There is something noble and enduring and magnificent about the forest.

That sense of wonder disappears though, the instant I see them. There are spirits here. And the ghosts mar the peacefulness for me. They hang from branches and loiter at the base of tree trunks. Their eyes are open and their skin is gray, and they watch me as I pass. I don't know what kind of people they were in life, but they seem faded and insignificant in death.

Okiku watches them but takes no action. These are not the people she hunts. They don't attack us because they're not that kind of ghosts. Most of them, I intuit, aren't violent. The only lives they had ever been capable of taking were their own.

I'm not afraid, despite their bloated faces, contorted from the ropes they use to hang themselves or the overdose of sleeping pills they've taken. If anything, I feel lingering sadness. I can sympathize with their helpless anguish. These people took their own lives, hoping to find some meaning in death when they couldn't find it in life. But there's nothing here but regret and longing.

And there's that tickle again, so light it is nearly imperceptible. Something in this forest attracts these deaths. It lures its unhappy victims with its strange siren's call and then, having taken what it needs, leaves their spirits to rot. A Venus flytrap for human souls.

Something is wrong here, and suddenly, the forest no longer looks as enticing or majestic as when we arrived.

The faded ghosts bow low to Okiku as she drifts past, and she nods in turn. Many bow their heads to me too. I gulp.

"What's wrong?" Callie whispers, tugging at my hand.

Telling her about the ghosts would be counterproductive. The last thing I want is for Callie to hyperventilate in this middle of nowhere. So I say, "Nothing. This place just gives me the creeps."

"I don't know." Callie looks around. "If there weren't all those stories about the suicides, I'd think it was a lovely place to visit."

"That's how it pulls you in."

My cousin shoots me an odd look but doesn't push it.

Shouts ring out from the other side of the woods, and the volunteers break into hushed murmurings. "I think one of the dogs found a body," I translate for Callie, fear rising in my chest.

We wait tersely for several more minutes before the word reaches us. It's the body of an unknown hiker, most likely a suicide.

The search resumes, pausing only for a brief lunch break. I estimate we're about three kilometers or so past the nearest hiking trail, and there are still no signs of Kagura or any of the film crew. We're only allowed to search until the five-kilometer mark, with the more experienced professionals exploring the rest of the 3,500-hectare-wide forest. It will take weeks, possibly even months, to cover the whole area—if that is even possible. I doubt Aokigahara will ever be fully explored. As the day wears on, hope that Kagura is still unhurt in these woods sinks like the sun.

A halt to volunteer rescue efforts is called at four in the afternoon. Parts of Jukai are already too dark to search, and some other groups have reported stands of trees where darkness was nearly absolute.

Callie and I are bone-tired, our clothes dirty and our hands scraped and bruised from climbing and sliding. I'm sweaty, and my muscles ache from the exertion and the weight of my bag. Bringing my backpack turned out to be a bad idea after all.

"We'll come back tomorrow," Callie says, ever the optimist. "And the police and rescue teams are going to keep searching, so they might find something too." The others in our group are already starting their retreat, heads bent and eyes downcast.

"Sure," I say, but my heart's not in it.

As Callie turns away, my eyes catch sight of something on the ground, almost hidden among the leaves. It's only several feet from where we stand.

"Hey, Callie. Look at this." I walk over and crouch to get a better look. Then I let out a whoop of excitement. Staring back at me is a handheld video camcorder. It's a little the worse for wear but still intact. For all I know, some careless tourist with a hankering for expensive gadgetry dropped it, but most tourists don't head this far out. It could belong to one of the *Ghost Haunts* crew.

"Callie, I found something!" I call out again, but Callie is nowhere to be found. She's gone. For that matter, so is everyone else. I'm all alone. Even the ghosts have disappeared.

Crap.

"Hello?" My voice bounces off the trees, loud but futile against the growing darkness. I shout again, aware of the panic in my cry, but the trees are silent. No one is there. I grab my whistle, but the shrill sound yields no response.

Oh crap. Oh crap. Oh crap. Oh crap.

"Okiku?"

When she appears, relief cartwheels through me. She doesn't react when I close the distance between us and throw my arms around her, though her hollow eyes look startled. "Ki, where is everyone?"

She shakes her head.

"Callie was standing literally three feet away from me. There is no way she could have vanished—"

"There is something here."

"A good something or a bad something?" I ask her.

Okiku shoots me a look.

"Of course. Why did I even bother asking?" I wheel around. The light is fading fast, and I'm going to have to act quickly before it gets too dark to see, much less find Callie and the others.

All my misgivings about lugging my heavy backpack are forgotten. I drop to the ground and rummage through it for a flashlight. I flick it on and splay it nervously across the trees, trying to find any other signs of life. But other than me and Okiku, who technically isn't really any kind of life at all, there's nothing.

The darkness in this place no longer creeps on me; it rushes at me with a well-placed headbutt. But what chills me to the bone is the sudden hushed stillness, which is different from the silence. It's the feeling that no one else is meant to be here—but something is. I swallow hard, trying to keep my voice from squeaking. "Okiku, any idea where to go next?"

Okiku hesitates. "Something is here," she says, her voice very soft. "It limits what I can sense. We can travel the woods forever with no end in sight. But I can sense something else. There."

"Doesn't sound like we have a choice then."

I reach out and take her hand. It's not something I usually do with her—Okiku tends to shy away from physical contact—but after a moment of hesitation she squeezes my fingers.

The flashlight keeps me from tripping over most of the foliage, but without an actual path to follow, progress is painstakingly slow. I try checking my phone, but the lack of signal makes it an expensive paperweight until we get out of Jukai. Even the clock isn't working. The numbers skew wildly. It tells me it's 7:00 p.m., and then 8:31 a.m., and then 76:92 p.m., before settling into what I can only presume is a default error code.

My anxiety has been growing ever since Callie and I got separated. Now, after this voodoo trick with my phone, it's peaking into the higher registers of panic.

Okiku is my sole compass, leading the way. Her steps never waver, the direction she chooses unerring, and I find solace in her confidence. My hand grips hers tighter. It feels like we've been walking for hours, but she never lets go.

Finally, we burst into a clearing, and what we see makes me stumble.

It's a village.

A village that looks to have been abandoned for some time. The wooden gate entrance has splintered in several places, as if something large and fearsome crashed through. We've left the tight choke hold of trees, but a thick fog rises, settling protectively around the little village like an evening cape.

"Okiku, is this Aitou?" I whisper.

Okiku frowns. She doesn't know what it is, only that we're not alone here.

I'm scared, but I don't see what choice I have. I step past the broken barrier onto a rough path, a better alternative than the jungle we'd been wandering through. If Kagura's in here, if any of the ghost-hunter crew is here, then I will find them.

I'm tempted to call out, hoping someone can hear me, but caution stills my tongue. I know better. This is not the kind of place where you want to attract attention.

The houses are lined up on either side of the path, and none show signs of recent habitation. Everything looks truly abandoned, and the only color I can see is the glint of gold up ahead. There's some kind of temple in the distance, with a curved roof and pillars. It looks strangely familiar, though at the moment, I don't know why.

But the best place to start looking for answers is the camcorder I'm dragging around. Now that we've broken through the woods, it's a good time to check it out. I hunker down beside a stone bench next to the nearest house. In the meantime, Okiku slowly spins around as she takes in our new surroundings.

I find the button and the camera flickers to life. I scroll through the menu to access the data. There are only four recorded videos, and I start with the first. I push Play. Kagura shows up on screen, sitting on a chair and looking remarkably self-conscious. Garrick Adams is sitting across from her.

"Don't be nervous," he says.

Kagura tries to smile. "I'm sorry. I'm not used to being filmed."

It's comforting to hear my friend's voice, rich and warm, even if it is on a video recorder.

"That's okay. Ignore the camera. Pretend it's just me asking questions."

"Interview commencing," another voice off screen says, "in three...two...one...go!"

"Miss Kino, would you mind telling us more about this village?"

"There isn't much known about Aitou. Or the rituals villagers have been said to practice." Kagura clears her throat. "According to my father's research, a ritual took place in Aitou every three years. Certain girls in the village were chosen to take part in purifying the supposed hell's gate and to appease the spirits therein. What roles the girls played aren't very clear, but my father believed that the girls might have been sacrificed."

"How does he know this? I haven't found any corroborating evidence from any other historian. You admit as much."

Kagura's voice takes on a slightly defensive edge. "My father was very thorough. He extensively researched the *onmyōji* practices of the time and found the memoirs of many contemporaries of Hiroshi Mikage, the exorcist believed to have founded Aitou. Their writings prove that it was a ritual commonly believed to close all hell's gates. Mikage himself wrote about it, and I believe my father read what little of his works were available."

"Had your father kept any of this Mikage's writings?"

"If he did, I could not find them among his belongings."

Adams questions, "Is there any way your father might have mistaken the ritual for the many suicides in Aokigahara?"

Kagura shakes her head, still huffy that her father's research is being questioned. "Absolutely not."

"Why not? It seems plausible."

"Don't badger her, Garrick." Stephen Riley's voice comes from somewhere off screen, sounding annoyed as well. "Why do you think that, Miss Kino?"

"The spirits in Jukai are a consequence of the gate ceremonies, not its cause. The village predates most of the suicides. Something in the forest…seeks pleasure in death, and it affects many of those who venture in. Though the general ritual was known among the *onmyōji* of that time, the specifics have never been written about, as far as I know, so it would appear that this was a closely guarded secret, meant to prevent others from making such attempts at the gate."

"Tell me more about the marriages in Aitou. Is there any evidence that the girls might have been sacrificed?"

"A marriage between a village boy and the chosen girl was said to be part of the gate ritual. It was a means to protect the couple from the evil spirits they'd encounter when they left the village.

"Each girl was kept in seclusion for years before the ritual, and her intended was the girl's sole companion during her isolation. My father believes it was an attempt to forge a bond between them, so that their spirits would not return to the village to seek vengeance.

"It's a carefully guarded secret that the girls were being sacrificed.

None of the chosen girls were ever seen after the rituals. My father doubted that the villagers were even aware of the truth. They believed that the couple was sent away from the village after their marriage and the ritual. Aitou would then be safe from bad luck for another three years, after which they'd have to perform the ritual all over again."

"Where did he learn these specifics?"

"Again, I do not know."

"Did your father ever find out the purpose for these rituals?"

"It could have been as simple as ensuring a good harvest. There was the great Tenpō famine during the eighteen thirties in Japan, and many families starved."

"That sounds terrible."

"People have been sacrificed for less."

"Was there proof that any of the villagers protested this?"

"Only hints written in the diary my father found. The harvests were always bountiful in Aitou, and villagers probably believed the ceremonies were a cause of this."

"Did your father learn anything else?"

"He possessed a rough map, supposedly of the village itself. I can't vouch for its accuracy, but certain houses were marked with names—seven in all. These were believed to be the family residences of the seven girls who had been sacrificed, and—wait." Kagura pauses, stealing a flustered glance at the camera. "Do I show you a copy of the map at this point? Or will your people add it in later?"

"We can add it in later," Garrick says, smiling. "I'd like copies for all of us before we set out, if you don't mind. It might not be accurate, but it's the best lead we've got." Garrick looks into the camera as well. "That enough, Jerry?"

"Yeah, I think so," someone else responds, and the video ends.

The fog is thicker now, and I shiver at the encroaching chill. Before I can select the next video file, a hissing noise from Okiku makes me look up. She is staring off into the distance, and her fingers curl. Okiku is about to go on the warpath.

The creature is crawling on the ground toward us. It's a horrible, horrible sight. Long black hair covers her face, and her fingers end in bone rather than with nails. The remains of a kimono trail behind her, the robe slipping loose from one shoulder, which is completely devoid of flesh.

I don't sit around waiting for her to approach and strike up a conversation. I snatch up my backpack and the camcorder and race toward the nearest house.

"Ki!"

Okiku is with me as I enter the house and whip out one of the *ofudas* I had taken from Kagura's room. The last thing I hear outside before I slide the door shut behind me is the crawling lady's moan, a desperate cry that rings through the silent village, begging for blood.

CHAPTER TEN

THE EYE

At first, I'm worried that the *ofuda* won't stick between the two shoji screens that separate the rooms, but it stays up with little difficulty. It's more like a barricade than a weapon, but at least it will prevent any creatures from following me in. It occurs to me on hindsight that the *ofuda* could also prevent me from leaving with Okiku—and I definitely do not want that.

The room I stumble into is a safe haven, mostly ghost-free as far as I can tell. It smells of dry hay and is mostly bare, with a few rotting mats, a broken table, and faded wall scrolls. A small, dusty doll in a kimono, still remarkably intact, sits atop what must have been a family altar used for worship.

There's nothing here for me to hide behind or underneath in case another spirit shows up. I huddle in the farthest corner to wait things out, just in case the crawling creature is still wandering around. I fish out my tape recorder and an empty doll; I'd rather not take any chances.

Something scratches at the door. I can see a shadow moving

across the screen, and then a hand presses against its surface, forming claws where it pushes against the thin wall. There's a definite maliciousness in the deliberate scrape of the bone.

I know you're here, it tells me. *I know you're here, and the* ofuda *is a temporary inconvenience that can be overcome soon enough.*

The scraping tapers off. For several seconds, the shadow doesn't move.

I can feel it studying me through the semitransparent divider.

Then it crawls away, its silhouette slowly disappearing from view.

I still aim the doll at the screen, ready to switch on the recorder should the crawling creature decide to change its mind.

All the while, Okiku is quiet, but I can see from the corner of my eye the way the muscles in her shoulders bunch, her hands knuckled against the floor, poised to strike. When more minutes pass and nothing happens, she relaxes, sitting and tucking her legs underneath her. When she does this, I relax in turn, dropping the doll in my relieved exhaustion.

"Ki, what the hell was that?"

"A wandering spirit." Unlike when she's mentioned the ghosts we've hunted, Okiku doesn't sound eager or vicious or bloodthirsty. She frowns, lost in thought.

"How many?"

"Many. But there are—others. Other things. Vessels. Dolls."

"Dolls?"

"I… It is hard to know for certain. But I sense them all the same."

I dig into my backpack once more and bring out all the items I took from Kagura's room: a dozen *ofudas* and a dozen wooden spikes, each about three inches long. Then I take stock of my other supplies: my tape recorder, two dolls stuffed with rice, the sewing kit, a pocketknife, two bottles (one drinking water and one salt water), a flashlight, extra batteries, and the emergency medical pack they handed out to volunteers that morning, which had another sewing kit, bandages, some ointment, and a small pen. It's easy to see why I've been huffing and puffing for most of the day. Right now, I'm grateful for the self-imposed burden.

I slip the *ofuda* into the front pocket of my knapsack to make sure I can grab it quickly if I have to, which, given my luck, I probably will. I shove my tape recorder into my right pocket. I take a quick gulp of water, then return the bottle and the rest of the items to my pack, except for a flashlight and one of the spikes. Kagura never actually shared what I was supposed to do with the latter, but I've seen enough vampire series on TV to make a good guess.

The doll on the altar is still looking at me. It's creepy, and I turn it around so it faces the wall instead.

That done, I sit and check the camcorder. I'm not moving until I'm at least eighty percent sure that whatever was outside has moved on to prey on something that isn't me. Okiku hasn't budged either, still deep in thought.

I play the second video. It begins with an image of Adams smiling into the lens. "This is Aokigahara," I can hear him narrating, "one of Japan's most beautiful forests—and also one of its most tragic." The camera pans over to the familiar row of trees and unmarked trails where I walked earlier. "The deaths in the forest are well documented. Hundreds of suicides have been reported here, and the numbers only continue to rise every year.

"But the legend of the Aitou village within Aokigahara is a different case completely. There is literally nothing about Aitou in modern documents or personal accounts, and very few records about it have survived. If the village exists at all, Aitou has been very successful at keeping its secrets."

A pause, then his tone becomes more relaxed. "What do you think, Henry? That sound good enough to add in later?"

The camera leaves Adams to zoom in on one of the other crew members. "I'm the writer, Adams. Stop doing my job for me." Muted laughter. "But yeah, sounds good. I'll have Jacobs look it through at post."

The camera moves again, and my heart leaps when it focuses on Kagura, who was standing off to one side. "Miss Kino, where are we going next?"

"We'll need to go deeper into the woods, though I cannot guarantee the exact location. My father's map is very crudely drawn—mostly guesswork, I'm afraid."

"It's better than nothing, Miss Kino," says whoever is holding the camcorder. "You still got your photocopied maps, guys?"

A chorus of yeahs.

Adams says, "To be honest, I'm not holding my breath. If

nothing else, we can attempt to call out the spirits in the forest if we can't find the village. But hey, who knows?"

"Yeah," I mutter, "who knew?"

The video runs for another ten minutes. I don't glean much from it. The crew is mainly silent as they travel, with only a few warnings from Kagura about how to proceed whenever the terrain proves particularly tricky. When not in motion, the video cam tends to linger on Kagura, who pauses every now and then to survey the area with a worried frown on her face.

More often than not, Stephen Riley is by her side, talking and gesturing at things out of the camera's range. He sneaks glances at her when he thinks she isn't looking, and I can tell from the unguarded look on his face that the man has a huge crush on the *miko*. The faint snickers from behind the camera tell me that whoever's filming knows it too.

It's only when the video's about to end that I see the ghost.

What gets me is that, like Okiku, she's very young. Unlike Okiku though, she is grinning, lips distended and stretched over blackened teeth, and her eyes are wild with madness. Her skin is paper-white; her short-cropped hair is bobbed and cut in the style of a *kokeshi* doll's. She is clad in a heavy ceremonial kimono that leaves a silky trail on the ground behind her.

Her eyebrows are different. They're shaved off, with teardrop-shaped gobs of ink painted on in their place. From what I remember of the books I've read, it's a fashionable court custom called *hikimayu*. It was a popular practice among noble ladies, though it tapered off by the time the Meiji era rolled around.

The apparition makes an unnerving, ululating sound. I watch in horror as it flings its head back and jerks toward Kagura.

The video chooses that moment to end.

"Ah, damn it!" I frantically play the next one, but I needn't have worried.

"We found it!" The excitement bubbles in Adams's voice. Nobody else seems to have noticed the ghostly presence I saw in the last clip, and the sight of Kagura standing unharmed beside Adams helps me breathe easier.

"Oh my God, we actually found it!"

They'd found the village. Hope struggles with the despair growing inside me. Kagura and the crew must be somewhere around this place, but that also means they could have encountered the wandering ghost as well.

"I don't believe this," I hear Kagura whisper in Japanese. The others are too jubilant to hear her dismay.

"This is unbelievable," Stephen Riley is saying. "We have actually found the legendary Aitou village, a place no one has seen in more than a hundred years. This is almost like—like a ghost hunter's version of El Dorado. This is phenomenal."

"It has all the atmosphere you'd expect with this creepy fog and rows and rows of abandoned houses," someone else says. "It's the perfect place to talk to ghosts."

"Please stop." The camera swings back to Kagura. The *miko* is visibly distressed, and she's holding a wooden stake in each hand. "Please, please be silent. We are in danger here."

"In danger? I don't see anything, Miss Kino. There's no one left here."

"It does not matter," Kagura insists. "Please stay close to me and do as I say. Strange spirits still live here. Do not anger them."

"Kagura—" Riley begins.

"There is no time, Stephen! We must find the dolls and exorcise the ghosts immediately. My father's notes say it's the only way. Do not antagonize these spirits!"

"Miss Kino," Adams protests, "we make a business out of pissing off ghosts. That's the risk we take every time we're out on haunts like this."

But even as he says the words, a startled cry rises in the air. The camera turns to one of the film crew, who is trembling on the ground.

"Franz is gone!"

"What? But he was just standing—"

"I saw it. I saw her grab him from the mist. She dragged him into it." The man raises his arm, and the camcorder follows the direction he's pointing, away from the village. But the woods have disappeared into an unending swirl of fog so thick you could tap-dance across it. "Oh my God, she has Franz!"

"Run! Make for the shrine!" This time, the crew takes heed of the fear in Kagura's voice. The men scramble for safety, the camera bouncing at dizzying angles.

Then the camera sweeps back to Kagura, who had remained behind to face the ghost inside that mist. A few seconds before the video ends, I see something rising behind Kagura. I pause the film to study it. It's not the female ghost from the previous video. The spirit is facing away from the camera, so all I can tell is that her hair is longer and her head is set at an unnatural angle. My hopes fall. Had Kagura confronted it?

I view the last video. At first, there's nothing but black, and I wonder if someone forgot to take off the lens cap. But then a man moves into view. I assume it's the man who's been holding the camcorder all this time. His face is pale, and streaks of blood run across his face, though I can't tell if it's his own or someone else's. He's wheezing, as if he's having difficulty breathing. I don't know where he is. The camera seems to have a hard time focusing on his surroundings. The frame looks grayed out and blurred.

"If anyone can…suh-see this, puh-puh-please help," he gasps, struggling with the words, "don't let her…don't let hhhher take me. The shrine is the kkuuuh-key. The shri…"

He stops, eyes wide. Something has slithered up behind him. Pale hands wrap around his face. A dead girl's face rises on screen before the man loses his grip on the camera, and it crashes to the ground. In the distance, there is an odd, gargling sound.

The camera continues to record. I wait with bated breath, torn between my horror for the man and fear that there is nothing I can do. I know I'm too late to help this man. The next best thing I can do is to avenge him or put a stop to whatever spirit got him.

I regret the thought almost immediately. The girl comes back into view, her face so close to the screen that I reel away from the camera, hitting the wall with the back of my head.

It's not the same ghost who'd been tailing the crew or the one behind Kagura or *even* the one I'd seen crawling outside. Much to my shock, the ghost has the same teardrop brows, the same black, distended smile, but it's a different girl.

"He is not the one," the ghost whispers into the camera and then reaches out for me.

I switch off the camcorder, breathing hard. Throughout my misery, Okiku does nothing. Her eyes are closed.

I come to three conclusions from the videos. They confirm that the ghost hunters arrived at the village where I am now. They tell me there are at least four angry spirits here.

Now I remember why the temple I'd seen when I entered the village looked so familiar. It's the same one in the photograph Kagura sent me. And if she and any of the men are still alive, it's possible that they'll be at that shrine.

Which means I need to leave this house, whether I want to or not. *Argh*.

"There are many ghosts wandering," Okiku whispers, sensing where my thoughts lie.

"I know."

"There is one ghost wandering."

"Yes, I think she made that pretty clear when she chased us in here."

"No. There is one ghost wandering this house."

A cold chill takes over. I glance back at the sliding door in a panic, but the *ofuda* remains securely in place. There doesn't seem to be any malignant presence outside.

But then the thumping noises begin, and it sounds like the noise is coming from my left.

The furniture that remains in the house is in varying states of disrepair, with parts and disintegrating pieces bundled against one wall. The scratching sounds come from somewhere behind them.

I respond by scampering as far away from the noise as I can, but Okiku is built differently. She moves toward the pile.

"Okiku…"

She ignores me. "It is harmless, but you must end it."

"End what?"

Furniture tumbles down. Okiku sweeps the remaining debris away with one powerful swipe of her hand, revealing a strange cocoon-like being. It's the size of a full-grown adult, if full-grown adults wrap themselves like caterpillars and thump against the floor in mute agony.

"What is this?" I ask, appalled.

"A victim," Okiku says, her voice one of sadness.

"Are you going to…"

She shakes her head. "I cannot touch it. But you can."

"Me? Ki, I am not touching that thing even if it's a million dollars." A million dollars that's scratching its way across the floor.

"Wood will be enough."

I look down at the stake I'm holding in my hand.

"Please." Her voice is softer. "It is suffering…"

I don't want to. I really don't. But Okiku has never pleaded with me for anything before…

I swallow and step forward. The cocooned creature makes a noise that sounds like a whimper as I raise my hand.

The thing breaks open when I find my mark. It's like a brittle, desiccated coffin made of thread. Inside, there's a wisp of an image: a young man in worker's clothes, a look of indescribable despair on his face. Then he's gone. The cocoon crumbles into dust, and all that is left are cobweb-like strings splayed on the ground.

"Silkworms," Okiku murmurs.

I shudder. I know a lot of rural villages used to be established in the silkworm trade, but just how big do these things get in Aitou? "Ki, was that a man in there?"

She nods. "He was suffering. The village still suffers."

"But why would anyone do that to him?"

"There is a hunger here. There is a need to feed."

"Why couldn't you free him?" The words come out sounding petulant, but I can't help myself. The thought of whatever killed and entrapped these villagers is an unsettling reminder of the kind of place we're stuck in.

"It is a creature of earth."

That might sound cryptic to anyone else, but I understand. Certain elements can nurture or destroy others, according to *wu xing*, a Chinese philosophy often associated with feng shui. Metal weakens wood; wood weakens earth; earth weakens water; water weakens fire; and fire weakens metal. I suppose it's why the wooden spikes worked so well on it. I now realize why Kagura brought them with her and insisted that the ghost crew bring the same.

It seemed odd of Okiku to flee from the crawling creature when she'd always stood her ground before. Or that she'd ask me to kill the cocoon. Okiku has always wanted to deliver the killing blows so I won't have to.

She's standing so *damn* still, as if she's afraid she might break if she moves. I take a step toward her and she sags forward, the rattle in her throat no longer a warning of impending death but a sound of pain. I catch her before she topples forward. And then I realize.

"Ki, if these are all creatures of earth, then you're—"

Earth weakens water.

"It is of no consequence."

I wish she'd stop saying that. "'Of no consequence,' my ass. Ki, you can barely stand. If staying in this village makes you weaker, then I want to get us out of here as soon as we can.

"Look, do you want to—do you want to rest for a bit? I'll miss the company, but it'll help keep your strength up."

She looks at me.

"No, I'm not kidding. I've got these—" I make a halfhearted wave at her with the spike. "And I've got flashlights and *ofudas* and everything. Come on. The sooner we find Kagura and get out of here, the sooner we can find another hot spring to annoy you with."

She finally smiles at my lame attempts at humor. She draws near and touches my face. Her fingers are cold but not as chilly as the fog outside. "Be vigilant," she says before stepping into me, and—

—she isn't breathing. She is fighting her way out of the

find him seek him take him

dank cold, bloodless fingers clawing at unforgiving stone, and she isn't breathing. It takes so long, so long to find her way out of her water grave, and she isn't breathing. Her mouth is screaming, the things inside her head are screaming, but the night around her feels strangely silent, unconcerned and

little deaths whisper whispering claws and bone find him

unforgiving as she reaches the top.

Her tangled corpse rises out of the well. Horrible noises rumble in her throat. She isn't breathing. Her fingers, talons now, swipe at the thin air with growing ferocity, leaving grooves in the wind.

Her first decision as a dead woman is vengeance. She crawls up the walls of the castle, the castle that should have meant something to her, but it is a luxury she can no longer remember, because she

creatures flit blood and bone blood and bone

ashes lift find him take him find

him

isn't breathing. She is looking for him. She is looking for him, because she isn't breathing, and he is her

vengeance.

He is looking out the window, and he cries when she looms before him. For all his deformities, he is a soldier. He scrambles for his sword and draws it. She shrills her laughter when he slices through her body and finds no resistance, because she isn't breathing and he can no longer

seek destroy kill feast kill feast kill eat kill eat kill

touch her.

For the first time, she sees the boy on his back. Wide-eyed, trembling, more skeleton than youth, the crumble of his clothes older than his age. She was not his first, and the rage

kill eat kill feast kill eat kill feast kill FEAST KILL FEAST KILLFEAST

grows that he could not even accord her that privilege.

The retainer begins to

KILLFEASTKILLFEASTKILLFEASTKILLFEASTKILL FEASTKILLFEAST

scream.

And when it is over, she—

—I sink to the floor, forgetting momentarily that I have legs.

I need a few seconds to catch my breath while trying to blink the images out from my eyeballs. I'm usually treated to snippets of Okiku's old life when we merge, but this was the first time I've ever been privy to snippets of her life after she died. I could feel the retainer's fear and her gleeful satisfaction as her hands dug into his eyes. Viewing his death—however much he deserved it—leaves a foul taste in my soul.

I close my eyes and wait until the shaking passes. There will be more questions to ask Okiku later.

I retrieve my backpack, but I need a few minutes to marshal the nerve to peel the *ofuda* off the doors. Nothing comes screaming through the shoji screen, so I slide it open slowly, still expecting the worst. But there's nothing waiting for me on the other side—pun intended.

"Here goes, Ki," I mutter under my breath and start running.

I make sure to keep within the shadows, uncertain if any spirits can find me by sight alone or if they're using some other preternatural sense. I don't give them much opportunity, skirting from house to house while working my way toward the shrine. I can see it silhouetted against the dark night, and the rest of my trip is, thankfully, free of any mishaps.

I see a couple more of the human-sized silkworm cocoons along the way. I know Okiku would insist, so I dispatch them as well. The first carries the soul of a young mother and her child, and the second is a little boy's. I'm not sure if this gives them peace, but at this point, I can't do much else for them.

Several of the houses I pass are no longer habitable, though a few remain upright. The exterior of every house also seems to have a cabinet-like enclosure with multiple dividers along the outside walls, though I also see similar structures in the outdoor sheds beside these residences. I wonder briefly what they're for but decide I have bigger problems at the moment.

The biggest of these turns out to be the shrine itself. The main doors are boarded up. I can't find any other way inside, and I don't have anything that could help pry them open. Ironically, I concede that a crowbar is probably the first thing Callie would have thought to bring.

Thinking about Callie makes my eyes sting. The idea that she could be trapped here as well terrified me at first. But there was nothing unusual in the photo I'd taken of her to show this, and that gives me some comfort, however cold.

She's going to be so pissed we got separated though.

"Now what?" I ask myself.

I circle the shrine as best as I can, but I can't find another entrance. I take a step back, studying the boards. They were nailed haphazardly and with little finesse, but there are small holes in the wood that I can peek through.

What I see makes my spirits sink even further. There is a large, gaping hole in the floor. Kagura isn't here.

I ponder using my flashlight, hesitating only because I don't know if this might attract more attention than I want.

A twig snaps somewhere behind me, and I whirl around. The road behind me is empty, and I don't see anything moving among the houses. Still, I grip the spike tightly in my right hand, the flashlight in my left, in case it's possible to bash a ghost's head with it. After all, these bastards cheat.

I resume looking through the hole and blink. The shrine's floor and the walls, in their varying shades of darkness, have disappeared. Now everything's blue, as if a blanket had been draped across the opening when I wasn't looking. In the center of that blue is a small black circle.

I still don't understand.

Until the black circle in that pool of blue dilates—and she blinks.

CHAPTER ELEVEN

PURPOSE

I don't recall how I made it from gaping at the ghost girl to cowering inside the nearest house. But I'm taping another *ofuda* across the sliding screen by the time I'm aware of what I'm doing. Then I sag to my knees, because if those ghosts don't kill me, a premature heart attack will.

I can feel Okiku stirring, concerned.

"No." My voice comes out hoarse. "I'm okay."

It's too early for her to have fully recovered, and despite all the evidence to the contrary, male pride insists I can handle the situation until she has.

I scan the room with my flashlight, trying to listen for any sounds of scratching and thumping, but I don't seem to be sharing the space with anyone else, incorporeal or otherwise. Then I devote a minute or two to rocking myself on the floor and whimpering, because holy hell, that was scary as fuck.

Blue eyes. The ghost had freaking blue eyes. I'm the only Asian I know with blue eyes, and my dad is to thank for that. Kazuhiko

Kino never mentioned any of the girls having a foreign mom or dad, which makes this even more confusing.

After I calm myself as best as I can, I take another quick look around. This room is much larger than the first one I entered. It's also more fully furnished with an assortment of tables and chairs that have stood the test of time. What catches my eye are the books strewn about—some still on makeshift wooden shelves and bookcases, others tumbled about the floor—as if someone left in a hurry and didn't bother to clean up before he went. When I examine one of the far bookcases, I find another writhing cocoon on the floor beside it, this time an old woman, which I take care of quickly.

A yellowed and moth-eaten old futon is folded in the room's center. A small Jizo statue, complete with its own mini stone grotto, is built into one corner. It's the only thing in the room that looks intact, though parts of its face have eroded over time.

The books are the obvious choice to look through, but I'm not sure how much information I can glean from these. Aside from being written in kanji, they are worn out and capable of crumbling into dust if I so much as touch them. There's nothing sadder than a book that hasn't been cared for, a book too broken to read.

Still, I try to thumb my way through the ones that seem most durable, hoping for an illustration or some clue as to where Kagura and the others might be. Some books look like they've been churned out of an old printing press, but others appear to have been written by hand. Those are the ones that I concentrate on. I find a book with a series of rough diagrams and a drawing I recognize immediately, given my previous scares.

Silkworms. The diagrams depict silkworms in varying stages of life, from egg to pupa to ugly flying insect.

I remember the white, shapeless mass thumping on the floor, and I shudder.

I find a few more drawings in other volumes—either raising silkworms was the occupant's hobby or Aitou trade centered around it. There must be a connection between this and the large creature I had to kill, because there was no way that cocoon could have been natural.

Remember my pet spider? It's back. I know even before I turn around that there's a presence behind me. The tape recorder is within reach, but I'd need to dig into my pack for the dolls I brought with me. The wooden stake is my best hope.

I gulp in a deep breath and then whip around, taking several steps back as I do, in case it tries to lunge for me.

It doesn't. It's not the crawling ghost or the ghost in the videos or even the shrine ghost.

It's an old man, and he doesn't attack. Instead, he stands there and looks at me with a sad, forlorn look on his graying face. He's dressed in a long, plain robe, and the *tate eboshi* cap on his forehead tells me he was someone of enough importance in the village to be given the right to wear it. Every textbook I've read on Japanese history always portrayed scribes with that tall, black hat.

He's staring at me—not in a bad way but not in any way I can call good either. He lifts his hand and points at a spot above my head and then vanishes before my eyes.

I turn in the direction he pointed. There are a couple of books on one of the upper shelves, collecting dust and cobwebs. I carefully take them down and slowly open one, trying not to choke on the dust billowing in my face.

It doesn't look all that different from the others I've tried to read, but the handwriting's a lot more legible and I can pick out maybe one word for every seven or eight. Some words, like *hitori-kakurenbo* and *kekkon*, jump out at me, because I've researched them enough to familiarize myself with the kanji.

Hitori-kakurenbo means one-man tag. The same game I played with Sondheim and Trish and the seven-armed, unfortunately named Dumbelina.

Kekkon is not a word I would normally find with it, but I know what it means—marriage. Kagura's father wrote about a ritualized marriage in the village, and Kagura mentioned it in the video.

I don't like where this is going. I'm not surprised that marriage is mentioned in connection with the village, but what does one-man tag have to do with all this?

I pick out a few more words, but the context is difficult to understand. I see "shrine maiden" and "dolls" and "companion," but the rest of the passage may as well be caveman drawings for all the good it does me. My frustration mounts. I know there's something important written in these pages, but I can't read it!

I turn a few more pages and a sheaf of paper slips out. I pick it up; it looks like a list:

梶原 冨士子	十六歳	明治三十四	平川 登里生
狐 美猫	十五歳	明治三十七	新田 明乃
森本 北	十六歳	明治四十	日髙 明彦
紺野 成子	十七歳	明治四十三	三宅 丈夫
平野 蘭	十五歳	大正二	花壇 栄武
内山 幸子	十六歳	大正五	岡村 真琴
甥御門 佛	十七歳		

I don't recognize most of the kanji, but I know the third column is a list of dates based on the Japanese calendar, with the last entry in the same time period as that in the girl's diary. This could be important.

I turn my attention to the book's cover. It's blank, except for a name scrawled along the bottom. Japanese names are even harder for me to understand than words, because one additional stroke of the kanji can completely change its meaning. But the owner of this house was clearly an important person—possibly the man whose ghost directed me to the book.

"Are you still here?" My voice quavers. Helpful or not, he's still a ghost, and I'm still not sure what his motives are. I'm not actually expecting a reply, but I'm disappointed by the silence.

"Tarquin?" I hear Okiku whisper. I feel her step out, stronger now than she was, another sign that there are no other spirits nearby—malignant ones anyway.

"I need some help." I show her the book. "Any idea what this is all about?"

Okiku studies the pages and turns them rapidly. She could soak up a library in minutes if she wanted to. "It is a ritual," she says softly.

"What kind of ritual?"

"A sacrifice. A foul sacrifice."

I swallow, my sense of foreboding rising. I'm trying to put together all the information I've gotten so far. "What does it say?"

"That girls are given to boys in the village for marriage."

"The ritual marriages, right? I guess one part of Kagura's father's research has been verified. Anything else in particular?"

"For three years, she is given only the boy for company. At the end, she is willing. At the end, he will also be willing. She will be chosen."

"So it's a nicer way of saying she'll be killed. I get it. Did Kazuhiko interview some of these boys before they were... No, I don't think so. It would have been too important not to have been mentioned in his research, and Kagura never said anything about it. Do you know what this list is for?" I show her the page.

"Girls," Okiku says softly, touching the first column. Her finger moves across the rest. "Ages. *Nengō*." I nod. *Nengō* are Japanese eras—often named in accordance with the emperor in power—that were used in place of dates on the standard Western calendar. The dates in the girl's diary were marked the same way. Based on how these *nengō* were written, I estimate that three years have passed in between each name, which makes seven names over twenty years. Okiku nods in confirmation, then explains the final column. "Boys."

"Do you know what this means? Are these the girls who were sacrificed? Why does the last entry only include the girl's name?" I pause, staring at the last line. Then I take the book back from Okiku and look at the cover again.

"Say, Ki… This name has some of the same kanji as the one on the cover."

"Oimikado Hiroshi." She touches the book, then returns to the loose sheaf. "Oimikado Hotoke."

"They're related? Like…father and daughter?" Did incomplete information mean that the girl managed to escape and the practice was discontinued? That didn't sound likely. I know from firsthand experience that botched rituals can lead to hauntings and curses. And I'm beginning to think the ghosts who haunt the village are the sacrificed girls. Was that what the man's ghost was trying to do? Show me how to break the curse somehow?

What had Kagura's notes said again?

Should any of these rituals fail, then the sacrifices shall be released back into the world of men. Those who face their wrath are doomed.

Well, damn.

A cry splits the air from somewhere outside, all the more horrifying because I recognize it as a human sound. I spring for the door and edge it open, careful not to dislodge the *ofuda* and wary that this might somehow be a trap, though I think it would be hard for any ghost to mimic the absolute terror I hear in that voice.

A man is on the ground, his shirt caked in blood and grime. There are several cuts on his face, and one of his legs appears to be broken. His eyes widen when he sees me. "Help!" he gasps, turning to look over his shoulder in fright.

I don't need to see why. The crawling ghost is back, and she is closing in. I know he will never make it into the house by himself.

I tear out the *ofuda* to open the door all the way and lunge forward to help. The man has thirty pounds or so on me, and lugging him inside is both exhausting and terrifying, because the ghost is gaining on us. For a brief moment, I'm tempted to leave this man to his fate and save myself. But the ghost makes a horrific clacking sound, and every muscle in my body screams at me to stop thinking and bring him in, *goddamn it*.

We make it inside, the ghost only a few yards away. I all but toss the poor man into the center of the room and slide the door shut, though the force makes the screen bounce open a couple of inches. I yank out another *ofuda* and slap it onto the screen, right in the gap between the two—just moments before the girl's ghastly white face appears, clacking her teeth at me.

I freeze, ready to pee in my pants and expecting the *ofuda* not to work. We stare at each other, and the girl's smile only widens, like she's enjoying the game I'm letting her play. She lifts her hand and places it on the shoji screen. Her smile shrinks when Okiku looms up behind me, matching her stare for undead stare. The other ghost eventually retreats but only partly because of Okiku. Her filmy eyes flick to something to her left, and she emits a furious snarl before vanishing into the mist—but not before I get a better view of the bloodied green kimono she's wearing.

My blood freezes at the sight. It's a selection of cranes—how did that girl's diary describe it?— "looking out through the bamboos and plums."

Another ghost flits across the opening of the door, head tilted to one side, hair thankfully covering her face and sparing me the horrifying sight. Unlike the first, this one prefers to stand, passing me without so much as a glance. Her focus seems intent on the other ghost, and when she disappears, I am too glad to question her indifference.

Shaken, I sag to the floor before remembering I have a wounded guy with me. Up close, his injuries are more serious than I thought. There are angry red gashes across his chest, the tip of one extending all the way up to his cheek. As far as I can tell, his right leg is useless. I don't need a medical degree to know he won't be using it ever again. He's making harsh sounds, nearly unintelligible in his agony.

At best, I can do something about the lacerations on his chest. I pour some of my water onto the wounds and wrap the deeper gashes with the strips of bandages from the medical kit. The man sinks into unconsciousness, still sobbing. From the ragged remains of his shirt, I can see the *Ghost Haunts* logo, and there's no doubt in my mind that he's one of the film crew. The knowledge brings me hope—because Kagura and the others might have survived too—but also fear that they all encountered the ghost that did a number on this guy.

Okiku is perched atop a small pile of rubble, eyeballing the man the way she might a poisonous snake. I shoo her away, because a competent nurse she is not.

"You're not going to die," I tell the man, trying not to sound too grim about that statement. I don't really want another death on my conscience, and if I want to find his companions alive, that revolves around keeping him breathing so I can ferret out as much information as I can.

The man revives again after a few minutes, and I help him drink from the bottle. The thought crosses my mind that this place doesn't look like it has access to clean drinking water, and with mine now more than halfway depleted, I'll need to figure something out later on.

"You're not a ghost," the guy whispers after one last swallow.

I bite back the urge to be sarcastic, lowering my voice instead to try to sound soothing. "No, I'm a friend of Kagura's. You're with the *Ghost Haunts* crew, right?" A weak moan is his answer. "I've been looking for you guys. Do you know where the others are?"

"The shrine. They're heading to the shrine…"

"I've been to the shrine. It's boarded up."

The man tries to shake his head, but he mews in pain again. I take the rolled-up futon and prop it behind his back. There isn't much in the way of blankets, so I'm relieved the house is sturdy enough to stop the cold drafts from outside.

"A...nother way," the man gasps. "There's another way..."

"Another way into the shrine? Where is it?"

"The dolls," the man sobs. "Miss Kino..."

His strength gives out, and he lapses once more into unconsciousness.

I stare at the overhead ceiling, scowling, like maybe the answer is going to leap out at me from there. Then I look through my backpack and bring out the camcorder. My skin crawls at the thought of the video, but I can't bring myself to delete it, under the absurd, twisted notion that it might still have useful information that I missed the first time.

I play the second video again, fast-forwarding through Kagura's interview until I come to the part I'm looking for. "He possessed a rough map, supposedly of the village itself. I can't vouch for its accuracy, but certain houses were marked with names—seven in all," Kagura is saying. "These were believed to be the family residences of the seven girls who had been sacrificed—"

I hit the fast-forward button and release it. "I'd like copies for all of us before we set out, if you don't mind," Garrick says this time. "It might not be accurate, but it's the best lead we've got."

Bingo.

Pawing through an unconscious man's pants while he's still

wearing them does not rank up there as one of my greatest moments, but given what's at stake, I mumble an apology and dig into the sleeping man's pockets like my life depends on it. I find a lighter, his wallet (driver's license puts his name as Alan George), and a piece of paper that I unfold eagerly.

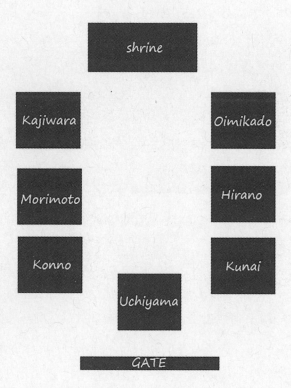

A "rough sketch" is right. The only houses listed on the map are the girls' residences, but based on my last exploration outside, I know there are a lot more houses than this, and none of them had any family names written on their front porches. Okiku seems to be able to detect where the ghosts are, so I figure I'll let her do the guiding if I need to.

All the houses look the same to me anyway, so I focus on the shrine to get my bearings, then work from there. If this map is accurate, then the house we are in must be the Oimikado household, which explains a lot. The ghost I saw earlier must be the elder Oimikado, and his daughter the last to be sacrificed.

But what happened to her? The list implies that the seventh ritual hadn't been completed. Where is the girl now? Is she one of the spirits roving this village, or did she manage to escape?

I scan the map again to compare it with the list. The kanji of the girls' family names match the houses mentioned, which bolsters the credibility of both. But is there something in these houses we're supposed to find? And for what? Hiroshi Mikage's residence isn't marked, and I'm assuming the most important man in the village gets to have a palace of sorts. Why isn't it indicated here?

All girls eight through twelve shall bring their hanayome ningyō, *each in their likeness. When the door closes, the sun shall die. When it is reborn anew,* she *whose doll is honored shall be chosen, and* she *must be willing.*

I'm pretty sure that was how they selected the girls for the ceremony. If the families in Aitou village were as traditional as they sounded, they would have kept their daughters' dolls. They would have found places of honor for the dolls in family shrines, where they would have been protected and worshipped along with the other gods.

It also meant that if these daughters are still prowling the village, the only vessels capable of containing them will be these dolls, if any of them still remain.

"Oh shit." I whisper. To close the hell's gate, seven rituals are required, and at least six have already been carried out. Six girls meant six dolls. I now understand the purpose of one-man tag in this village. To contain their ghosts, I'll have to play with each of them.

"Oh shit," I say again, just because I can. The thought of playing another game of one-man tag is enough to make me weep, let alone six more.

"Okiku, can you tell me her name—right here?" My finger hovers on the sixth name on the list.

"Uchiyama Yukiko."

"Uchiyama Yukiko," I echo. The Yukiko-chan referenced in that unnamed girl's diary that Kagura kept. The same Yukiko-chan to have worn a kimono of cranes and plums.

She had been chased away by that other ghost and for no reason I could think of. Are they possessive of their respective territories? It's something to remember at least.

The man coughs weakly and opens his eyes again. I'm by his side within seconds. "Listen, Mr. George," I begin, trying to make myself as precise as I can, wanting to learn as much as I can without pushing. "My name is Tark Halloway. I'm looking for Kagura and the rest of your crew. Do you understand me so far?"

The man blinks at me but nods.

"Good. I know you're in pain, and I'm sorry, but this is important. I want you to tell me everything Kagura told you about this place. Do you know where she is or where the others are? What did she tell you to do?"

Alan gulps, his eyes flicking toward the shoji screen.

"No one is coming in, Alan." I try to sound reassuring. "There are wards on the door to prevent anything from coming in. Please, I need to know."

The man's lips move. "The dolls," he croaks out. "The dolls are the key."

"The key?"

"The key to the shrine below. Miss Kagura…" He coughs again and struggles to sit up. I help him back down, not wanting him to see the extent of his own injuries. "Miss Kagura took…the ghost. It…went *into* the doll. But there were more of them…"

"What doll was this?" I persist.

"She found it. In one of the huh-houses…" His voice trails, losing strength again. "She called it a…a haname…hayome…"

"A *hanayome ningyo*." A bridal doll, just like Okiku had said. Just like the doll that had been staring at me in the first house we snuck into. I'd dismissed it as a simple child's toy.

Then there must be other dolls like those, scattered in the houses around us.

That settles things. George's account cheers me up, as odd as it may seem. Kagura's alive. I know it. She's stuck here in this strange limbo, and she's done what I would have counted on her to do: seal these ghosts away. If I investigate the houses, I can possibly find the bridal dolls and find her.

The downside is that to do this, I'll have to brave going outside again. Out to face the ghosts and whatever creatures wander in that dark.

Decisions, decisions.

"I can sense them," Okiku says.

"The ghosts?" I ask, ignoring the man's confused expression.

"No. The dolls. They are still in the village."

"Are they intact? I mean, can we use them?"

"As long as the ghosts wander, the dolls remain." Okiku purses her lips.

"Good to know."

"It is strange. They feel…"

I wait for her to finish, but Okiku's train of thought ends there. Instead, she stands by the shoji screen, frowning to herself.

I give the man more water to drink and adjust the futon behind him so he's as comfortable as he can be. "I am going to leave," I begin and then keep him still when he bolts up to protest. "No, listen to me. I've placed wards on the doors. As long as you're here, you're going to be safe. I mean, we've been here for a while and we have been, right?"

I fish out a few of the *ofuda* and press them into his hand. I add a couple of the wooden spikes as well. "Keep these close to you at all times. They can protect you. I'll ward the doors again when I go out. Do not open them to anyone else. As soon as I find Kagura and the others, I'm coming back for you."

"You're going out there? With all those…things?"

"Somebody has to. I must find Kagura. I'm…her apprentice."

A small shudder goes through the man, but after a moment, he nods again, firmer this time. "Be careful."

Probably not, I think grimly, as I finish my preparations and slide open the door, knowing I am exposing myself to the terrors with that simple action. But hey, I've got nothing else planned tonight.

"Let's go kick some ghost ass, Ki."

CHAPTER TWELVE

MATERNAL BONES

Okiku tells me the names of the young girls on the list, and I scribble them down before I steal out of the house. I'm trying to commit them to memory.

梶原 冨士子 *Kajiwara Fujiko*	十六歳 *sixteen years old*	明治三十四 *Meiji 34th year*	平川 登里生 *Hirakawa Torio*
狐 美猫 *Kunai Mineko*	十五歳 *fifteen years old*	明治三十七 *Meiji 37th year*	新田 明乃 *Nitta Akeno*
森本 北 *Morimoto Kita*	十六歳 *sixteen years old*	明治四十 *Meiji 40th year*	日髙 明彦 *Hidaka Akihiko*
紺野 成子 *Konno Nariko*	十七歳 *seventeen years old*	明治四十三 *Meiji 43rd year*	三宅 丈夫 *Miyake Takeo*
平野 蘭 *Hirano Ran*	十五歳 *fifteen years old*	大正二 *Taishō 2nd year*	花壇 栄武 *Kadan Abe*
内山 幸子 *Uchiyama Yukiko*	十六歳 *sixteen years old*	大正五 *Taishō 5th year*	岡村 真琴 *Okamura Makoto*
甥御門 佛 *Oimikado Hotoke*	十七歳 *seventeen years old*		

The precious map is in one pocket and my tape recorder is in the other because I know I've got a long night ahead, and I'd rather keep my hands occupied with things I can use to stab or exorcise.

The mist is thicker now, and it makes my skin crawl. But Okiku forges on, floating into the fog like we're strolling through Disneyland. I follow her lead, trusting she'll spot anything untoward long before I can.

According to Kagura's map, the Hirano residence is the nearest to where we're standing, so we make for that. I'm hoping to take a clockwise route through the village, both to systematically search out Kagura and the other men and also so I won't need to retrace my route back to the shrine. When I loop back, hopefully it will be with all the possessed dolls in tow so I can figure out a way to burn them all at once.

I've noted that Yukiko Uchiyama was prowling the area near her family residence, so I presume these ghosts don't wander too far from where they lived during their lifetime. Most of the ghosts anyway, I correct myself, remembering the ghoul who chased Yukiko away.

One-man tag takes on a whole new meaning here. I won't need much preparation to lure in the ghosts. I can't scrub down the walls and floors with herbs or holy water for protection. I can't mark small circles on the floor with salt. But the dolls should be enough to attract the ghosts, which is a good thing.

But I won't have any kind of personal protection either, which is a bad thing.

"There," Okiku whispers as we enter. The house is worse off than the previous two. Parts of the roof have already caved in, and there's debris and dust everywhere. I'm pretty sure I would never have found the doll by myself, but Okiku, ever the trusty meta-phorical bloodhound, leads me to a large pile of rotten wood and torn fabric at the center of the room. I wish I'd brought some kind of hazmat suit, because if the ghosts won't kill me, the mold prob-ably will.

I grab my shirt's neck collar and lift it over my nose, trying not to choke on the dust. Everything here is so deteriorated that I'm surprised anything is left standing. But I see a dusty mirror, the glass still intact; a smattering of broken crockery and dented cook-ware; and the remains of what appears to be a tea set.

My ghost walks around the heap of rubble, which is almost as tall as I am. She keeps her distance. Technically, Ki is made from the same stuff as these other spirits, distinguished from them by only a conscience and willpower the size of Tokyo. She never touches the dolls I've used before, because they could be used against her too and because I suspect doing so would be like touching your own grave.

I set to work dismantling the mound, clearing away the bigger rocks and wood before digging my way toward its center. Fifteen minutes later, I've made some progress, though my hands are bruised and cut in a few places from the occasional unexpected splinter.

"Nothing out there yet, Ki?" I grunt, manhandling a three-foot plank out of my way. The way Okiku has been staring at the wood-pile, I'm surprised it hasn't spontaneously burst into flames.

The reason for her intense scrutiny soon becomes obvious. I pull out one last piece of timber, take a look at what I've uncovered, and nearly drop the whole damn thing on my foot.

There's a corpse at the center of the heap, more skeleton than flesh. It's a woman, because scraps of kimono are still clinging to what's left of her frame and strands of black hair are spread out around the bits where her head used to be.

Nestled within its shrunken arms is the doll I'd been looking for. It's grimy, with parts of its kimono frayed at the edges, but compared to its owner, it's well preserved. A little too well preserved, in fact, for something that has been decomposing for years. I remember from Kagura's notes that most girls in small villages played with paper dolls, because most wouldn't have been able to afford any other kind. Villagers didn't buy these ceremonial-looking dolls as a hobby.

This has to be the *hanayome ningyō*. It looks like it could easily have come out of the expensive doll collection my mother used to have.

The corpse's arms are wrapped tightly around the doll, like it was never letting it go. Eye sockets gaze up at me, daring me to approach.

"This," I say because I really don't want to do this, "sucks."

I draw as close to the remains as I can and, with shaking hands, reach for the doll. I don't want to touch the corpse. I could be infected with all sorts of bacteria and disease and madness. As a compromise, I snag a kimono sleeve, gently lifting it and the bony hand inside it up and away from the doll. Then I do the same to the other arm.

"I'm sorry."

The corpse's hand springs up and catches mine just as I am lifting the doll away from its chest.

I am not ashamed of shrieking. My arm whips back, and the doll follows its momentum, landing on its head a couple of yards away. I sit hard on my ass as the skeleton tries to rise to its feet, bones rattling. The rotting body twists its head in my direction and groans.

"Ki!" I scramble for the doll, my fingers finding it just as something finds my ankle. I'm dragged a few feet but retain my grip on the doll. A bad time to choose the stake for my primary weapon, considering there isn't much flesh to stab anymore. "Ki! What are you waiting for?"

Okiku hovers beside me, a concerned look on her face as another fierce tug drags me toward the creature. I kick at its arm, and it shatters, but the corpse is beginning to crawl.

"I promised."

"What?"

"I promised not to attack without first speaking to you."

There's a skeleton clinging to my ass, and Okiku chooses this moment to quibble over semantics. "Okiku, I take back whatever I said! You have my permission to kill it!"

"Is this what you truly—"

"*Okiku, kill it.*"

She stomps down hard on the skeleton's wrist. There's a sickening crunch, and the whole hand dissolves into fine black sand. The rest of its body twists and then collapses onto the floor. Okiku hovers over it, waiting for it to rise again.

A rustle of cloth behind me. A low, moaning sound. A sudden movement catches my eye.

I turn and spot the dirty mirror again, my own face barely recognizable underneath all the cobwebs and grime.

But I see enough to realize there's something behind me with wide, dark eyes staring out of its head.

I scramble forward on my hands and knees. I feel a swipe at the back of my neck, a harsh snarl. The bride ghost reaches for me again, all hair and groping hands. It lifts its head, and I see that we have not yet met. From what I can see of her torn face, she's younger and slighter in form—but with the same distorted grin, the same ink-black brows as the other brides.

Okiku reacts. Her fingernails bite into the ghost's yellow kimono, but the ghost shrugs off the grasp and leaps to attack. Okiku slides out of the way, barely. The ghost attempts to strike back, her rotten teeth snapping.

I fish out the tape recorder and hit Play. The sonorous chants that fill the room have never sounded so good.

"Hirano Ran," I croak. "Hirano Ran. Hirano Ran."

The ghost bride pauses and turns to me with a low hiss. Okiku takes advantage of her distraction to score another hit across the face, and the ghost staggers back. I hold the *hanayome ningyō* out, repeating the ghost's name.

Ran.

The whisper does not come from me or Okiku. I swallow, turning to the skeleton at the center of the room.

It has lifted itself but makes no move to harm us. Its eyeless sockets are trained on the Hirano ghost.

Ran. The name rattles from between fleshless jaws.

For a second, the ghost bride wavers, and another face emerges from behind its hair—not another creature of blood and squick but that of a young girl.

Okaasan. She draws the word out, as if she's no longer used to speech.

The emotion in her voice transports me back to Washington, DC. I'm at the old motel on First and Third, watching a little girl cry for her scumbag father.

"Hirano Ran," I say again, my voice raw.

She looks at me. There is nothing gruesome about her appearance. The horror is gone. Now she seems unsure, almost fearful.

Ran—the skeleton clatters—*follow him.*

I'm not going to argue, so I hold out the doll to her, the recorded mantras still playing, and gulp. I wait for her to sprout teeth and claws, but she doesn't. Her feet begin to slip and slide across the floor, the chants pulling her toward the doll in my hand. For a moment, she resists, and her face darkens again. But then her eyes close, allowing the chants to wash her away—

There are eighteen dolls in the room, all seated around a small altar. Candles burn in every corner, throwing heavy shadows on the dolls' expressionless faces. She sets her doll down to complete the circle and takes a step back, unable to tear her eyes away from the strange sight.

"It's okay," her mother says from behind her, a faint tremor in her

voice. *"Come here now, Ran-chan. Let us leave the gods to decide." The words are followed by a queer, hacking cough.*

She takes in the room one last time before returning to her mother. The door closes behind her.

In the morning, she hovers by the doorway with the other children. The gods decided. Seventeen dolls are strewn across the room, no longer in their perfect circle. Only her doll remains untouched.

Behind her, her mother begins to cry.

The gods have chosen her—

—and I double over, hacking and sputtering. I stagger back and cling to the wall, hoping the dizziness passes. The look on Okiku's face tells me she's seen the vision too. Nothing gets past my brain that she doesn't see. The doll pulses in my hands, its eyes a familiar, wretched shade of black. I position the spike. It only takes a second to ensure the ghost won't be going anywhere.

There's still one more unauthorized ghost in the room, and I raise the recorder again, clawing behind me for one of the dolls I'd brought along.

"Wait."

I pause.

"Wait," Okiku says again, this time with more urgency.

With great reluctance, I switch off the recorder. The skeleton remains immobile. Then the skeleton bends and kneels in the formal *seiza*-style, her legs tucked underneath her. As she does, she takes on a flimsy, transparent appearance—the figure of an elderly matron wrapped around her bones.

It's an unnerving sight. I see how she would have looked when she was alive, yet it is like seeing her through an X-ray. Her eyes, however, are on Okiku, who has assumed a similar sitting position beside me. I remain where I am, my heart hammering, because I don't know what the hell is going on.

The old-woman skeleton is weeping. The threat of battle is in the air but with all the outward formalities of a tea ceremony.

Cozy.

Okiku speaks first. "She was incomplete. Her soul remains in this village still."

The response comes, dull and hollow, as the ghost continues to weep. "Yes."

"Why was this so?"

"The *kannushi* chose the path for her."

"It is a perilous path."

"Yes."

"Your daughter is different from the others."

"She is not completely *aragami*. She is not completely corrupted. I am not like the other mothers. But it made little difference." The grief is evident in that worn, hopeless voice. "I stay for her. She is a good daughter, dutiful and obedient.

"I wrapped her in spells and charms before her sacrifice to help her on her journey. I did not know that the *kannushi* lied when he took her. When the last ritual failed, she and the chosen brides were caught in the chaos, and I died with the rest of the village. I cannot leave while she is here. She cannot leave while I am here."

"You can leave now."

The ghost turns to look at the doll, which I'm still holding in a death grip.

"Yes." Some animation enters her voice, pathetic with longing, as her gaze meets mine. "He is different."

"Yes," Okiku agrees.

"The *kannushi* will seek him out."

"Yes."

I interrupt with "I'm sitting right here, you know," but they don't listen.

"Do not let the *kannushi* take him. There is great risk."

Okiku's reply brings an ache to my chest: "I risk all for him."

"Good. Please—you must free the villagers. The girls. They are trapped by the silkworms. Give us peace."

The old woman says nothing more, only gestures at me to continue my ritual. I oblige, and the chants resume. The ghost stands and bows low to Okiku and then to me before closing her eyes. Her surrender is easy—

She sits in the darkness, cradling the hanayome ningyō *in her arms. She is calm.*

Outside, the world is ending. Insanity hurtles through the small house, rattling the screen doors. Peal after peal of wild laughter echoes, interspersed with the screams of those still living, still running. The force is enough to knock over her meager possessions: vases break, wood splinters, and the ceiling comes down around her. Still she sits. Still she waits. She knows there is nowhere else to go.

The doors burst open, and things *crawl into the room.*

She recognizes some of them in their tangle of limbs, and her grip on the doll tightens, her mouth whispering prayers. One of the corpses inches closer, ever closer. She has been dead many years, but the woman knows who she is despite her face.

"Kaaaasaaan," it says in a singsong voice, "Mother, mother, mother"—

I'm not used to two exorcisms in succession, so it's at least ten minutes before I catch my breath, trying to understand what I have just seen.

"The visions of that ritual, that was the last in this village," I say with sudden clarity. "Something happened, and it freed the ghosts of all those sacrificed girls. We need to find out what went wrong."

"The old woman was strong," Okiku observes quietly, "to maintain her sense of self."

"I could tell. She didn't once try to eat my spleen," I say. "What does she mean by silkworms? And that Ran girl's vision—was that how they chose which girl to sacrifice? That's—this is insane. What did she call her—an *aragami*?"

"One who had been sacrificed in vain and returns for malice."

"In vain? But I thought the previous rituals were completed."

"No. The rituals make up a larger, more powerful one. It is not yet finished. He intended this all along." There's newfound steel in Okiku's voice. This is the angry, vengeful, justice-seeking Okiku I know and love. "The *kannushi* founded the village for this purpose alone. He intended to sacrifice all for the hell's gate. He cared nothing but for the power he could receive from it. The last ritual trapped the people in this village. But it is still incomplete."

"This was all the *kannushi*'s doing? The master of ceremonies? But why?" Then it hits me. "Do you think the *kannushi* is this Hiroshi Mikage person? The guy who was exiled from the emperor's court for dabbling in forbidden magic?"

"The woman does not know. She only knows that the *kannushi*'s magic took her daughter's corpse and breathed malice into it, as it did the other brides. Until the ritual is complete, they are bound here. What protection the woman had given preserved some of the girl's memories, and she stayed until her child could be vanquished."

"Some of the other ghosts might not be hostile, right?"

"She is likely the exception."

"I hate that the nice ones always have to be the exception." Very carefully, I remove the stake and place the doll inside my backpack. "So one down, at least six more to go. Where's the nearest one you can sense?"

"To the east."

"Alrighty then. But before that—"

Okiku does not move when I approach her. She looks puzzled. "I'm going to hug you," I say and then do just that, enfolding her in my arms.

"Why?" The rattle of her voice is muffled against my shoulder. *I risk all for him.*

"Because I want to." My voice still sounds scratchy. "You change your mind about hugs now?"

"No."

"Party pooper." I let go. "I guess there's nothing else for us here. Let's aim for that next house."

The Kunai residence is next on the map. As with the Hiranos', the house has suffered through the years, with gaping holes in the floorboards and caved-in walls, which makes putting up *ofudas* a useless endeavor. I keep my eyes on the ground, fearful the whole floor might give way with each step. I tiptoe along the walls, where the wood looks firmer and the foundation appears unscathed. Okiku, who likes being unfair, simply sails across the gaps.

The Kunai altar is located inside the inner room. The doll sits atop it, surrounded by discarded bits of incense and broken pottery that may have once contained food offerings to whatever deities the people honored. There is only one problem—the floor has collapsed into a gaping hole that splits the room in two, separating us from the doll by about eight feet of air—at least four feet more than I'm willing to risk jumping across. I try to peer into the dark chasm below, but all I can see is darkness. I play my flashlight back and forth over a stone path about twenty feet down. An underground cave? A collapsed tunnel?

"What the hell kind of architecture is this? Why would people build their houses over yawning pits like this?"

Of course, I get no good answer to that. Okiku—who I'm pretty sure hates holes in the ground more than I do, given that she died in one—just stares at it.

"Is there any way you can get it just this once for me?" I wheedle. She reluctantly moves across the room and attempts to do just that. Her hands pass through the doll like it's not even there. It's the same reason she couldn't touch the doll back at Sondheim's apartment—spirits of water can't touch vessels belonging to creatures of wood. Ghosts can't touch vessels made to entrap them either, which is the reason the ghosts haven't been able to hide their dolls. Most of the time, it's the only advantage humans have over ghosts.

Should the gate fall, only one hope remains: use the vessels to trap the sacrifices and perform a final ritual in their presence.

I can't help but give the *kannushi* some credit, albeit grudgingly. He'd read *The Book of Unnatural Changes* too. He must have told the girls' families to honor their daughters through these bridal dolls, knowing he would use these vessels to perform the eighth ritual—the one that would give him power to rule the gate.

"Guess not." I glance around, trying to see if there is any way to overcome the obstacle. There are a few long, wooden planks that don't look too badly decomposed—sturdy enough to walk across.

"I definitely did not sign up to be a trapeze artist," I complain, lugging one into place. I drag a few other planks beside the first, until half the hole has been covered. I figure if I don't put my full weight on just one, then there will be less chance of the planks giving way.

I take off my backpack and make a tentative step, balancing my arms out on either side of me as I begin to make my way across.

"If Callie were here," I continue to grumble, "she'd say this would be by far the worst idea I'd ever come up with, and she'd be right. I'm glad Callie isn't here."

Why would a village build their houses above what look to be deep tunnels? How was it even possible for them to build something like this?

And then another question: what's at the bottom of these holes?

I make it to the other side, retrieving the doll without incident, and start my return.

"There is something here," Okiku says.

I nearly lose my balance from that alone. "Goddamn it, Okiku, don't tell me that when I'm crossing a—"

And then something grabs on to my foot, and I really do lose my balance. The doll slips out of my grasp and drops into the darkness below. I lash out and succeed in latching on to the edge of the floor. I glance down and nearly faint at what I see.

A girl, clearly dead, has her hands wrapped around my ankle. She is covered from head to toe in dirt and slick, green slime, and her clothing is ragged beyond recognition. Her hair slicks down her face, and her wide, staring eyes are framed with the customary teardrop-shaped brows. The sudden smell of death and decay is overpowering. I gag and try to kick my way free, but she hisses and clings.

Okiku flies past me, catching the other ghost unaware and sending both of them tumbling into the black pit.

"Ki!" I scramble for safety, then turn and shine my light down, frantically searching for a glimpse of her. "Okiku!"

Fear seizes my heart. Weakened as she was by the miasma surrounding us, I know neither of us will have much of a chance if we are separated. But I don't see her anywhere.

I grab my backpack and steel myself.

"This is a stupid idea," I murmur to myself—and I jump.

CHAPTER THIRTEEN

THE CAVES

Don't let those action heroes in movies fool you—falling twenty feet onto a stone floor is a bitch.

I have enough sense to tuck and roll when I make impact, but it forces the air from my lungs all the same, and I don't stop rolling until I plant my face into the opposite wall. I lie there for a few more moments, wheezing like an old man and regretting the day I thumbed my nose at my local gym's annual membership.

There aren't any creatures lying in wait for me, but the downside is that neither is Okiku. I do see the doll lying a few feet away, dirty but intact.

"Ki?" I call, coughing but finding the strength to pick myself up off the cave floor. My right foot sends twinges of pain up the length of my leg, and I wince. "Ki?" I call out again. My voice echoes faintly down the passageway, but nobody answers.

I clamp the flashlight in my mouth and splay the light into the tunnel ahead of me, the spike raised in one hand and the doll in the other. If there are passages hidden underneath this house, then the same must hold true for many of the others. I'm no expert, but while I assume the caves are natural, some of these connecting passages look like they were dug by hand. How many people must have labored to do this? And for what purpose?

"Okiku?" It's not going to do much good to panic, but without her, I don't stand much of a chance at getting out of this village alive, much less spearheading a rescue. I close my eyes and try to sense where she went, ignoring the mild nausea of my fright. I can walk despite the pain, though I know I can't put too much pressure on my right foot.

"Better than breaking my ankle," I console myself.

Okiku has been weak, and I start to worry that the reason she hasn't returned is because she's in trouble herself. I start off down the passage, walking as quickly as I can.

Something scratches at the rock behind me.

It's probably nothing.

Just to be sure, I speed up, forcing down the increased discomfort in my leg.

Scuffling noises pick up behind me.

Don't look. Don't look. It's the mantra in my head as I quicken my pace even more. It's nothing. It's probably the sound water makes when it's trickling through rock. Or some small insects buzzing. It's definitely not something following you. Fingernails are too brittle to make that clawing sound.

Aren't they?

Crap. Now I can't get that image out of my head.

Don't look behind you. Don't look behind you. That's how people die in movies. Don't look behind you.

I look behind me.

The long-haired girl slithering toward me makes me forget about my foot. I run, eyes focused on the path ahead because falling now would be very bad. I can feel Okiku's presence growing stronger, as if she's sensed me too and is heading my way.

I run faster. The scratching behind me has increased in volume, but I can't tell whether it's gaining on me or whether it's just getting angrier.

There's a strange hissing next to me.

The glow of my flashlight catches Okiku bearing down on me, hollow eyes all afire and mouth stretched wider than possible for a normal human. I'm accustomed to how Okiku looks but not to encountering her in an abandoned tunnel with another ghost at my heels.

I throw myself to the ground as Okiku launches herself at the spirit dogging at my tail, the force of the crash sending them both tumbling into the wall.

The flashlight rolls away, but I spring to my feet, fumbling for the tape recorder. Shrieks ring out around me, but I can't place where the sounds are coming from. "Hey!" I yell, lifting the recorder, and soon, the sounds of chants intertwine with the horrific cries.

It doesn't always work like this. If a spirit's too strong, it won't take to the chants immediately, and then a fair amount of wrestling is needed to get it down and docile.

Both girls sail by me, inches from my head, and hit the ground. The other ghost has Okiku pinned, nails raking into her face.

I don't even think. I swing the spike and impale the spirit squarely in the chest, pinning her against the rock and keeping her immobile.

"Ki!" I drop to my knees and drag her away from the squirming, shrieking ghost. Okiku's eyes are closed, and she isn't moving. Her face is drawn, far more desiccated than she should be.

On the wall, the dead girl hisses out her triumph and tries to lunge forward, the stake sliding a bit when she does. I slam a second stake through her midsection, right in the center of a pink flower woven into her white kimono, and she screams. A third and a fourth keep her shoulders restrained. I stumble back. The ghost scratches at the air, clawing in my direction, but I hold up the doll and let the recorded incantations do their work.

She screeches more unintelligible sounds at me, but I keep the doll leveled in her direction until she feels the inevitable tug. Before my eyes, she melts like vapor, seeping into the doll I'm holding until all that remains of our encounter are the four spikes still embedded in the wall—

"I'm scared" is what she finally manages to say. "I want to see Akeno."

They're walking down a dank, dark tunnel. Her hands are bound, and there are guards to prevent her from escaping. It doesn't matter, because she feels too faint to break away. Her movements are sluggish, and she reels from side to side, unable to walk straight.

No one listens to her. The silent procession continues, and she does her best to keep in step. She feels lethargic, as if her mind is slipping away from her despite all her intentions.

Up ahead, she can see the back of the kannushi's *head, the rattle of beads as he walks. She does not recognize the other priests because they are all dressed in white robes, faces hidden beneath masks. She and the head priest are the only ones dressed differently—he in his ceremonial garb and she in her favorite kimono of coral peonies.*

"I'm scared," she says, but it's a ghost of a cry, and no one listens.

The passageway leads to an underground cave. As they approach, she sees snatches of light streaming in from above, and her eyes widen when she sees the magnificent tree before them. It reaches up to the rock ceiling. The tree is clearly dead, its branches black and leafless. And yet, it seems very much alive. The withered gnarls of its branches curl and uncurl like spindly fingers beckoning at them. Shadowy shapes hang from its branches, some wriggling, but her vision has become blurry, and she cannot focus to see what they are.

The priests file into the cave, but the kannushi *does not move and neither do the two priests at the girl's side.*

"We must do something first," the kannushi *tells her, and she can only nod dumbly before she is ushered into another tunnel.*

She must have dozed off while walking, for she recalls little until she finds herself standing before a yawning pit. Her mind shrinks at its size.

"Would you like to see Akeno before we begin?" The kannushi *asks. She nods and does not know why she grows more afraid when he asks this.*

"Then come here, Mineko. Here. Look."

He leads her to the edge of the pit. Shaking, she looks down and sees—

—and I come back to myself. I'm still corkscrewing the spike into the doll's chest, though this is no longer necessary. For a moment, I can see the spirit juxtaposed onto its face, gnashing sharp teeth in the hopes she can score one last blow. But her image fades, and she recedes into the doll, which watches me with burning midnight eyes.

The *kannushi* didn't need the boys for his rituals. Nothing in *The Book of Unnatural Changes* or Kagura's notes ever mentioned their importance beyond their marriage providing another layer of protection for the girls. But Kazuhiko's research did mention one other thing:

> *To rule the gate, it is important that the last sacrifice must be willing.*
>
> *But to close the gate, all seven sacrifices must suffer to slake hell's hunger.*

Was that the *kannushi*'s intention all along—that the boys' fates increase the girls' suffering?

Danger averted, I crawl back to where Okiku is still prone on the ground. "Ki," I plead, lifting her in my arms. I need her to be all right.

I've seen Okiku wounded in action before. There was a particularly nasty earth spirit lurking near a small shrine in Kyoto that surprised us both. It took weeks for her to recuperate, despite my fussing over her and her wounds that didn't heal. They only went away after she spent two weeks hibernating inside my body, curled up beside my heart. I'm reminded once more that being immortal doesn't mean Okiku can't be dealt a mortal blow from a power stronger than she is.

She opens her eyes and looks at me. Her face is impassive, but her eyes are painful to see. "I am tired," she whispers.

"I'll handle this," I promise. "You need to hide here for a while," I say, tapping my chest. "I'm not taking no for an answer."

She shakes her head. "Not yet."

"Not yet? What do you..." I trail off because she shifts, death draining from her features to reveal human Okiku with several small wounds dotting the side of her kimono, which is ripped and shredded from the fight, exposing a part of her abdomen. "Pull them out."

I look closer and see several bits of wood and—I blanch— fingernails piercing the skin. I nearly throw up a little in my mouth, then get to work.

Okiku doesn't flinch at every splinter and nail I pull out, though I do most of the flinching for her. Her injuries would have been severe had she been human, but when I pull out each offending piece, her wounds seem to close up a little, and the blood ceases.

Once I'm sure I've gotten everything out, I pull her closer to me. "Are you okay?"

"No. I am angry."

"Not a surprise. You were angry at me long before we got here."
My grin fades when I see her brows draw together. "Okiku, you're
not still angry at me, right?"

"I am not."

"We never really got around to talking the other night, did we?"
I'm deliberately changing the subject—anything to get her mind
off the pain I know she's feeling. "I knew you were angry at me
even before McNeil. We were going to talk and then I opened my
big mouth and you…" I try to decide a nicer way to say "stormed
off in a huff."

"…and you stormed off in a huff."

Okiku works herself into a sitting position. The color returns to
her cheeks, if you count pale white as a color.

"I do not like her."

I blink. "Her? The ghost, Mineko Kunai? I don't like her either."

"No. The human girl."

"Callie? I know she's still a little wary when it comes to you, but
I don't think she means anything by—"

"No. The *girl*."

"The… Kendele? You don't like Kendele?" It feels a little ridiculous to hear her make this confession when I haven't thought much
about Kendele since arriving in Japan.

"Yes."

I wait for her to explain, but she's not forthcoming. She just
looks at me expectantly.

"Uh, okay. Why don't you like her?"

Now it's her turn to frown. "I do not know. I only know that I do not wish to see you with her. It…upsets me."

I have never seen Okiku jealous. I am aware of the heat climbing up my face. Okiku is watching me again with that puzzled look on her face, and I realize that *she* doesn't even know why. So it doesn't seem fair that I'm the one feeling embarrassed.

"Kendele is just…a friend, okay? Like Callie, except we're not related."

"Callie does not kiss you the way she does."

My face feels like it is on fire. "It's nothing! Don't think about it too much." Maybe I'm overthinking this, but… "Ki, you're not jealous, are you?"

"Jealous of what?"

I am definitely overthinking this. "Never mind. I'm just saying that it's normal for me to, um, have…friendships with other people. It doesn't mean that anything about us has to be different. Okay?" I catch the look on her face. "There's something else, isn't there?"

"I am sorry."

Mood swings aren't usually her thing, but now her voice is so very, very soft, the way she often gets when her own odd sense of depression sets in.

"Sorry for what?"

"For depriving you of a normal childhood when you should be at…parties. To find other people who do not ask you to hunt for strange prey."

I can't help myself. I start to laugh.

She eyes me like I'm losing my mind.

"Okiku. First, I'm not a fan of parties, so it's highly unlikely I'd be going off to one even if you weren't around." I pause before making my next point, because I'm not sure how to explain it.

"And secondly—I really don't know how I feel about Kendele. I mean, I like her. She's the only one I talk to on a regular basis at school, and that's kind of pathetic. But regardless of what I think about her, I promise you that nothing will ever change between us. Hunting bad guys might churn my insides every now and then, but that doesn't mean I regret it. It's not just because you saved my life either. I want you to be happy, Ki, because I feel happier with you.

"Now, come on. The sooner you step in, the sooner you get to recuperate."

The smile on her face grows with every word I say, and when I finish, she leans over to touch my face with her fingers in her usual display of affection. Then the smile recedes, her mouth twisting into a look of determination. She takes a step forward—

"I have done nothing wrong," she says, her voice unsteady despite this assertion.

The young lord does not listen to her, and even if he did, he would not believe her. He looks back once more at his prized collection of plates. Where there had once been ten, only nine remain, but she is not to blame.

"Count them, Okiku," he commands angrily.

Helpless, knowing what the outcome will be, she counts again. The lord's retainer stands to the side and watches her, smiling.

"Nine," she whispers. "I have done nothing wrong."

"Do not lie to me, Okiku!" her lord roars.

Tears prick at her eyes. He softens his tone almost immediately and places a hand on her shoulder. "Okiku," he begins again, gentler this time, "if you confess now, then I promise you I will treat you fairly and you will not be punished."

For a moment, she is tempted to take the easy way out, to say she stole the plate and be done with it.

But she cannot not lie. Not even for him. He trusted her once, and it had saved his life. Surely he will believe her.

"I swear on my mother's grave, my lord," she says, weeping, "that I have done nothing wrong."

She watches his face change, feels his hand leave her shoulder, watches as he turns away toward his retainer.

"You are right," he says. "Do with her as you will—"

"You bastard," I hiss, getting back my bearings, salt stinging my own eyes. "You stupid, fucking asshole."

I hate that man whom Okiku loved so dearly, sometimes almost as much as I hate his goddamn retainer. Okiku tends to shield me from her harsher memories, but when she's weak, the filter isn't there. Seeing for myself how he'd betrayed Ki sends my blood boiling, and I have to remind myself that dwelling on the urge to strangle long-dead Japanese nobility is not my priority at the moment.

My foot feels better by the time I stand, the hurt reduced to mild discomfort. I pry the wooden stakes from the wall—not only was the tree that crafted these things sacred, but the stakes are surprisingly sharp and durable—and stash all but one and the bridal doll inside my knapsack. That done, I splay the flashlight along the walls of the tunnel once more. I don't sense any more malingering presences in this part of the cave, and I'm hoping it stays that way until I find the next doll.

Which is why it comes as a surprise when the beam of light illuminates a figure up ahead, clad in robes. I backtrack quickly, not sure if I should risk trying to run past the specter or if I should hide and wait for a better opportunity to pass. I'm pawing behind me in my pack for an extra doll for additional protection when the figure turns his head and watches me sadly. It's the same old man from before, the one I first met at the Oimikado household.

He holds out his hands. I interpret it as a sign that he holds me no ill intent. He gestures down the passage and starts walking in that direction without waiting for my response. I follow because I don't have a better choice.

The old man does not seem to mind my flashlight trained on his half-transparent figure and keeps moving at a steady pace until stopping at a nearly hidden path that I might have missed on my own. The passageway ends at a small staircase carved into the ground, which looks like a dead end. I'm puzzled until the old man traces a pattern on the wall, and the large stone edifice gives way, rolling to one side. Cold, misty air greets me. It's a way out!

I would hug that old man, but I'm afraid he'd misinterpret things. He's already fading out, the barest silhouette of him lingering a couple of seconds before he vanishes.

Just to be sure I'm alone and no other ghosts are wandering nearby, I stick out my hand with the tape recorder. Finding none, I emerge cautiously and assess my surroundings. I see only more rubble and rot. I'm in a completely different house.

After a quick look at my map, I determine I must be in or near the Kajiwaras. How many underground passages connect these houses, and what purpose have they served? The more answers I pick up, the more questions they seem to pose.

The stone edifice the old man had moved turns out to be the back of a small Jizo shrine that I would have sworn was carved right into the rock. I can feel Okiku, who isn't completely resting within me despite my insistence, tugging me toward the opposite side of the village. I comply, picking my way past the wood and debris and still keeping an eye out for anything untoward.

I'm beginning to sense a pattern among these odd girl-ghosts. If the previous two were any indication, these girls tend to stay close to their shrine dolls and don't wander, in the same way Okiku isn't able to go a long distance before being drawn back to me. I'm like Okiku's doll in a lot of ways, I realize with some consternation.

And like the girls in this village, she'd been sacrificed too, in a fashion. It's hard not to compare her to them, given their similarities—unavenged spirits betrayed by the people they trusted and made to suffer—so a part of me feels sorry for these ghosts, even when I know they're trying their best to rip out my throat.

I debate about returning to the village elder's house to check up on the *Ghost Haunts* crew member I left behind or foraging for more ghosts. There's still no sign of Kagura anywhere, and my spirits sink again as I entertain the possibilities of her—or anyone else—surviving for this long.

One more doll, I decide. I remember the diary entries of that unfortunate girl, the way she talked about a Yukiko-san. I remember the first ghost I'd spotted, the aggressive little bugger that chased me nearly all the way into the house, barred temporarily only by the *ofuda* I'd placed in her way.

On a sudden flash of insight, I peruse the list of girls' names. Sure enough, I recognize one of the kanjis on the list as being the same as the kanji on the girl's diary and remember her describing with perfect accuracy the kimono the other girl had worn before she was sacrificed.

Yukiko Uchiyama. The second to the last name on the list. But that would mean that the writer of the diary must be...

I glance down at the last name on the page. Oimikado Hotoke. The ghostly old man trying to help me must have been her father, Lord Oimikado, since he was in the Oimikado house. It all fits together.

"Thank you," I murmur. I've been able to piece together what scant information I have because of her diary, and I feel like the only way I can repay her is to find out if she managed to escape the village...or if she was sacrificed like her predecessors.

The fastest way to do that, I figure, is to find the ghost of Yukiko Uchiyama, the only girl Hotoke referred to by name. I let Okiku tug me to the right house. The Uchiyama residence is near the village entrance, confirming my theory that these ghosts tend to wander near the houses they grew up in. Unless they are chasing someone, I think, remembering Alan with a wince.

Still, I can't help but feel wary as I slide the shoji screen open and peer inside. This particular ghost is more upfront about being antagonistic than the rest, and with Okiku occupied, I'm not sure how well I'll fare.

"Here goes," I mutter.

I barely have a foot through the doorway when I freeze at a sudden, frightened cry from inside. It's followed shortly by a litany of familiar sutras and chants, and my eyes widen. I recognize that voice.

"Kagura!"

CHAPTER FOURTEEN

A REUNION

She's still got her *hakama* and her *haori*, though the former's been ripped around the hem and the latter's become a makeshift bandage around her upper arm, now stained red. A canvas bag is strapped to her good shoulder, and her hair's loose instead of in the ponytail she usually wears. There are scratches and dirt on her face, like she had to force her way through some man-eating thornbushes. Given the circumstances, I think Kagura looks perfectly composed—for someone who's been lost inside a haunted village for days.

Her eyes widen when she catches sight of me, and her voice wavers. Her chanting stops, and Yukiko Uchiyama takes advantage of it, springing forward and all but bowling the *miko* over with one timed leap. I run to Kagura's aid, my recording picking up where her chant left off, and take a well-aimed kick at the ghost's head before her teeth can close on the *miko*'s face. She rears back, and I thrust the stake at her. Yukiko's quicker than I expect, dodging it, but she backs away from Kagura, who's sprawled on the ground and trying to catch her breath.

The apparition tries to approach once more, but the recorder makes her wary enough that she never quite closes the distance between us. I make sure to keep myself between her and the *miko* until finally, with one last baleful look at us, she backs into a wall, disappearing from view.

"Well," Kagura gasps, pulling herself to a sitting position, "I'm glad to see you've been taking your training seriously."

"I'm glad to see you!" I fold her into a quick hug, making sure not to put pressure on her injured shoulder. "What happened? Where's the rest of the crew? How the hell are we going to get out of here?"

"All questions that are rather difficult to answer at the moment." She smiles wanly at me. "Where's Okiku?"

I point toward my chest, and her smile fades. "I knew it," she says, sighing. "I was hoping you wouldn't be here. These are creatures of earth, and the strain on Okiku might be too much to bear. What are *you* doing here?"

I put forward a quick summary of events, starting from our search in Aokigahara, and she shakes her head. "Oh, Tark."

"You and Callie both," I retort. "You're here and I'm here, so there's no use dwelling on that. But I'd really like to know what's going on." I scan the room, just in case the ghost bride wishes to return. "I found the camcorder one of the crew was using. I watched the video when you guys first arrived. How did you even escape the...whatever it was chasing you?"

"I'm not quite sure myself." Kagura winces. "I think we would have been doomed almost as soon as that first ghost attacked if not for her."

"Her?"

"There was another ghost. As odd as it sounds, she…defended us from the first *aragami*." Kagura exhales noisily. "I've never seen anything like it before. Except Okiku, of course. I don't know who this ghost is, and I don't know why she came to my aid, but I didn't have time to ask—not with the others scattered and injured."

"Was there anything unusual about the ghost?"

"Yes. She had blue eyes." At my sharp intake, she glances in my direction. "What's wrong?"

"I've seen her before. She was lurking inside the shrine, and I think she may have helped repel an attack by another ghost too.

It looks like we have an ally in Aitou, at the very least. But one thing is clear—we need to find the dolls, Tark, and use them to exorcise these spirits. There is a chance that the curse might lift the moment they are all contained, and we can leave."

"I'm way ahead of you." I produce the two *hanayome ningyō*, not without some smugness. Kagura looks surprised and pleased. I quickly relay all that happened—from Callie and me finding the notes Kagura had left behind to my adventures inside Aitou.

She frowns when I tell her about the old woman and the *tate eboshi* wearing scholar, and she insists on a more detailed description of the latter. "He could be one of the ceremonial assistants of the *kannushi*," she concedes.

"Whoever he is, he seems like he wants to help."

"I hope so. I have exorcised two of the ghost brides myself." She opens her bag and shows me two more dolls not unlike the ones I have, their beady eyes dark. "Nariko Konno's and Kita Morimoto's." She holds up another. "I have found the doll belonging to Yukiko Uchiyama, but as you could see, she's been a little harder to catch. Counting Yukiko, that leaves only three more." She pauses. "How long have I been missing?"

"Two weeks, give or take. Auntie's worried sick, and there are all sorts of television reporters and searchers out looking for you."

"Looking for the *Ghost Haunts* crew," Kagura corrects me with a rueful smile. "I should have trusted my instincts and refused to allow them access to my father's work."

"I think they would have found another way, regardless of whether or not you helped them. They're not…dead or anything, right?"

"I do not know. We were all supposed to head for the shrine, but it's been boarded up. I brought them to a house beside the Konno residence and told them all not to step outside until I said so. It was the most structurally sound of all the remaining houses. I warded the room as much as I was able to, but when I returned, they were all gone." She rakes a hand through her hair. "This is all my fault. I was responsible for their safety—"

"You were responsible for providing them with information about Aitou," I interrupt. "They're grown men who chase ghosts. They knew what they were getting themselves into. At any rate, I found one of them—Alan George. I got his map and left him in one of the houses, having *ofuda*'d what I could. He's pretty banged up."

"That is some consolation, at least, to know he is alive. I have not had much luck in finding the others. Oh, Tark—I wish you weren't here!"

"Don't worry about that, Kagura," I tell her with as much confidence as I can. "I chose to come here. I gotta say that it's been a crappy vacation so far though. I think I've had enough of the sights Aokigahara has to offer. What do we do next?"

"I need to tell you the rest of what I know about Aitou. My father disappeared in Aokigahara, Tark. I fear he knew more than what he let on and that Aitou holds his grave. But he also knew more than I thought about the ritual. It was very much like him to keep secrets, especially if he thought they might worry me or Mother."

"I saw some old photos of him, back in your room. You look a lot alike."

"Thank you. He did not like having his picture taken, and those are all I have of him." She smiles faintly. "He always wore a small *magatama* around his neck. Someone very special gave it to him when he was young, and he believed it afforded him protection against spirits. Did you read the old parchment I had in my trunk?"

"I remember reading something from an old red one, but it was more like a riddle than anything."

"It was his proof, I think. Proof that he had been inside Aitou before and had survived. He was never clear on how he found the village in the first place, but I have no doubt that on his last trip, he wished to find more evidence. But"—a flash of pain crossed her face—"toward the end, he was so obsessed with finding Aitou and proving himself right that he didn't always make the best decisions, and I fear he paid the price for that.

"I do not intend to do the same. The only recourse open to us is to find the other ghost brides and see that they are laid to rest. And to do that, we must gain access to the shrine."

"But it's all boarded up."

"This shrine is merely a front; the real shrine is underground. There are passageways underneath some of these houses. I suspect they were used by many of the ceremony masters to gain access to the shrine without being seen by the common people. My father's notes indicated that these caves existed long before the village came into being and that its layout had been planned to accommodate what lies below." She sobers. "And somewhere within those caves, I imagine, lies the hell's gate."

"Please tell me we don't need to go there." I don't want to go anywhere with "hell" as part of the description if I can help it.

"We must if we are to find the shrine. How many of my notes have you read?"

"All that I could find. I read the diary, the odd parchments your father kept, and about the rituals." I frown. "I didn't know about the shrine being underground though, or about some of the other rituals mentioned in his research. Why isn't Hiroshi Mikage's house on the map you gave the *Ghost Haunts* crew? He's the village priest after all. I thought your father would have concentrated on finding his house first."

"I don't know where it is either. It was never mentioned in my father's accounts."

"Is it possible that Hiroshi Mikage is the *kannushi*, Kagura? There isn't much information about the head priest, and being the master of ceremonies and in charge of everything, he's the most likely culprit."

Kagura considers it. "That does make sense. The *kannushi* would have overseen all the village rituals, and that would have made him the most important man in Aitou."

"And the ritual must be performed underground?"

"Yes. The place where the rituals first began is also the place where we must end it. You told me you found one of the passageways."

"Yes, but parts of it were caved in. The path I took led from the Kunai residence into the house to the left of this one."

Kagura nods. "The Kajiwara house, I think. My father's account states that the Kajiwaras were heavily involved in the ceremonies and rituals here in Aitou. It would explain why their house would be one with underground access to the shrine."

I groan. "Figures. Let's get this over with then."

"Let's start here. I don't know about you, but I would like to get rid of that ghost before we do anything else. I've been trying to track her for some time, but she's been very clever—and stronger than many of the others."

"Tell me about it. She's the first one I met, and she welcomed me with moldy open arms."

Ever cautious, we move through the rooms of the Uchiyama

residence. I don't know about the other ghost brides Kagura hunted, but it is clear that whatever glowing accounts the Oimikado girl had written about Yukiko Uchiyama in her diary, Uchiyama was also at the top of her class in the crazy department.

Although the other residences show signs of disrepair and disuse, this ghost bride has pulled out all the stops to let visitors know that a madwoman haunts here. Chairs had been thrown into mirrors, bits of wood still sticking out of the frames. Pottery is shattered on the floors, and some of the walls are riddled with deep fingernail scratches. The rest of the structure has been liberally splattered with rough kanji, using what I'm pretty sure is not red paint. Had I been her intended fiancé, I would have broken it off by now.

"'Don't drink the tea,'" Kagura translates, looking at one wall.

"That's a little tamer than what I was expecting."

"I don't think you can choose what to write when you're insane."

I concede her point and move on to the next room, where we encounter more writings, ranging from "'Beware the beautiful death'" to "'The monsters are here.'" I stand before the first of these, frowning at their familiarity and trying to recall where I've heard these phrases before.

Kagura finally urges me on. There's no sign of the ghost anywhere. "There's no point in lingering around here," Kagura says after we've looked through the rubble. "I don't want to leave her behind, but we don't have much choice for now. Let's try the next house over, the one with the passageway."

The temperature has dropped and my breath leaves my

mouth in puffs as I jog to keep pace with Kagura. She's already hurrying to the Kajiwara residence. Here, some parts of the walls are missing, allowing the winds to swoop inside and making me shiver all the more. Despite her bare shoulder, Kagura doesn't seem to feel the cold.

Although the room has been open to the elements, the bridal doll is where we'd expected it to be—by the makeshift family altar and looking none the worse for wear.

What we don't expect are the dozens of other dolls strewn around it.

Most of the dolls are unfinished or half made. Some are missing hair and eyes and facial expressions. There're piles of arms and legs gathering dust and rust. Time has done a number on all of them, but their states of decay only make this more horrifying.

"I was right," Kagura murmurs. "If the Kajiwaras were the doll makers of Aitou, then they would have been extremely influential. That they were the masters of ceremony might have made them the predominant family in the village after Mikage. They were very likely conspiring with the *kannushi* in exchange for a share of the power. Remember that he left Edo with a handful of followers after he was exiled. Some of them could have been the Kajiwaras."

"I am so glad I found you" is all I say. I take a step forward, but Kagura stops me. "Be ready. The ghosts are irrevocably tied to their *hanayome ningyō*. Take the doll, and its ghost bride will most likely attack."

"I wish I'd known that two dolls ago."

Despite our situation, Kagura grins. At her instruction, we circle the room first, trying to ignore the profusion of doll heads and appendages. It's the largest room we've seen, which only highlights the *miko*'s assertion that the Kajiwaras must have been very rich or very well-respected to afford this rural luxury. That didn't seem to prevent one of their daughters from being sacrificed in the ritual, and I wonder if they resisted or simply accepted her fate.

Kagura scours one side of the room while I circle the perimeter in the opposite direction. Then she places a finger to her lips, signaling for me to stop. Her hearing is sharper than mine. I need a few seconds to detect the strange humming from the room in front of us, coming from the other side of the shoji screen.

As we watch, a shadow rises from behind it—a profile of someone with long hair streaming behind her. The silhouette rocks back and forth for several moments, and the humming continues. And then, much to my horror, I watch as it lengthens and expands, the neck rising, rising, *rising*, until it's stretched several feet above from the still-reclining body.

The rising head turns. It is looking at us.

Despite my shaking knees, I manage to take several steps back. Kagura is made of stronger stuff. She glides toward the screen and yanks it open in one hard movement. The screen slides back easily, but no one is behind it, just a tatami mat and a moth-eaten kimono strung along a small clothesline.

Farther into the room, however, is a small closet.

"Kagura," I whisper, sweating now despite the cold.

"You might want to stand behind me." The *miku*'s voice is terrifyingly calm. "Grab the bridal doll as soon as I give the order."

I obey, and she steps into the room. Back by the altar, hand poised over the doll, I watch Kagura. She must have nerves of steel. She isn't trembling, and every step she takes toward the closet is made with such preternatural calm that she could be strolling down a street of shops in Akihabara.

Kagura's hand slowly reaches for the door, and I brace myself for the worst. With a deft flick of her wrist, she sends the door sliding open.

There's nothing there. Kagura swears, a rare occurrence for her.

"Language," I chide, not sure whether to be relieved or terrified.

She turns to scowl at me. Then her face pales. "Tark!"

A voice giggles in my ear.

I snatch the doll from the altar and dash away, but I'm too slow. Pain blooms along my upper back as nails score my skin. I hit the floor hard. Instinct tells me to crawl away as fast as I'm able, and that's what I do. There's a heavy *thunk* and a brittle shriek. I risk a look behind me. A stake has found its mark, sinking into the ghost bride's chest. Kagura is an excellent shot. The ghost ripped into my knapsack, tempering the blow before it could reach me and saving my life.

The sacred stakes have weakened her, but she closes the distance between us. Her eyes are too large for her face, her mouth too wide, and she is screaming.

Kagura runs toward me, the familiar chants leaving her lips even as she raises her arm to throw another spike. The pain in my back is getting harder to bear. I don't think she's going to be able to save me.

But the killing blow never comes. I *feel* instead of see Okiku reaching up from inside me to deflect the clawed hand. There's a sickening crunch followed by a shrill scream.

I turn my head to see the ghost staggering back, her wrist hanging uselessly off her arm. Ignoring the pain in my back, I lunge with my own stake and catch the ghost bride in the stomach. The momentum sends her to the floor, with me nearly on top of her. More wood splinters as the spike lodges itself in the floor, leaving her squirming in agony.

"Stop moving," I growl, but the ghost isn't interested in commands. She reaches for me with her uninjured hand, but I roll away. Kagura is close behind and sends two more stakes into the ghost bride's shoulders. All the while, she recites her sutras, so when I drag the doll in front of Kajiwara's livid, blackened face, it doesn't take long.

"Tark, wait!" Kagura gasps. "Let me take the doll and—"
Too late.

She hangs suspended from its branches and knows that she must flee. But her arms and legs refuse to comply with the screaming in her head. They remain motionless, unable to struggle. She feels tired and exhausted, as if she gave up control of her body a long time ago.

Her feet are tied together, her arms stretched above her and bound by the wrists. She tries in vain to move again, to think, to free herself, but there is a low voice telling her that everything is going to be all right, that she must only fulfill her intended purpose.

She wishes Toreo was here. No. Toreo cannot be here, *she remembers. Toreo cannot be here with her, because…because…*

It is getting harder to think, to will words into her mind.

Her vision clears for a moment, and she sees the kannushi *standing solemn before her. His attendants—her father and her brothers—stand on either side of him, carrying long yards of cloth so white and pure that it looks nearly invisible in their hands.*

"Sleep well, Fujiko." The kannushi's *voice is gentle. "Sleep, and protect this village from what comes."*

Her father and brothers carry the cloth so that it is stretched in front of her, brushing against her kimono. She tries to look at her father, not quite sure what is supposed to happen next.

She hangs suspended from a lower branch of a large tree. It is dark and dying, yet magnificent, though it no longer has leaves to shed.

A curious beat of drums starts nearby, and her father and brothers begin to circle her, wrapping the cloth around her midsection. Their speed quickens, until her chest and lower torso are bound in the silky material, and she is finding it hard to breathe.

Now her lower legs are constrained so tightly that she could no longer move even if she wished to. The material twines around her chest—her neck, nearly choking her—and her mouth. The last thing she sees before the thin gauze wraps around her eyes is the kannushi, *watching her from behind his mask—*

I am only barely aware that my face is planted onto the floor when I surface back into consciousness as Kagura frantically shakes me awake. There is ash in my mouth. It tastes bitter and grainy. I gasp for air. I feel like I was the one being strangled in Fujiko Kajiwara's place.

The ghost bride is long gone, the holy stakes on the floor the only evidence she was ever there, but I'm still clasping her *hanayome ningyō*, those now-familiar black eyes large against that placid, porcelain face. Kagura's hand clutches at its leg.

"Kagura, did you…?"

"Long enough to see." The *miko* bites back a sob. "Those poor, poor girls…"

In light of what we've just seen, the girls' attempts at murdering anyone who enters Aitou now seem pretty justified. But there is one more thing we have to do for Fujiko Kajiwara, and Kagura finally delivers the coup de grâce. Her eyes brimming with unshed tears, she yanks one of the wooden stakes from the floor and sends it straight into the doll's chest.

CHAPTER FIFTEEN

LAST WORDS

"I'm fine, Kagura. It barely even hurts anymore. See?" I rotate my shoulder to prove my point, then disprove it when what feels like fire ants come dancing up the length of my back. "*Owwww.*" The wound turns out to be only a scratch, but that doesn't stop it from hurting.

"I don't recall you being this petulant before," Kagura chides lightly, placing gauze on the wound on my back. With hindsight, I realize I didn't bring as many first-aid supplies as I should have, but thankfully, Kagura also came prepared.

"I don't recall ever being clawed by a ghost before," I say grumpily and then flinch again. The upper part of my knapsack is shredded, but some quick work with my needle while Kagura works on my back ensures it's intact enough to carry most of my belongings. The thick cloth, along with Okiku's timely intervention, kept the ghost bride's fingernails from digging in too deeply.

"You should have let me finish the exorcism, Tark."

I give Kagura's shoulder a pointed glance and then sober up. "Hey,

Kagura…I read as many of the notes you left behind as I could, and nowhere did I read how the ritual was performed. Do you know?" The idea that the girls were potentially killed via suffocation, spun slowly into the cloth like trapped insects, is a sickening revelation.

"I wasn't sure of it myself. Father's account gave no details of it, just generalities."

"They were weaving the girls into cocoons." It fit with the earlier vision from Mineko Kunai's ghost when, through her eyes, I saw that massive, horrifying tree and that wriggling cocoon hanging from its branches. "Your father said that the ritual only takes place every three years. So if something inside the cocoon was still moving, then at least one of the girls had been alive inside it for…" I pause, shocked by the very idea.

"…for three years, at the very least. Yes." Kagura rolls up the rest of the bandages, and I gingerly pull my shirt down. "Mikage dealt with some very dark magic, Tarquin-san—the kind of magic that could sustain life, of a sort, though its victim would suffer very much from it. But it is not true life as you would know it, Tark. It's an existence much like Okiku's, where one can exist and yet still be dead at the same time."

Great. Schrödinger's ghost.

"Did you read what my father wrote about the silkworm-raising techniques?"

"Not really. I didn't know then what they had to do with Aitou."

"More than even Father suspected, unfortunately. Once silk-worms reach a certain age in their larva phase, they begin to spin silk cocoons. Eventually, when they become moths, they bore holes through these prison walls, and the silk is destroyed in the process. As a result, silkworm breeders boil the silkworms before they reach that stage."

"I take it that's not very good for the silkworms involved."

"No, it isn't." Even now, Kagura is oblivious to sarcasm. "The cloth they used for the ritual—I've seen evidence of silkworm hatcheries in more than a few of the houses. Aitou was self-sufficient by all accounts. I think they took the best of these silks and wove them to make the ceremonial cloths used for the ritual, to bind the girls—"

"But for what?" I burst out. "It doesn't seem *sane*. Why go through all that trouble? If they were going to sacrifice those girls, couldn't they have at least gone about it in a more humane way?"

"Suffering is the most important aspect of many of these kinds of rituals, Tarquin-san. The more suffering involved, the more successful the ritual." She smiles sadly. "I had hoped against all hope that you would never find your way here, Tarquin. Despite everything you've been through, your heart's too kind to comprehend the evils man can do when he is afforded the opportunity. You must not think about these things. We should plan our next move."

"And what would that be?"

"Exorcising Yukiko Uchiyama is still my priority. Failing that, we must gain access to the underground shrine to find those cocoons and purify them if necessary. And we must learn the fate of the last girl sacrificed."

"That Oimikado girl, you mean? You don't know what happened to her either?"

"Nothing I have read mentions her fate. Her diary is all I've had to go on."

"She had blue eyes," I say suddenly. Cold seeps through me, triggering a faint spasm of pain on my back. I hadn't thought much about the girl's eye color with the whirlwind of all that's happened, so I'm only now making the connection. "The diary said something about people who looked down on her because of her eyes. And that her mother belonged to the Ainu tribe."

"I remember that entry. The Ainu are frequently discriminated against for their mixed racial stock, for having Caucasian ancestry. Blue eyes would not be too unusual for them."

"I've seen her inside the shrine! When I was trying to get in. She must be the ghost helping us, Kagura! And if she's one of the ghosts here"—I swallow—"she must have been sacrificed too."

I feel a little sick. It's a long shot to hope that she got away safely, but it doesn't stop my anger and my disappointment.

Kagura is more pragmatic. "If she was sacrificed, there is little we can do other than to help her find peace. How is Okiku?"

"Sleeping—or as close to sleeping as someone like her is able to. I think that thing with the Fujiwara girl sapped more of her strength than she's willing to admit."

"The longer she can hibernate, the better. She cannot linger long in this village."

I know Kagura doesn't mean to, but her words make me feel

guilty all the same. Okiku made no complaint or protest when I decided to come here, though she must have known what kind of creatures lurk in Aitou—the ones she is weakest against.

"Kagura, what visions did you see when you caught those other two ghosts?"

The *miko* packs the rest of her first-aid kit back into her bag and hesitates at my question. When she replies, her tone is guarded.

"I don't think they'll be very important."

"I told you mine," I remind her. "Only seems fair that you tell my yours. We can compare notes better that way."

"I couldn't discern much information from my vision of Kita Morimoto. She moved as if she had been drugged, and her memories were of being fitted into her ceremonial kimono and being told that her companion—Akihiko, I think—was also being prepared for their wedding. And as for Nariko Konno—"

"Yes?" I prompt when she doesn't say anything for several seconds.

"Like Mineko Kunai, Nariko Konno was led to the edge of a very large pit, though I didn't see the large silkworm tree in that vision. She looked in and saw—"

The *miko* shivers. I can practically hear her debating whether or not to tell me before she gives in. In a perverse sort of way, I already know—or at least have made a very good guess—about what she is about to tell me. The fear and horror I felt from Mineko were enough to understand what she'd seen, even if the vision ended before I saw the complete picture.

"She saw bodies, Tarquin. Bodies of villagers—villagers she recognized as being the most vocal against the ritual and bodies of corpses that looked as if they have been there for years. She saw Akihiko's body, still in his wedding robes, among those of the dead. He had been killed before she arrived."

We're both silent for a while after that, trying to wrap our minds around the evil we're going up against. I think about the Oimikado girl's diary, about Yukiko's father, who demanded to know where his daughter and her fiancé had gone after their wedding ceremony. I suppose, in the end, he did.

I have some misgivings when Kagura insists on returning to the small grotto I found. She wants to be sure that there is no other way to access the shrine through it.

"Did you look for possible passageways, or were you focused on escaping?" she asks me. "The sooner we can find our way to the shrine, the better, and I'd like to know we have all our exits covered—literally."

She is, I reluctantly admit, being logical. I don't relish the thought of returning underground, but I'm surprised when Kagura takes that decision away from me. "I'm going to explore this on my own," she tells me, heading off any protests.

A closer inspection of the little Jizo statue reveals a lever on its back that makes it easier to roll, revealing a hidden entrance to the path that leads underground.

"You didn't see any kind of lever that could be pulled from the inside, right?" she asks.

"No, the old man was too far away for me to see what he was doing, and I wasn't sure I was supposed to ask him."

"Since we can only open this from the outside, you should stay here until I get back. I'd rather not get trapped inside."

"By *yourself*? Kagura, that's insane."

"I've been dealing with ghosts since long before you reached puberty, Tarquin-san. I've survived thus far, and I believe I'll be able to take care of myself for a little longer."

Kagura Kino doesn't actually have any balls, anatomically speaking, but I suspect hers are still bigger than mine.

"Wish me luck."

The *miko* promptly disappears into the bowels of the earth. I'm tempted to go after her, despite all my previous complaints, but what she said made sense. Kagura usually does.

"What are you laughing about?" I grumble at the stone figurine, then remember that Jizo statues served as guardians for children who died before their parents and also as a kind of patron saint for travelers. *Fat lot of good that did for the girls in Aitou—or us, for that matter.*

I haven't had much chance to explore this residence yet, but I don't wander too far from the statue, in case Kagura returns earlier than I expect. I take stock of what the rest of the room has to offer. Like many of the houses, there isn't a lot of furniture, but the books have survived a little better, which is an oddity in itself, given their fragile state. Some appear safe to touch, but others look in danger of crumbling to dust if they are so much as breathed upon.

There aren't any mirrors that I can see, which is a relief. Looking at mirrors always makes things creepier, and this place is already as horrifying as it gets. But there are more paintings here than in any of the other houses. Most are ink-wash landscapes. One attracts my eye, mostly because it is edged by what looks like a gold-leaf border. I've only seen that on expensive paintings in Japanese museums.

The painting itself is minimal in design. Four or five small clusters of sparse Japanese pines against a background of white snow. A closer inspection shows a lot of loving attention to detail.

There's something in the background, a small speck of moving dust. My first impression is that a fly is crawling across the canvas. Except this is no fly. Like a picture coming into focus, I make out the shape of a head, the outline of a body against a blinding snow.

This is the same shadow I saw in the photo Kagura emailed me of herself and the American crew. And just like before, it turns and opens its eyes.

Find me.

I take a sudden step back from the painting, and for a second, the background seems to move. Winds envelop the small black figure, reducing it to nothing more than a patch of white.

Knowing that we'd already captured Kajiwara Fujiko's spirit makes being alone in the Kajiwara house easier, but my skin prickles. That sixth-sense spider is scuttling underneath my skin in warning. I'm not alone. There's a presence nearby, but it doesn't feel malevolent. Not like with the ghost brides.

I can feel it behind me.

I turn.

The old man—the same old man helping me, the one I think is Lord Oimikado—is thirty, thirty-five feet away and staring at me. As before, he doesn't appear antagonistic. His hands are clasped as if in prayer, and he looks tired. He bows low to me. I'm at a loss for how to respond. Then he moves back toward a small bookcase, which houses the few volumes that have survived the village's death. His arm lifts and he runs a hand along the thin spine of one and then, just as before, he winks out into nothing.

I take an agonized glance back at the Jizo statue, note that Kagura has yet to surface—it's only been fifteen minutes at the most, but I still can't help but feel worried—and then retrace the old man's steps, slowly taking out the book he brought to my attention.

The bound leather, dry and crusty, is untitled. Its pages have definitely seen better days. There aren't many, and careful investigation reveals that there is only one entry—two pages in small, prim writing, handwritten in Japanese. It's a diary of sorts.

I feel Okiku stir and slowly detach herself from me.

"Okiku, you need to rest."

She shakes her head. She looks better than she did—at least as far as dead girls go. She's frowning deeply and looks almost anxious. "There's something wrong."

I ask her, not without some nervous trepidation, what she means by that, but she only shakes her head. She doesn't act like there's someone else in the vicinity though, so I show her the book.

"Can you make something out of this, Ki?"

She doesn't hear me at first, staring off into the distance, lost in thought.

"Ki? You okay?"

She blinks and settles her black eyes on me. "Yes," she says, though I'm not sure she believes it herself. She does little to explain. Instead, she settles herself on my right and slowly reads the words.

"'I am the last of the village.'"

Slivers of dread run through me.

"'It has all been for nothing. The sacrifice of my daughter, the sacrifices of those who have had daughters—we have failed. The dead walk outside, wearing the faces of those who have succumbed to the madness, the faces of those who have gone before them. Even my fellow priests have not been impervious to the sickness, but that is not the worst of it.

"'I have seen the face of my poor Fujiko, gone all these years, and there is nothing of the beauty, the humanity in her now. She is among the damned, and her shrine sisters walk beside her.

"'Oimikado Hotoke was brave. A victim like all the chosen brides before her—but the bravest of them. Ironic that she would prove to be his undoing.

"'They will not rest. They will never rest until the final ritual is performed.

"'It is all Hiroshi's doing. I understand that now. He did not perform the ceremony the way he should have. He did not seek to close the gate but to rule over it. He betrayed us, sacrificed everyone in his mad quest for power. When I think of what we did to those poor boys…

"'…the look my Fujiko gave me, dazed and drugged as she was, when she saw what awaited her in that pit…

"'But it is too late. It is too late. We knew not what we had done, though our hands are stained guilty with their blood. It will make no difference to the dead.

"'*Kami* willing, I will make my way back to the shrine. I hope to finish the ritual on my own and end things once and for all. I do not believe I will be successful—but I must try to atone for all my sins.'"

A muffled thump comes from somewhere nearby. I look around, wondering if it was Kagura or something else, but Okiku pays it no heed and continues.

"'And you, oh poor traveler who has happened upon the writings of this unfortunate man! Let my words serve as a warning—leave the village immediately or be prepared to share in our fate. If the way out is barred, then find the Jizo statues and travel to the silkworm tree. Free those poor girls from its clutches and burn it with their fires. And if anything interrupts your quest—then may the gods have mercy on your soul.'"

I groan when Okiku is finished. "I really, really hate it when they end letters like that." But I understand now. The writings in those mysterious parchments, the lingering ghost brides and their hate—even Yukiko Uchiyama's mad wall graffiti.

There's another muted thump and then a strangled noise that sounds like "shit" that comes from inside one of the closets. I rise to my feet, Okiku staring quizzically at me. I should probably exercise more caution, but I'm pretty sure Japanese ghosts don't swear in English.

My steps are confident as I cross the room and slide open the door where I heard the sound. The instant I do, I'm received with the most ungodly shriek, and I can't resist responding with a surprised holler of my own.

It's Stephen Riley. The man gazing wild-eyed at me is a far cry from the well-groomed, self-assured cohost of *Ghost Haunts*. His beard's scraggly, and his hair's unkempt. Unless the camera really does put on ten pounds, he's lost a considerable amount of weight, and the rags he's wearing could barely be called a shirt and pants. He looks like he's been picked up, kicked around, and then thrown down a flight of stairs, but at least he doesn't look dead, a feature most of the village inhabitants share.

"Whoa, whoa, whoa!" I hold up my hands as he scrambles away, arms raised in a futile attempt to ward off harm. "I'm Kagura's friend, okay? Are you listening to me?" He freezes, staring at me like I'm a mirage. "We're here to get you out, so don't flip out or anything. We're going to—"

A hand taps me on the shoulder, and I swear if I had jumped any higher, my head would have put a hole through the roof.

"What is going on in here?" Kagura sounds crabby, a clear indication that she hasn't found any new passageways. She gives Okiku a respectful nod and peers past me. Her eyes widen when she takes in Riley. "Stephen-san?"

"Kagura!" The man is nearly beside himself as he stumbles out of the small room, clinging to her hand like she is a flotation device. "I thought I was a goner!" he gasps out.

"Stephen-san, I am glad you're all right." Have I mentioned that Kagura is the queen of understatements? "What happened? I came back to find most of you gone, and Garrick and Henry..." Her voice shakes slightly.

"Garrick got impatient. He wanted to find out what was going on, so he removed the *ofuda* you placed on the door. I tried to talk him out of it, but by then that...that girl came inside, and we all started running. Garrick...Garrick didn't make it?"

"I'm afraid I don't know. I only found Henry's body."

Stephen's shoulders slump. Me, I'm just fervently glad I didn't break into the Konno house where the ghost hunters first sought shelter. I don't want to know what condition Henry's body was left in.

"Who are you?" Stephen asks, staring at me. "How the hell did you get here?"

"The same way you did," I say lightly, not wanting to frighten the poor man further. "Kagura, we need to go back to the Oimikado residence. We can bring Mr. Riley up to speed along the way."

"Why?"

"Because I know how to get into the shrine."

CHAPTER SIXTEEN

THE PIT

The Oimikado residence is the place where I found the list of brides' names and first encountered the old man, though he's nowhere to be seen. Kagura is a little skeptical about him, even when I show her the journal he kindly pointed out to me.

"It could be a trap," she says.

"Trap or not, it's not like we've got some other route out, right? He's telling us how to get into the shrine, and that's what we want to do anyway." I think Kagura would feel a lot better if we'd tracked down Yukiko Uchiyama first, but we haven't seen her lovely, grotesquely drawn face since she tried clawing my back off.

Stephen Riley is understandably reluctant to be pulled from his dark, musty closet only to traipse through some dark, musty caves, so we decide to bring him to the Oimikado house, where his fellow crew member is waiting. He brightens when I tell him I found Alan George, glad that someone else has survived, though the latter's not in the best shape.

It takes some time for Stephen to get the circulation back into his legs after crouching and hiding for so long, but despite his weakened state, he can walk on his own after a few false starts. Much to my relief, he doesn't seem to notice Okiku, even when she's practically standing next to him. I didn't expect him to. He's not a ghost hunter; he just plays one on television. Surprisingly, he's retained the holy stakes that Kagura gave him. If he doubted their value before, he seems ready to use them now, especially after what's happened to his crew.

I offer him some of my water, and Kagura has some dried beef on hand, both of which he finishes with relish. I don't know how long I've been stuck in Aitou, much less how long Kagura and Riley have—time seems to have its own rules in this village—but the fear of running out of food and water lurks at the back of everyone's minds.

That fear remains with us until the Oimikado house looms into view. Until I knee the door aside and discover that the *ofuda* I placed across it for protection is no longer where I left it but is now torn in half on the floor.

I raise my hand behind me to signal Kagura to stop and then pry the rest of the door open. The unmistakable metallic aroma of blood and earth and dirt clogs my nostrils. There was no pungent odor when I left. Alan George is not here, but there's ample enough evidence that he *used* to be and may not have left on his own terms. The wall where I remember leaving Alan is caked in soot and something congealed is scattered in lumps on the floor. One whiff tells me that I am better off not knowing what it is.

"Where's George?" I'm not sure Stephen Riley can take too many more hits, and it's apparent by the way he's shaking that he knows something came for his friend.

"I'm sorry, Stephen," I say, suddenly angry. "I told him! I told him not to take it off!"

"He wouldn't have if there wasn't good reason to," Riley insists, defending his crewmate. "We all saw what happened when Garrick removed the protection. He wouldn't make that same mistake."

"Then what the hell happened here? I should never have left him alone." My voice is hoarse with emotion.

"You didn't have much of a choice," Kagura reminds me, though her own face is grim, her lips thinning. She's quick to compartmentalize her emotions, stepping bravely into the room. I endeavor to follow, though with less calm. I bind the door with another strip of *ofuda*, though I'm not sure it will make much of a difference if the creature is already inside the house.

"You're not going to leave me here, are you?" Riley asks, panicked. I don't blame him.

Kagura takes a deep breath, and I suspect she is about to suggest it. "Alan-san took off the *ofuda* when he wasn't supposed to. You should still be safest here."

"You're going to leave me to become food for whatever creatures lurk around here? Hell no." Fear is a great motivator, and as weak as he is, Riley isn't backing down. "I'll go with you guys. I won't fall behind. Just don't…don't leave me here with the thing that got Alan."

Kagura glances at me, and I nod after a moment, still feeling guilty about leaving the man to fend for himself. May as well die together rather than alone.

"I think we need to go over this place, just to be sure," I say. Whatever tore the *ofuda* might still be lurking inside, and I want to make sure there are no more surprises. Kagura nods in agreement. Riley is less accommodating, but neither of us says anything as we begin the search. My back still aches, but adrenaline's doing a good job of helping me ignore the pain.

I find Alan George in the next room. His knees are drawn up despite his bad leg, his face buried between them, and his arms are wrapped around his calves. He is rocking back and forth, and he doesn't seem to hear me when I call out gently to him.

I take a step back, turning my head toward where the others were. "Kagura, I found Alan. He's—"

The screen dividing the two rooms slides shut inches from my face, barely missing my nose and cutting off the rest of my words, as well as access to Kagura. Startled, I yank at the screen, but it refuses to give.

"What the hell? Kagura!" I hear pounding on the other side and know it's the *miko*, but she's having just as much luck as I am at prying the door open, which is none at all.

I rear back, raising my foot and slamming my heel into the wood. "Alan?" I say as I kick the door again. The man is barely fazed by the loud noise and the unexpected poltergeist activity. He's too catatonic to notice. "Hey, Alan, are you all right? We found

Stephen Riley. We're gonna get you both out, just as soon as—" I kick hard; the wood wheezes again but doesn't give.

I stop in my tracks. Now that I'm not banging on the door, I can hear a strange hissing sound coming from behind me. It doesn't sound normal. In fact, it doesn't sound human at all.

I swallow hard and force myself to speak. "You're not Alan George, are you?"

The spitting, croaking rattle that responds is answer enough. "*No.*"

I can feel Okiku rising, ready to do battle, but I gently push her back down. This one's on me.

"Alan George is dead, isn't he?" I grip the wooden stake, hard enough that I could have squeezed water from it.

I hear the rustle of movement behind me, and I don't wait for a reply this time. I drop to the floor, relying on my tried-and-tested habit of playing dead instead of mustering a defense, and the clawed hand flies uselessly over my head. I aim for the feet, figuring that a bum leg is a bum leg, whether its owner's been possessed or otherwise. The trick works, and Alan George's body hits the floor beside me, my stake through his ankle preventing him from doing more than flail around.

One look at him tells me that we're too late. His face looks like it no longer believes in adipose tissue and is decomposing rapidly. Cobweb-like threads gather at his neck and wrap around his head, and I can tell this was the initial metamorphosis the villagers went through before they were finally spun into cocoons.

Kagura and Riley are still attempting to break down the door, but I can't wait for them to finish. "I'm sorry," I tell Alan's body. It's one thing to stake down ghosts, people you consider dead and gone. It's another thing to confront someone you just talked to, who was alive and breathing when you left him.

"I'm really, really sorry." I'm sure the man's past the point of feeling anything now, but I cringe as I hammer a stake through his hand. Alan rolls his eyes until only the whites show. His cheek sags. I steel myself, croak out another "sorry," and shove the final sacred spike into his chest just as Kagura and Riley burst through the door, armed with what look like the remains of a chair.

George's body jerks and his muscles lock, as if rigor mortis has finally remembered to set in. I see a brief vision of him as I first remember him, minus the bone-mangling features. And then his whole being crumbles into dust.

"Holy fuck," Riley says, staring at the spot where his friend used to be.

The look of horror on Kagura's face makes me feel worse. "It's my fault." I tug at the stakes on the floor. "He was on my watch, and I didn't take enough precautions. I didn't think he'd take the *ofuda* off…"

"No, the fault is mine. I should have never…" The *miko*'s voice catches, and Riley's hand finds her shoulder.

"I think Adams and I were the fools here," he says thickly.

We don't say much. There's little left of Alan to remember him by, so we stand in a semicircle for a moment of silence before Kagura tells us we have to go.

Whatever trespassed on this property and possessed George appears to have left. I lead the way to where I found the Jizo statue. There's a lever on this one too, in almost the exact same position, which saves us time. It pulls to the side in a similar manner, revealing another set of stairs leading down to a dark tunnel below.

I can practically hear Riley reconsidering joining us, but to his credit, he doesn't make a sound. Kagura insists on leading the way, shining her flashlight into the dank depths and being careful to keep her pace slow in case anything jumps out at us. Okiku and I take up the rear. There's another lever artfully tucked to the side that will allow us to move the statue from inside, so we don't need to leave anyone to guard the entrance, which also makes me breathe easier. We might be eaten and torn to bits by whatever creatures we find wandering these passageways, but at least we won't be trapped.

As before, the tunnels are devoid of light, so we have only our twin flashlights to guide us. I keep close to Okiku, not wanting to be overprotective but also not able to stop myself. She looks a lot better than she did, but I know she's not up to her full strength yet. Her exhaustion pulls at me, mingling with my worry.

"You could stay hidden within me, you know," I murmur to her as we inch our way down the musty-smelling path, the cave glittering from the way the beams of light hit the mold and the uneven walls. I make a note to add a flu mask to the list of essentials to bring next time I find myself in a ghost-ridden town. "You don't need to physically be here."

Okiku eyes me like I've just spoken in Klingon. "I am fine. I am—curious."

That's an odd thing to say. It's on the tip of my tongue to ask what else she is curious about, but Riley gives me a funny look, so I shut up. After all that time spent hunting ghosts on his show, you'd think he'd know if one was nearby.

"There is something here," Okiku whispers.

"A fork in the path," Kagura calls out in front of us.

A small path branches out to the right, and another tunnels straight ahead. There's nothing to distinguish one from the other, no way to determine which route will take us to the shrine.

"I surmise one of them leads to the Kunai house, which has been blocked off, and the other should lead us to the shrine. The problem is figuring out which one is which." Kagura bites her lip. "We were facing east when we entered the caves, and the shrine's due north. If the ritual was being performed directly underneath it, then the path to the right should take us there."

The words are barely out of her mouth when a loud sonorous chanting booms out, echoing against the walls and hitting us from all directions, so we're not quite sure where it's coming from. All I know is that it's not Kagura and it's not from my recorder.

"What's going on?" Riley's voice is rising.

"Stay calm, man!" I bark at him, spinning and trying to figure out if the voices are coming from the path before us or to our right. "Kagura, what kind of chants are they?"

"Nothing that I've ever heard before—I don't even know what

they're saying. Let's move out of their range if we can." The *miko* strides down the forked path, and Riley and I follow. It isn't until we've gone about a hundred yards that we finally find out what's been making the racket.

A spectral arm shoots out from one of the walls and attempts to paw at Riley. The ghost hunter leaps to the side and strikes at the glowing limb with his stake, impaling it at the wrist. There's a faint rumble of outrage, and then the arm fades to nothing.

I can't help myself. "You still have some moves, old man."

Riley grins weakly at me. "I may not look it right now, but I do know how to fight."

I have no time for a comeback. More arms appear from the walls, some reaching so far into the corridor that they reveal their long robes and hats. I grunt when a hand snags my hair and drive my own sacred spike into the forehead of a phantom that's lunging at me with bulging eyes and moaning piteously. Kagura uses her stake to cut through the forest of arms the way a woodcutter might use a hatchet to cut through a tangle of thorns, creating an opening. We rush through before any more arms can manifest.

"Did you see that?" She pants, still running.

"I didn't see anything," I huff behind her, not tired enough not to be sarcastic.

"I recognized some of their outfits. They're ceremonial priests, Tark. In the emperor's court, they were tasked with performing the most sacred of ceremonies. This must mean we're getting close."

"Close to what?" I grunt, but Kagura's running faster, and Riley and I work to keep up.

Something lands a blow on my weak ankle, and I pitch forward, putting my hands up just in time to prevent my head from bouncing off the rocky ground. One of the damned old priest-ghosts has latched on to my foot, and it takes a couple more thrusts with the spike before he's persuaded to let go. I hear the moans of his brethren not far behind, but Okiku is already there, claws ripping limbs from ghostly sockets and buying me enough time to scramble upright. When I'm back on my feet again, both Riley and Kagura have disappeared from view, and I redouble my efforts. I take another look behind me, and what I see nearly makes me trip again.

Not content with reaching for us from the walls, the men in robes are scrambling to free themselves from the rock. The overall effect is that of a mass of flailing arms and heads moving through the rocks at growing speed as they come after us. I tear down the tunnel, calling out for Kagura, though I receive no answer.

Then I come across another fork in the path. There's no sign of Kagura or Riley on either path, and I swear loudly. Sounds of our pursuers draw closer. I have to make a decision—fast.

"Forward," Okiku whispers.

Her instincts are better than mine, so I don't question her and plunge on ahead. I keep hoping for a glimpse of my companions, but every time I swing my flashlight down the tunnel, all I can make out is more darkness. The narrow passage feels like it stretches for miles, though it can't be more than a few hundred yards before the path widens without warning, and I stumble into a large cavern.

The sounds behind me are silenced; the priests have abandoned their pursuit. This part of the cave leads to a dead end, but it only takes one look for me to understand why Okiku wanted me to take this route.

The large silkworm tree I saw in the girls' visions isn't here, but this part of the caves has been witness to another kind of ritual altogether. A large stone statue, standing more than twenty feet high, has been carved into the wall. Looming over this stone edifice, also chiseled into its rocky surface, is the most horrifying face I've ever seen. It's easily ten feet across and twice as tall.

Its eyes are sunken so deep that they resemble nothing more than hollows, and two horns rise, one on either side of its head. Its cheeks are gaunt, twin skeletal protrusions only heightened by the shadows. A mouth is stretched in the same distended curl as the ghost brides' lips. How they were able to carve this using only rudimentary village tools, I don't know. But I wish they hadn't been so artistically talented.

I have seen Buddhist altars and offerings before but never one like this. It mocks the meaning of worship, twisting it until it is nothing short of a personal perversion.

Surrounding us are human-sized cocoons. In the beam of my flashlight, they writhe in their silk prisons, pushing and prodding against the threads binding them. My encounters with them tell me that they're not dangerous, but that doesn't stop me from wanting to bolt out of the cave all the same, even if it means running into the ghost priests again.

Okiku stares intently at the massive demon effigy above us.

"Okiku, do you know what this is?"

She doesn't answer. Instead, she continues toward the stone shrine, still entranced by the face looming above us. The altar is stained a rust color, and by the time Okiku speaks again, I realize why.

"This place is a killing field. This place begs for blood."

Okiku stands to one side of the grotesque chantry, looking at something behind it. I move to follow her line of sight. There is a large pit behind the altar, and the smell of rot and decay grows as I approach.

There are bones inside the pit—enough that I cannot see its bottom, only the pile of yellowed cartilages and skulls that serve as its bedding. I don't doubt that I am looking at the villagers who defied their leader, Hiroshi Mikage. And then I shudder, knowing that among those bones are the remains of the unfortunate men who were betrothed to the ghost girls. This was the vision Kagura saw from the Konno girl and the vision I saw at Mineko Kunai's.

But there is something else in the pit; another corpse is sprawled atop the bones. Its head is tossed to one side so that it is looking straight at me, and what is left of its arm is raised parallel to its chin. Bits of flesh still cling to its bones. This man hasn't been here as long as the others, and in this cool, damp cave, who knows how long it would take for him to putrefy.

A long, jeweled dagger is thrust into the corpse's body between its ribs. None of the other skeletons show any evidence of how they were killed, and none of the ghost girls I've encountered favor stabbing their victims with knives—though I can vouch that their fingernails are sharp enough to do the job.

"He is not one of them."

"I think so too. His clothes look different from the other ghosts'." As I shine my flashlight into the pit, a glint on the body catches my attention. A small jewel is tied to the corpse's neck by a piece of string. I know what it is!

"Ki, that's a *magatama*." I swallow, now knowing who the poor man is. I've seen the necklace in Kagura's photo. "That's Kagura's dad. Kazuhiko Kino. It has to be."

Okiku's silence is all the affirmation I need.

I can almost hear Kazuhiko telling me what I need to do, and I know I can't leave until I do it.

"I don't suppose you could retrieve the *magatama* for me, Ki?" The last time I tried to pillage from a skeleton, things didn't go according to plan.

Okiku shakes her head. Spirits can't handle certain holy objects, and I suppose the *magatama* falls into that category.

"Right. Help me find some rope."

I find a lengthy piece coiled up in a corner, making sure to avoid the squirming cocoons while I'm at it, telling myself I'll deal with them later.

The altar is the closest immovable object to the pit, so I tie one end hastily around its leg and then dump the rest of the rope into the hole, giving it a few tugs to ensure my knot won't unravel. I relinquish my backpack, setting it near the edge of the pit, then use the rope to lower myself into the hole, trying not to focus on the death around me, the smell of the open grave, and the sickening noise my feet make when they came into contact with a hapless skull. I tread warily toward Kazuhiko's remains, wincing whenever the cushion of bones can't handle my weight and I sink in ankle-deep.

I slip on a bleached head that's smoother than I expect and land on my hands and knees, hovering above Kagura's father. A tiny white maggot chooses that moment to crawl out of the corpse's eye sockets, and I draw back with a shudder. Not wanting to linger, my fingers find the *magatama*, and I lift it from his neck. At the last minute, I snatch the jeweled dagger as well, because I figure any added protection would be welcomed.

The invisible spiders crawling up my spine have multiplied and wriggle over every inch of my skin. I'm familiar enough with that feeling to know something's about to happen, and I don't want to be in the pit when it does.

I am halfway up the rope when I hear the scuttle of bone, the angry slide of femur against rock. The clacking sound only makes me quicken my pace, and for once, I'm smart enough not to look back until I've hauled myself to the side of the pit, flailing a little with my arms so that my chin hits the ground. For a brief moment, I swear something brushes against my leg, but I grit my teeth and kick back, then crawl the rest of the way out.

Okiku is perched on the edge, coolly assessing the situation. "Brat," I growl at her but not with much grumpiness. If she's not attacking, the ghosts are not hostile.

My hand clenched around the tiny jewel, I make sure I'm completely intact before looking at what I just got myself out of.

It's like a horror movie. The dead are rising from the graveyard's trenches, clamoring toward the side of the pit and me and Okiku. The skeletons scratch futilely at the rock. At least none of them look capable of scaling the hole. Only Kazuhiko's body remains inert. However he died, he's not part of their curse.

I look down at the *magatama* in my hand. The skeletons began to move almost as soon as I started my climb, and I wonder if something in the polished stone kept them immobile. There is a hole in the pendant where the necklace cord runs through, but it's bigger than it ought to be—an inch across in diameter by my estimate.

I peer through the hole in the *magatama*, straight into the pit, and nearly drop it at what I see.

I no longer see skeletons. I see men and women—villagers, judging from their clothes—pale and frightened, their arms raised in supplication, begging wordlessly. I see a few robed priests, parts of their heads bashed in, pleading with at me with missing jaws. But the pit dwellers that hold my attention are the unhappy-looking boys who would be about my age, with their throats slit from side to side, blood still running freely down their chests.

I pull away from the *magatama*, and the villagers are reduced to skeletons again.

I understand now what the *magatama* does. At least that's one mystery confirmed.

Okiku lets out a quiet hiss. She is no longer watching the skeletal mosh pit, her gaze now focused on something behind us.

Standing over the altar is Hotoke Oimikado, the last ghost bride.

CHAPTER SEVENTEEN

THE SILKWORM TREE

She is clearly dead. She is made up like the others, white-faced and strange-browed, and her kimono is the same as she described in her diary—adorned with wisteria and cherry trees, if no longer a pristine white. But unlike her sister ghosts', Hotoke's eyes are the vivid blue that I saw when I peered into the boarded-up shrine. And unlike her sister ghosts', her lips are not stretched across her face like a homicidal marionette's. Instead, her mouth is pursed, thin and colorless.

Also unlike her sister ghosts', Hotoke's head has nearly been taken off her shoulders. Her neck is slit from ear to ear, blood dripping onto her clothes.

I cringe, taking a step back before remembering the mob of skeletons behind me. Okiku thinks differently, positioning herself between us. I grab her hand.

"Ki, *no*." I don't want her to face the ghost, though I can't think of another alternative. I'd rather risk using my recorder and my last remaining Kewpie doll in lieu of a *hanayome ningyō* to trap the ghost than see Okiku helpless again.

She squeezes my hand. "It is all right."

"But—"

"Look."

The ghost circles us, blue eyes trained on my face, but she doesn't attack. If anything, she's hesitating. A vengeful creature would be trying to gnaw my face off by now.

"She has not been sacrificed," Okiku says.

Slowly, Hotoke nods. It takes a moment to process what they both mean. "She hasn't taken part in the ritual," I say, trying to puzzle my way through. It explains how the manner of her death— obvious enough—isn't consistent with the suffocation that the others succumbed to.

I remember my visions, the sluggish way the other girls walked to their executions, as if they had little control of their bodies.

The tea Father gave me is getting cold, Hotoke had written in her diary, *so I have set it aside.*

That explained all the research Kazuhiko Kino did about the use of belladonna. I had glossed over most of it, but a few things stand out in my mind. Belladonna is a poison, one that can have a paralyzing effect, and it was known as "the beautiful death."

Even Yukiko Uchiyama's mad scribblings had a grain of sanity to them.

Don't drink the tea.

Beware the beautiful death.

"There was something in the tea," I say, understanding. "That was why the other girls didn't resist. They wouldn't have been willing to be martyrs, so there had to be a way to keep them docile before they were sacrificed to meet the ritual's prerequisite. But you didn't drink the tea, did you, Hotoke-san? You weren't docile when they came for you once you realized the truth. You interrupted the ritual."

I refusssed. Her voice gurgles from the never-ending stream of blood flowing out of her neck.

"Tomeo told you what really happened to the other girls. He suspected that they and their companions were killed, right? And when he was killed, you tried to stop the ritual by killing yourself, thinking it would all end in your death." I struggle to remember what *The Book of Unnatural Changes* had mentioned. "Except it didn't. Instead, the ritual failed. Whatever was keeping the hell's gate stable fell apart. The gate wrested control away from the *kannushi* and condemned the whole village."

Sssuffering. Amendss.

"Is that why you helped us? To avenge Tomeo's death and to help the village?"

No.

In spite of her cut throat, she moves fast. She's in front of me in a blink of an eye, dead face lolling against mine. I fall back, but she's already reached a hand out and laid it against my cheek.

And I—

"You'll never win," she says, triumphant.

She does not resist when the men take hold of her arms, because she knows she cannot escape. That does not matter. Beside her, Tomeo's face is dirty and smudged. He too is being restrained by an assistant priest, but she draws comfort from his nearness, mustering all the strength that she will need. He looks over at her and tries to smile—

—Wait. I know that boy! I know—

—The kannushi *stands before her, and she knows that he is angry, even through his mask. Small torches flicker in the cave, casting an eerie light over the silkworm tree.*

"We will."

"You will not."

"You can escape again, and we will still find you," the kannushi *repeats, unrepentant. "Your attempts are futile. Now, we shall finish this." He gestures and the men obey. They force her toward the altar, and still she does not struggle. A long ceremonial knife lies in the center of the slab, the blade's dark gleam bright and beckoning.*

"I am sorry, Hotoke," the kannushi *says. "There is no other way."*

"There is always another way." She sobs bitterly. "I trusted you! Everyone in the village trusted you! You cannot do this!"

"But I can, my child." The man lifts his mask and smiles at his daughter. "Imagine what we can do with this power, Hotoke! Imagine how we can change the country, fostering a new age of prosperity and strength! I have the vision and the will to see it through, unlike the emperor's sycophants. Once we control the gate, Hotoke, I will bring you back, bring the whole village back! I will bring your soul back with the Hundred Days ritual. I swear on this!"

She does not answer her father at first, instead focusing on Tomeo. "Swear to me," she says, "swear that you will escape from here. It is the only way."

He knows it is futile to pretend that he could save her. His eyes fill with tears. "I swear."

"Now." With a sudden burst of energy she tears herself from her captors' grasp and snatches the knife. Tomeo shoves the assistant priest aside, taking advantage of the confusion to dart away.

Before anyone can stop her, she presses the knife to her throat.

"You lie, Father," she says, and—

"That is enough," Okiku interrupts sharply, ending the connection between the ghost and me. I stagger back, my hands clasped over my eyes. I had lifted them without thinking, an instinctive bid to shield myself from the sight of Hotoke Oimikado slitting her own throat, though it is hard to avoid if it's happening inside your mind.

I look up. Okiku hovers over me protectively, glaring at Hotoke's ghost.

"I-I know the boy," I manage to say, trembling, "I know Tomeo."

I've seen his face among Kagura's belongings—in the faded photograph of the kid with the solemn, sad smile, and then again in his twilight years, posing with his daughter, Kagura.

Tomeo is Kazuhiko Kino. It explains how he claimed to have been to Aitou, though he never told Kagura how he accomplished it. It also explains why he was so obsessed with returning to lift the curse. When Hotoke killed herself and unleashed the hell's gate, he must have found a way to escape the village.

As I struggle through this newfound epiphany, Hotoke is silent. Of all the spirits who reside in this tiny purgatory, she is the only one who has remained unaffected by the hell's gate's malice, but she has still been forced to endure years in this place, waiting for someone to lift the curse.

"She cannot enter the *kannushi*'s territory as she is," Okiku whispers. "The tree will entrap her if she does."

"Then how do we make this right?"

She indicates the *magatama* I hold. With a sudden burst of inspiration, I raise the jewel to my eye again.

The apparition staring back at me is no longer a figure of nightmares. She is a sad-eyed young girl, staring back at me with a combination of regret and determination. *You must perform the final ritual before he does,* I hear her say in my head. *Do not let him do it.*

I know who she's referring to. The *kannushi*. Her own father. I do not know the extent of the *magatama*'s power—if it shielded Kazuhiko from the bride ghosts or if it kept him sane during his time here—but it was not enough to protect him from the priest's wrath. If even Hotoke hadn't been able to save Kazuhiko, then the *kannushi* would be difficult to get rid of.

Even worse, I recognize the *kannushi*'s face. He guided me out of the underground passage and showed me the books in his library.

The mob in the pit is still scratching at its sides, but now that I know the truth, they no longer seem as malevolent, only beseeching. I watch as Hotoke drifts toward them, stopping by the corpse of her boyhood companion, the man who survived the first culling, only to succumb many years later to the fate he once escaped. I watch as she stoops to lay a hand along the man's sunken cheeks, fingers tracing a pattern across the withered skin.

"Will you help me?" For us to leave, I have to finish the ritual. And to finish the ritual, I need a sacrifice. I ask.

Hotoke doesn't answer, doesn't even turn to look at us, but I can hear her reply, loud and clear.

"Thank you," I tell her, but she continues to stroke the dead man's face like she hadn't heard. I feel Okiku's hand on my sleeve.

"Do you trust me?"

"Of course I do," I respond, appalled that she would have to ask, but when her eyes don't meet mine, I understand. Keren McNeil's death still hovers between us, and she's thinking about my previous accusation that she was no better than the woman in black who haunted my life for so long.

I cradle Okiku's face with my hand. "I trust you with my life, Ki. I will always trust you."

Her rigid mouth relaxes slightly. "She needs something from you."

I glance at the ghost. Hotoke kneels beside the remains of her fallen love while skeletons cluster around her, a mass of spectral memories venerating their queen. After a moment, she rises and moves toward me. I shrink back despite myself. "Do you trust her?" I ask Okiku.

"Enough for our purpose."

It's not the most comforting answer, but I nod. The specter studies me almost curiously, and then I feel the lightest of touches in my mind again—

It is late in the afternoon when a group of woodsmen encounter the half-delirious boy, too weak to resist as they carry him away. From the gates of the cursed village, the ghost watches until they are gone, the stillness of the woods muting their footsteps.

"Do not come back, Tomeo," she whispers. "Do not come back—"

—I don't quite understand what happens next, but when I resurface, Hotoke is gone. With her departure, the other ghosts have also lost their mobility, their bones lying scattered as they were when we first arrived.

"She wishes to be left alone," Okiku says. I decide not to argue with her. Kagura and Riley are still somewhere in these tunnels, and I need to find them quickly.

But first, I hang the *magatama* around my neck and attend to the cocoons, which contain the essence of more villagers and a few of the lower-ranked assistant priests who'd been too innocent to really understand the kind of ceremony they were taking part in.

The last cocoon reveals the image of a familiar face, and my heart lurches in sympathy.

I've found Garrick Adams. I don't know how he found this place on his own—if his past experience with ghosts enabled him to get this far—but I'm sorry to discover one more person we couldn't save.

***

The old man is waiting for us when we return to the fork where I lost Kagura and Riley. It is as if he's been expecting me all this time. He tips his head and gestures toward the other end of the tunnel.

"Cut the bullshit, *kannushi*," I snap. Hotoke's memories are still as clear as a cloudless day in my head, and her hatred for her father mingles with my own disgust. "Or should I say, *Hiroshi Mikage*. Stop pretending to help me. We both know finishing the ritual is all you're interested in. Where are my friends?"

If I'm hoping to somehow intimidate the man, I'm wrong. A tiny, almost mocking smile appears on his face. It was the same expression I saw when he lifted his mask and condemned his own daughter, using her life to strengthen his.

My previous hunch is right. Hiroshi Mikage is the Lord Oimikado, the *kannushi* of Aitou village. *Mikado* means "emperor" in Japanese, a clue I should have noticed sooner. Given the accounts of him before his exile from the emperor's court, Mikage wouldn't have stooped to using some lowly peasant name.

Without saying a word, Oimikado walks down the passage. I follow; I already know where he's taking me.

When we step into a cave even larger than the one containing the altar, the silkworm tree is what first catches my eye. It's every inch as imposing and as terrifying as in the girls' visions: a stunning monument to decay and aberrance.

There is no need for torches here; a queer light emanates from somewhere above our heads. I can't tell if the ceiling opens to the sky or if the light is from some luminescent mold.

Kagura stands below the silkworm tree, her hands tied above

her head, much the same way the bride ghosts were bound. My hands clench when I see that the lower part of her body is already cocooned in a long silk cloth. Her bag is on the floor, and the bridal dolls she's acquired circle the tree. As I draw closer, I see the cocoons surrounding her and realize, to my revulsion, that some of them are *moving*.

Riley kneels beside Kagura, his hands bound behind his back. Two specters—both assistant priests, judging from their clothing, and still loyal to the *kannushi* even in death—stand behind him. The *Ghost Haunts* host looks visibly frightened, uncertain of what is going to happen next, but Kagura is calm and composed. She spots me, and her gaze hardens.

"Please get out of here, Tarquin-san."

"I won't, Kagura." I don't think I could have, even if I wanted to. There is only one way to end all this, and that is to face Hiroshi Mikage and all the demons he's freed from the hell's gate.

The *kannushi* does not need to ask me for the terms of my surrender. I can already imagine what he wants me to do. "My life in exchange for hers, right? And if I refuse, you'll kill them both, huh?"

"Don't do it, Tark!"

"He's been planning this from the very beginning, Kagura. Why else would he go through all this trouble to be helpful to me? He wants me here. Showing me that old book in his house, helping me through the tunnels—he wanted me to learn about the ritual, to come to this silkworm tree. I am meant to be a part of the sacrifice."

Because I'm exactly what he needs: a boy with a particularly strong attachment to a young ghost girl who, if not actually killed by the ritual Lord Oimikado or Hiroshi Mikage began, nonetheless meets all the requirements for it.

Okiku *does* meet all of the *kannushi's* requirements. I am to her the way Tomeo was to Hotoke, and Okiku doesn't need to have spent three years in an isolated room to strengthen our bond. She's rife with spiritual energy. To rule the gate, one must suffer. My death would cause Okiku to suffer, just as the ritual demands. And Mikage clearly intends to rule the gate.

That is the reason he has waited so long without performing the seventh ritual. He was willing to wait as long as it took for an eighth sacrifice to come to the village—for the eighth ritual to be performed as well. Kagura must have seemed like a viable candidate until he set his sights on Okiku.

"But you can't do that just yet, can you, Lord Oimikado? Or Hiroshi Mikage or douche bag or whatever the hell you call yourself nowadays." I reach behind me and produce one of the *hanayome ningyō*. "There are five dolls here, but you still need a sixth." I point to one doll lying by its lonesome, some distance from the circle— Yukiko's *hanayome ningyō*, still uninhabited by its owner.

Should the gate fall, only one hope remains. Use the vessels to trap the sacrifices within. Perform a final ritual one last time in their presence. Wasn't that what *The Book of Unnatural Changes* instructed?

"You have no control over the ghost brides, or you would have found a way to bind them years ago. For all the power you claim to possess, you can't even control your own failures. In fact," I add, with a sudden burst of certainty, "you don't go out much, do you? All those ghosts crawling the village scare you. They don't like you, do they? It's why I only see you inside your own house or here, underground. Hiding."

I didn't intend to bait the *kannushi*, but I guess it's just my personality. His face hardens and the gentle, almost compassionate features twist. The monster inside him comes out. It's like Keren McNeil all over again. Mikage's own incompetence obviously grates on him, and my barbs are hitting home.

I risk more of his wrath by walking over to the empty bridal doll and picking it up. Faint movement above us tells me I've got more to worry about than just the priest, and I struggle to keep the same composure as Kagura. I don't have much of a choice; the circle of ghost brides needs to be completed in order to pull this off the way I hope to. The problem is that Lord Oimikado–Mikage–douche bag needs for it to happen too.

Another problem is the ghost lurking in the shadows above— Yukiko Uchiyama in her kimono of plums and bamboos and cranes. Kagura and I never did catch her, but the *miko* banked on the fact that Yukiko's ghost would be attracted to the spiritual energy surrounding the place, to the dolls and the ghost brides trapped inside. To her own doll that we'd taken, the one I'm holding at the moment.

I can feel Okiku breaking away from me, her attention focused on the cave ceiling. The action is all I need to prepare myself. I slip my recorder out of my pocket, still holding on to my wooden stake.

The hissing, inhuman noises above me are my signal. I glance up.

Yukiko Uchiyama's ghost crawls along the rock, trailing blood and other sorts of crazy. For once, the dead girl's focus isn't on me. Her gaze is trained on Hiroshi Mikage, the man responsible for her years of torment, and her wide-lipped grin is bright with the promise of bloodshed.

That's the problem with collecting too much energy in one place. There's the energy that the silkworm tree possesses and the dolls multiplying it further. Just as I attract spirits to me when Okiku isn't around, the tree attracts spirits eager to feast.

Good thing there's one other person Yukiko despises more than a budding exorcist.

A thin, earsplitting wail breaks through the air, and the ghost attacks. Her claws sink into the *kannushi*, driving him to the ground. I sprint toward Kagura and Riley. The assistant priests hesitate, torn between protecting their master and preventing their prisoners from escaping. Finally, they abandon the duo and race to defend their head priest.

"That was dangerous," Kagura whispers after I use the jeweled dagger to cut her bindings, then do the same for Riley.

"Put that in my annual performance review." Yukiko is still going to town on the *kannushi*, but as neither can bleed, I don't know how much damage Mikage is sustaining. The assistant priests reach his side, but Yukiko doesn't even blink. Her hands tear through one of them like he is made of paper, and the glowing figure collapses, falling to his knees.

One negligent toss of Yukiko's hand, and we're treated to the sight of the man's head bouncing across the ground before the head and his prone body vanish into smoke, swallowed by the darkness. I remember Hotoke mentioning in her diary that Yukiko had the ability to become a powerful priestess in her own right, which is proving to be correct.

The *kannushi* disappears in the ruckus, but I don't have time to see if it's because Yukiko has finished him off. I flip the switch on my recorder, and the sounds of Buddhist chants fill the cave, bouncing from wall to wall in melancholic resonance. Yukiko beheads the second assistant and turns toward me, her teeth gnashing. She lunges, and I swing the *hanayome ningyō* like a baseball bat, braining her—but the momentum carries the ghost forward, and I wind up underneath her, treated to a close-up of her rotting, grinning face.

She hesitates, her fingers hovering inches above my face. I feel a surge of heat on my chest. The *magatama* is throbbing like it has its own heartbeat. The ghost stiffens. She attempts to rake her nails down the front of my shirt but is stopped by a barrier I can't see.

Then Okiku barrels into her, slashing and scratching. She tears into Yukiko with her own brand of savagery, slicing at the bride ghost's flesh. Yukiko hisses and delivers a few blows of her own, sending Okiku's head snapping back. I sense her initial advantage is waning. Earth trumps water, and here, deep underground, Yukiko has strength in reserve.

Yukiko is distracted when Kagura appears. The *miko*'s aim is true, and she drives a sharpened spike through one of the bride ghost's hands. Without pause, Yukiko throws off Okiku and turns to swipe at Kagura, who dances back just in time. Riley tries to get in on the fight too, though he's having no luck getting close enough to score a hit.

Even pinned to the floor, Yukiko drags herself across the ground. The embedded stake actually drags *through* the rock, creating small cracks in the otherwise solid ground. Her other hand blurs through the air, and Kagura winces when it catches her unaware. Deep cuts appear on the front of the *miko*'s already ruined *haori*.

I lash out with my own weapon, trying to restrain the revenant, and manage to drill through her foot. Yukiko stumbles, but persists. She lunges at me, and I recoil, biting back a cry of pain as her nails scour at my face. If I'd been half a second slower, she would have sliced through my neck instead.

Okiku isn't out of the fight yet; she tackles the other ghost again. Yukiko swipes, and Okiku lets her. Those knife-like fingers sink into the center of Okiku's chest.

A red mist settles in my vision, and I'm aware that I'm shouting at the ghost, but I don't know the words I'm saying, just that they are filled with anger. I dimly recall ignoring Kagura's own yells as I leap at Yukiko. By the time I come back to myself, Yukiko is on the ground, froth dripping from her bared teeth. A wooden stake sprouts from the center of her forehead and black is oozing out of that terrible wound. Her hand has been ripped from her wrist. Okiku must have done that.

Okiku is in my arms, bleeding black from the wounds she's sustained. I press my hands to her chest, trying to stem the flow. I don't realize I'm crying until I feel the tears dripping down my chin.

Yukiko screams horrible curses at us. She tries to lift her head, the stake pulling a few centimeters from the ground.

And then it's Riley's turn. Before the ghost can dislodge the spike, he sends his own into her chest. The horrid, gurgled screech she emits will always haunt my nightmares. Still holding Okiku, I lift the doll. It's now or never.

"Rest in goddamn peace already!" I snarl. It's not the invocation Kagura would have chosen, but it does the trick. The stakes pinning Yukiko Uchiyama begin to move again but this time not of her volition. They pull her toward the doll I'm aiming in her direction. Yukiko's struggles are frantic. Her severed hand clings to the floor, creating deep grooves along the rocky surface as it is yanked along with its owner. The ghost wails one last time—

"Please, no more," she begs.

Makoto's face is a grotesque puzzle, his features nearly unrecognizable. He hangs suspended over the pit. The ropes holding him twist as he writhes in pain. He has been stripped naked, and the priests have carved symbols into his skin that can never be washed away. His blood runs down his body and gathers at the tips of his toes, creating a steady drip, drip, drip as it is cast into the darkness beneath him.

Makoto is still alive. She wishes he was not.

"Please, no more," she sobs.

"You are the strongest of them so far, Yukiko-chan," the kannushi *says.*

Yukiko hangs from the silkworm tree, the long strips of cloth already binding her up to her waist, but he forces her to face the suffering boy before her.

"You are the strongest, Yukiko-chan, and it is you who must suffer the most—"

The doll shudders in my hand, and I drop it, unable to hold it any longer. It hits the floor and flops onto its back before finally stilling, baleful eyes staring upward. Riley stabs at it again, completing the exorcism.

"The dolls," Kagura says in between gasps. Yukiko's ghost is stronger than the others, and it's possible that even these dolls can't hold her for too long.

Riley understands. With shaking hands, he takes it, runs to the ring of *dolls*, and places Yukiko's vessel among them, completing the circle.

"You little idiot," I choke, cradling Okiku in my arms.

She smiles up at me, the expression strange on her face.

"No protests this time," I tell her. "None of that 'it is of no consequence' crap. You're going to rest." The flow of blood isn't as heavy as it was minutes before, and I know Okiku heals fast. I blink back my tears. "You're going to rest, then we're going to finish the ritual, and *then* I expect to see neither hide nor hair from you until we're out of this damned village."

"You are angry at me."

"Damn right I'm angry at you. But we can talk more about that later, when you don't have that hole in your chest." I bend and brush my lips against her clammy forehead, ignoring the weird looks Riley keeps shooting at me. From his viewpoint, I must look to be cradling air. "Now get on with it, and I'll go check on Kagura."

Okiku makes a soft sigh in acquiescence, and I feel her start to slip—

—*and when it is over, she finds herself crying.*

She flees from the body, the cursed, bloated corpse of the man she has killed. She should feel triumph for killing him, should feel vindicated by his death, but all that remains is the strange emptiness she abhors. The voices that fill her head with their enticing promises of vengeance have been silenced, and for the first time, she knows she is truly alone.

Nearly blind, she claws at the walls. Parts of them crumble away from the strength she now possesses. She wants to leave Himeji Castle, this smell of live flesh and human hearts. This is no longer her home. This is no longer a place for the dead like her.

She sees the lord of the castle before he sees her. He is clothed in his evening robes, a candle held aloft to investigate the curious noises. His eyes meet hers. Then he recoils as shock and fear stamp themselves across his features. His voice is no longer swift and sure; now it quavers.

"Okiku?"

She should slay him as well. He gave the order. He turned her away, for all her useless pleading...but he falls to his knees with a low cry when she approaches, and he begins to weep. She has never seen the lord of Himeji Castle vulnerable before.

"Forgive me," he sobs. "Forgive me!"

She cannot.

She turns from him and wills the shadows to swallow her up, to take all the memories of her past life here. Instead, when her eyes open again, she is standing outside Himeji, with nothing but the stars above to bear witness to her sorrow. She feels warmth in her hands and opens them to see the small soul she saved when she killed the murderer, which floats up to graze her bowed head and then flies into the dark sky to mingle with the night.

Take me with you, *she says.* Do not leave me here with nothing.

But the heavens do not answer.

On her knees, she begins to weep—

"—there is something wrong," Kagura is saying.

"What?" I switched off the recorder after Yukiko was exorcised, but the chants continue. It's not the harmonizing of Buddhist monks but one lone voice speaking in a language I have trouble recognizing. I feel sluggish, and I don't understand the urgency in Kagura's voice until it's too late.

Sudden, agonizing pain tears through my head. It's the last thing I remember before the blackness consumes me.

CHAPTER EIGHTEEN

THE EIGHTH RITUAL

You do not belong here.

My head feels unnaturally thick, like someone packed a plane-load of cotton wads into a thimble-sized cranium. There is granite on my tongue, and the taste is disgustedly informing my brain that I'm facedown on the ground again. I turn my head to the side and try to spit, but my mouth refuses to work. My sense of hearing is the next to return.

You are too weak to face me.

It's a man's voice, but it isn't Riley's. I open my eyes and wait for everything to stop swimming around. I'm still inside the cave and can see the silkworm tree and its cocooned inhabitants, swaying in some unknown wind. A gasp escapes me when I spot Okiku facing the *kannushi*. She hasn't had time to heal. Her body is bent over like she can't even carry her own weight. The ground around her is dark with her blood, as black continues to spill from her wounds.

Kagura and Riley are sprawled on the ground nearby. Whatever hit me got them as well. Riley is unconscious, but Kagura's awake, though in no shape to move.

The *kannushi* is smiling at Okiku like he's already won. I try to lift myself off the ground, but I can't move either. There is only the boy, the *kannushi* says through his mask, and Okiku is listening.

"Don't" is what I want to say, but it comes out as a gurgle. The only way to close the hell's gate is to perform the seventh ritual. Six have successfully taken place. And Okiku knows it.

Nothing about the ritual says that you can't use a ghost for a sacrifice if she meets all other requirements.

You have only the boy. Without him, what do you have left?

Okiku turns to me. Her face softens until the beautiful girl she is looks back at me. Her smile is sad and ripe with yearning.

"Nothing," she whispers,

"Without him, I am

nothing.

Do not take him away."

"Kiiii," I gasp. Something feels warm against my chest. The *magatama*.

I can free you. I will spare him.

He's lying. He's going to bind her soul to the ritual, not set it free. I know it, Okiku knows it—but she doesn't have a choice, or else he'll kill me immediately. That's why she's going to accept.

This wasn't part of the plan. Hotoke should have been the seventh sacrifice. It all should have ended with her. Okiku wasn't supposed to be a sacrifice. But she's going to accept, because she trusts me—even at the cost of her own life.

I risk all for him.

I need to move. Now.

"Kiii." The *magatama* grows hotter. Heat curls down my back, toward my arms and legs. It concentrates there, and almost instantly, I feel my limbs thaw. The sensation of pins and needles prickles my skin as I begin taking back control of my body. But there's something else—I feel the stirrings of a strange presence inside me. I have experienced this countless times with Okiku, but this is different.

Okiku steps underneath the silkworm tree, and a swath of cloth gathers around her. I'm still too weak to do anything other than watch as the silk binds her hands, wrapping swiftly around her legs and waist, climbing up into her chest. The *magatama* brands my flesh.

"Okiku!"

She smiles at me one last time, and then she disappears amid the swirl of cloth, binding her form forever.

The *kannushi* is chanting, but the sound is lost in my screaming. She knew. There are two more rituals that can be performed—one to control the gate and one more to rule it. The sacrifices must be willing. To save my life, Okiku gave hers.

While droning on, the *kannushi* turns to me and picks up the ceremonial knife I brought. He'll kill me anyway—if not only to increase her suffering but because he can.

And then two hands rise up from my back and something forces itself from my body. Hotoke Oimikado emerges like a contortionist crawling out of a box, her face and throat still horribly mutilated, leering at her father's apparition through sunken eyes.

The *kannushi*'s chanting breaks off. He had not expected his daughter's ghost to use me as a hiding place. *Dumbelina, you're it.*

But I wouldn't care if Satan himself spawned out of my back. My eyes are locked on the seventh silkworm cocoon. I frantically search with my mind for a sign that Okiku's presence is still there—and find nothing. I reach out, frantic, and encounter emptiness. In that moment, I find the strength to move.

The recorder must have fallen when I did. It's lying a few meters away. I hit the play button, and monks' chanting fills the air. When a faint metallic clatter sounds to my right, I crawl toward the noise as soon as I'm able to. Kagura's still immobile, watching through frightened eyes.

I close the distance between me and the ritual dagger and stagger to my feet. I understand now why the knife was in the other cave instead of in the *kannushi*'s possession. When his daughter's ritual failed and the malice overwhelmed him, the *kannushi* became a creature of wood, just like the hell's gate, this silkworm tree he worships. So he has become susceptible to sacred metal, even his own.

Kazuhiko, Kagura's father, must have known this and used the dagger to fight him, but he was too old or too weak to succeed. As if I could access Hotoke's memories, I can almost see the *kannushi* fleeing the cavern in my mind's eye, weak from the knife's use and leaving the vile dagger behind just as the ghost bride arrived, too late to save her beloved.

Hotoke isn't as strong as Yukiko was, and the *kannushi* deflects most of her blows. But his mask has been ripped off, and his eyes are wild with the power so close to his grasp. I still feel a touch of Hotoke's presence within my head, and while her thoughts are nothing more than a jumble of emotions—fear, anger, rage, a tinge of madness at being dead—I sense that her father always underestimated her, even in life. He thinks he's winning; without Okiku in the fight, it feels like he will.

That doesn't stop me from plunging the dagger through his back, sliding it into what little heart he has left.

This time, the gurgling comes from the *kannushi*'s throat, and I withdraw and stab, withdraw and stab, withdraw and stab. He doesn't bleed, but the knife cripples him and causes him to stagger.

I want to see him suffer. I want to see him fall, to bring him to his knees using the very weapon he used to cause so many girls such grief and torment.

My final blow skewers him by the throat. I should be nauseated by that, but I'm not. The anger and sorrow of losing Okiku are still too much. I switch on the recorder and press my hands over his face.

"Tarquin-san!" Kagura screams at me, but I don't listen. I'm breathing hard, sweat dripping out of every pore. I can feel the priest struggling. His nails are doing a number on my hands, and he bites at my palms, but I barely feel the pain anymore.

I'm a moving, living, breathing doll—maybe not of the same aesthetic as the *hanayome ningyō*, but close enough. Kagura explained that enough times. All one needs is a vessel to contain malevolent spirits—*ningyō* dolls, Kewpies.

Or me.

I've been a vessel since I was five years old.

It's hard to explain what it feels like to have a hostile ghost bottled up inside you—it's worse than my experiences with the masked woman in black of my youth. I had tattoos stitched into my skin to keep her from breaking free. With the *kannushi*, and without the inked seals to lock him in, it's a wrestling match to stop him from using me as his own—a hand here, an eye there—when my defenses are down. He sends nightmares into my head, trying to frighten me, but I shield my mind and heart with memories of Okiku.

I don't need to hold the *kannushi* long, just long enough to finish what he's started—but on my own terms. I turn the tables on him. Now I force myself into *his* head and access *his* knowledge.

I tap into his mind, into everything I'll need to know to rule the gate and wrest the control away from him.

Seven to close and eight to rule.

I drag myself to the altar. Hotoke floats toward the silkworm tree, her arms outstretched. The silkworm cloth finds her easily, wrapping almost lovingly around her spread limbs. She's willing too.

The obscure mantras I need come easily to my lips, but they're not in my voice. I hold the ceremonial knife to my arm, pressing the blade against me. The *kannushi*'s presence leaps away from its touch, stilling him long enough for me to reap the words from his mind. The hymns dip and flow, bending the air around me, and for the first time, I welcome it.

The priest screams inside my head. The cloth wraps around Hotoke Oimikado one final time, and she disappears into the flowing silk.

A terrible noise whips through the air, like the crack of thunder. My breathing quickens, my lips moving faster as the chants quicken, and I watch the silkworm tree slowly split open, and its malice, a black shapeless form, begins to wriggle through the gradually widening entrance. I feel its heavy touch against my mind, its presence so overpowering that my first impulse is to get away from it.

I take a deep breath and embrace the darkness.

There is

nothing

here

Just the scrolling endless

dark of for

ever

So

easy

to let

go so easy

to let

It

overcome

you

no.

Okiku in the morning light.

Okiku, smiling at me for the first time in the glow of a lone lamppost.

Okiku as the fireflies stream past, my fingers tangling in her hair.

Okiku before the silkworms took her away.

No.

I won't let it take my memories of her.

I

won't.

I won't.

I

won't!

I rip my mind free before I go in too deep, before the tree ensures I can never go back. I can hear the tree snarl as I slip from its grasp.

I won't!

I delve one last time into the priest's mind, forcing my way through his insanity to find what I need before the darkness claims from him what it could not from me. I begin a new hymn, breaking the seals containing the area's power, allowing it to surge through me. I force myself to look through the dark gateway at the center of the tree, and I see the hell's gate in its true form: never-ending emptiness and despair. I feel the priest breaking free, yowling and shrieking, as the darkness pulls him into its gaping maw and to his fate.

With all my might, with thoughts of Okiku in my head as my sanctuary, I take in everything the gate has to offer, absorbing its power. For several moments, I'm sure I won't survive the onslaught, but I push on and on and on until it has nothing left to give.

I am ruling the gate. The power is so immense that I understand why the *kannushi* was willing to kill so many people for it, and my head spins at all I could break and bend to my will. I could move mountains, bring down lightning from the sky.

I could be like a god. I could *be* God.

No, I hear someone whisper in the darkest corners of my mind—the part of me that contains all that's left of Okiku. It's enough.

I feel the darkness's eagerness, its hunger.

I close my eyes. I take the energy channeling through me and wrap it around the malice. It does not expect this and struggles. For an instant, it nearly overwhelms me, its hatred overpowering. But I hold on to my memories of Okiku and slice through the blackness with everything I have.

The resulting backlash tosses me on my butt. A million screams of pure agony ring in my ears as the gaping hole in the tree explodes—and then, like a dark supernova, it abruptly collapses into itself.

***

When the world stops moving, I lift my head and cough out a mouthful of dust. The silkworm tree remains standing, but where it once thrummed with energy, it is now still. Half of its branches are gone, and the silkworm cocoons...

I brush past Kagura, who's finally achieved some mobility but isn't quick enough to stop me. I dash toward the silkworms. In the aftermath of the explosion, they've scattered and I don't know which one holds Okiku.

The dagger in my grip, I tear through the nearest cocoon and am rewarded with the faintest whiff of an image—a girl in a peony kimono. Ran Hirano. I move toward the next, the blade flashing quickly. Fujiko Kajiwara. Mineko Kunai.

I find Hotoke Oimikado inside the fourth cocoon, but unlike the others, she doesn't dissipate. She's so transparent as to be practically invisible, but she lingers—expectant, anticipating.

The fifth cocoon is empty, but I sense her, that faint scent of eucalyptus, the sensation of morning light on my face.

"*No!*"

I paw at the silken shell, scavenging for any trace of her, but there is nothing. Okiku is gone.

"*No! No, no, no, no!*"

I don't recall much of the minutes that followed, but I remember trying to cradle the bits of the silk threads around me, as if Okiku would return if I held them long enough.

She can't be gone. There's no way she could leave me behind with nothing but the memories of what she had to sacrifice for me.

Because it isn't fair. I didn't realize the consequences. It's only now that we've won the fight and the aftermath of the ritual has settled over us like dead skin that I feel truly afraid. I have to leave Okiku here with that terrible tree for her tombstone.

It doesn't deserve her. No grave deserves her.

I hear Kagura calling my name, but I don't answer. I feel her arms surround me, but I remain rigid and bent. My grief won't allow for comfort.

I'm crying when she lets me go, taking the ceremonial dagger from my hands. I'm crying as Kagura moves toward the godforsaken tree and slides past the twisted branches and the cobwebs spun across the floor like brittle blankets. I'm crying as she lifts her slender arms, the blade glinting in the unnatural light, and drives it violently into the tree's rotting trunk. Pools of frothing black gush out. The *miko* circles the tree, the knife flashing in and out, in and out, scoring new holes into the gnarled surface and spilling more blood.

No longer fattened by the blood of its cocooned prey, the tree succumbs. What is left of its branches thin out, and the bark sloughs off its limbs. Smoke rises from the tips, thatches of kindling consuming the rest of the wood in flame as if it had been nothing but an illusion all along. Within the space of a few minutes, the tree rots away until only a protrusion of stump remains.

And I am crying.

There is movement beside me, and I know who it is. I do not bother to turn around, because I no longer care. But Hotoke Oimikado forces me to look at her. Her fingers are cold, but the *magatama* glows when she takes hold of it. Fog curls from its center, rising in formless wisps to take a more concrete shape, until the ghost of Kazuhiko Kino stands before me, no longer an old man, but the watchful, defiant boy of his youth. I recall his sunken corpse in the pit. Unlike the other villagers and the ghost-hunter crew, he had not been woven into a cocoon. The *magatama* might not have saved his life, but at the very least, it kept his soul intact.

The boy turns toward Kagura, who watches him, awestruck. He kneels before her, smiling, and then she starts to weep.

Around me, the cocoons wriggle. Their motions become frantic, desperate.

As we watch, fireflies burst out of their silken prisons, wings whirring, taking flight into the darkness. The tiny fireflies surround me. As one, they venture higher, and I reach out without thinking, my hand knowing what I want before my mind consciously does.

I catch one of the glowing insects in my palm, and Hotoke's hand moves toward my forehead—

—I am no longer in a dark cave with a dead tree but in some nameless field on a bright morning. I am on my knees, and the silken threads of Okiku's cocoon that once bound her to me are gone. Fireflies soar overhead. Some stop to nuzzle against blades of grass, bracing against a restless wind. Others bat wings against my cheeks, wiping away the tracks my tears have taken.

Okiku is beside me. She is no longer garbed in death. There is color in her cheeks and brightness in her eyes, and she wears a plain brown yukata. Her face is tilted up, examining the sky with wonder, as if seeing it for the first time and wondering why she never took the time to observe such beauty before.

"Okiku!" I take her hands, but I have a hard time holding on to them. They keep slipping from my grasp, her skin sliding against mine, though she does nothing to pull back, does nothing to push me away.

"It is beautiful here." Her voice is hushed.

"Yes," I agree, wishing I could stay with her forever. "Do you remember when I took you firefly hunting in DC? You always loved that."

"I love any place where you are with me."

Air fills my lungs—too quickly. I choke, finding the words to say, "Don't leave me, Ki."

"I've come," Okiku says, "to say good-bye."

"No!" Fireflies spin away, startled by my forcefulness. "Okiku, I can't let you go!"

"I do not want to. But I must." She's happy and beautiful, but the regret she always wears about her lingers in her voice. "I cannot stay with you."

"I won't allow it. There has to be a way."

"It is beyond my control."

A small procession of people comes into view. I recognize them: Yukiko Uchiyama, no longer malicious but clothed in serenity and white. Like her, the other ghosts are in their bridal kimonos, and their betrothed stand by their sides. The old mother whose skeleton we unearthed in the Hirano house is with her daughter, both with joyous expressions.

Other villagers stream past us, talking and laughing. The burden of the Aitou curse has been thrown off their shoulders, and they are ready to ascend to something better. Hotoke and Kazuhiko trail behind them. They smile at me and Okiku, and then the fireflies surround them, wrapping them in frenzied flight, a hurricane of bright lights and promises that spins faster until their lights blur, a whirlpool of stars.

And then just as suddenly as they came, they slacken and fade.

"Tarquin." Okiku's soft, warm lips press against my forehead. She moves lower to kiss my nose, and somewhere in the space between us, my heart breaks.

"I lied," she whispers. "I am sorry."

"Lied about what?"

"I know why I do not like her. The girl. She is the life you should have led if I had not been selfish. But it is not too late." She rests her forehead against mine. "Think of me sometimes—"

—on its knees, the dead body that once knew itself as Okiku weeps bitterly for what life demanded of her, for what she had been unprepared to give.

Something brushes against her forehead. A pulsing brightness streaks past her, and when she raises her head, she sees a multitude of fireflies. Their wings brush against her forehead in gratitude, spinning around her until she is at the center of their maelstrom. They are tiny souls that had been lost, and in their glow, she sees a purpose. She sees a glimpse of the future and the souls she could save. An endless tide of children and innocents, one with a shade of black hair and unusual blue eyes…

She has nothing here.

But for now, she is not alone and that is enough—

The meadow fades to black, until I am hugging the floor of the cave once more. My tears could fill these open spaces soon, for Okiku is gone.

CHAPTER NINETEEN

UNNATURAL CHANGES

I don't remember how we stumble out of that accursed cave and back into the sunshine.

I am aware of Kagura at my elbow, keeping a firm grip to give me balance, and of her curt orders to Riley to do the same on my other side. I know they're speaking, but I'm not paying attention. Snatches of conversation and "in shock" filter to my ears. They're surely talking about me, but I find that I don't care.

I feel strange. I've learned to recognize the signs of possession: a feeling of sinking into your own chest, as if something else has laid claim to your insides. Its claws dig into you and sap you of your strength when it goes against your wishes, like the masked woman who lived within me for years. It gives you sudden bursts of energy when you're a willing partner, the way Okiku always was.

This presence is not being overt, but it's lying on the edge of my awareness—letting me know it's there but doing little else. For now.

In the meantime, my body is lead and sweat runs down my face.

Once or twice, Kagura commands Riley to stop and checks my temperature and listens for my pulse. Her lips are pursed, but she says nothing each time.

They carry my arms over their shoulders while the rest of my body slumps against theirs, a rag cloth hung out to dry. I'm mindful of us moving past the silkworm hatcheries and their rotting wood, past the houses and their rotting souls. At the back of my mind, I remember that before all of this decay, there were dolls on altars, cared for by those who had been left behind. I remember a diary and a mother's love.

It's easy to look around and forget there was life here once. That there was love here.

The gate leading out of the village looms before us. Kagura and Riley fight to pull it open while balancing me between them. As we exit, I start to struggle.

"I can't, Kagura." I've run out of tears, and I'm short on words. I repeat them over and over, as if saying them enough times will make a difference. "I can't, Kagura. I can't."

As irrational as it sounds, I don't want to leave *her* behind.

"I am so sorry, Tarquin-san," Kagura murmurs gently, "but we have to go."

They pull through the creaking gate, and we are once more in the thick of the woods. I am weak. In the end, I can do little more than flail and whimper, so the *miko* gets her way. The ground is spoiled with twigs and rocks, but for all their own injuries, both Kagura and Riley hold me tight and don't let me fall.

I blank out for a bit. I don't know how long we wander before we're found. It starts with a thrum of noise, a series of calls and whistles that penetrate Aokigahara's silence.

Riley runs madly ahead, whooping and hollering and waving his arms in the air. I blink, and then I am on the ground on my back, and people are lifting me onto a crude stretcher. I can see Kagura being carried on another stretcher despite her protests, and then my vision is full of Callie, who has swooped down from somewhere in the noise to envelop me in a tight hug that robs me of the rest of my breath.

"You nearly gave me a heart attack!" She weeps, our combined weight forcing the medical personnel to lower the stretcher to the forest floor. "Where did you go? Why did you run off like that? I told you never to do anything like that to me again. You liar!"

I can only manage a halfhearted "Callie…" before the men lift me again and carry me through the woods on a babble of excited voices and cheers.

When I wake up next, it is to the sticky-sweet, sanitized smell of the hospital. Callie is huddled at my bed and dozing off, her hands clasped around one of my own, but my faint movement is enough to wake her. She lifts her head, her eyes red-rimmed, but the smile on her face is the widest I've ever seen.

"H'llo," I mumble.

"Hi, yourself." Callie dashes at her eyes with the back of her hand. "You have a cut on your back, but it looks worse than it actually is. They said you're just mostly exhausted, and they can send you home tomorrow. But they wanted to keep you under observation tonight to make sure you didn't have any other injuries. Which is why I can do this." She gives me a light thwack on my nose, a swat one might use to belittle a puppy, and I yelp. "Whatever possessed you to run into the woods like that?"

"I didn't—"

"You've been gone for two days! I thought Auntie was going to have a heart attack. Even Saya joined the search for you. We were all so worried. Every time the rescuers found a body, I kept expecting it to be yours." A sob bubbles from her throat. "How did you find Kagura? And what happened to the rest of the *Ghost Haunts* guys?"

Something that doesn't feel like me coils inside my body, wishing to move, but I force it down. I don't want to talk about it. "Can we do this some other time?"

She softens. "Oh, of course. I'm sorry, Tark. I got a little wound up. Rest for as long as you want, okay? I'm just…" Her eyes brim up again. "I'm so glad to see you."

"I'm glad to see you too, Callie." I hug her back, grateful for her warmth and her closeness. But a strange burning curls inside me. It's been plaguing me ever since we left Aitou.

"Is Kagura okay?"

"She's banged up but mending fast. The doctors are having a hard time getting her to rest. The ghost-hunter guy's going to pull through too. Search parties are still looking for the others."

I close my eyes. They can look all they want, but the rest of the ghost-hunter crew will never be found. Guilt comes crawling back. Yet it doesn't dull the burning that wraps around my insides.

"Don't worry." Callie's tone is encouraging. "I'm sure we'll find them soon. We can talk later, when you're better."

But I don't get better. Not where it matters most.

As soon as I get a bit of my strength back, I start pacing in my room. Callie and a nurse come in and badger me into retreating back to the bed. But I can't sleep. I feel too restless, and I'm not sure why.

I'm discharged from the hospital the next day, and Callie talks me into going back to the Kamameshi Ryokan instead of waiting for Kagura to be released. There, I resume pacing, too restless to do anything else. The news outlets had me pegged as an unimportant member of the search party who got lost, so I've been spared the media attention that poor Kagura and Riley are no doubt enduring. I saw Riley being interviewed twice on television but not the *miko*.

Callie returned to the hospital almost as soon as I'd settled in—to fend off the worst of the news vultures and to look after the *miko*. There's nothing I can do but wait. As I pace for hours on end, I stare at the hot spring outside my room, remembering how much Okiku enjoyed the steam and the waters. Every so often, I would turn my head to ask her something, only to realize she's no longer here. The pain only worsens as time ticks by.

Okiku's presence is gone, but a strange one remains. I can feel it move. It whispers: *we are power*.

"Shut up," I snap, and it does not speak for the rest of the night.

On my second night at the inn, Auntie visits my room. I haven't told her about all that happened, and I'm pretty sure Kagura hasn't either. She gently wraps her arms around me.

"I am so sorry for your loss." I can hear her grief.

Maybe she could infer what had happened from my state of mind or maybe it's because an affinity for spirits has always been strong in Kagura's bloodline. Either way, I finally break, crying like a baby against her shoulder at losing Okiku. It's a good release, and I pull myself together, although I'm probably only a little better off than I had been. Dad calls the next morning, frantic to know if Kagura is all right.

I learn then that Callie has been sneaky, because she didn't tell him I'd been missing. For his peace of mind, I don't enlighten him. Because the news says nothing about my and Callie's involvement but is throwing Kagura's name around liberally now that she's been found, I don't even need to fib too much. I tell him about Kagura's current condition, playing down her injuries, and promise him that Callie and I are all right.

"I'm not so sure, Tark," Dad says uneasily. "Every time you're in Japan, strange things happen to the three of you."

"You're not going to stop us from visiting, are you?" That's the last thing I want. "This isn't Kagura's fault, and you know what they say about Aokigahara…"

"I know. I'm not blaming Kagura, of course. I just feel terrible not to be there to help her. The local police should restrict access to that forest. If even an experienced film crew can get lost in there, there's no telling what could happen to the average tourist. It doesn't feel right to not even be in the same country with you when something like this is going on."

"You worry too much, Dad. I'm almost eighteen, remember? I can take care of myself."

"I know you're more than capable, Tark." I can hear him smiling. "But that won't stop me from being a worrywart. You're my son."

"I know." I'm smiling too. "I guess I'm just going to have to live with that."

I dream of Okiku that night—of happier times together, all the little things I took for granted. I miss our hunts, the long silences when we had no need to talk, and sitting in our special field of fireflies. And then I wake, and the knowledge of what I lost returns, stronger than ever. There's something else I'm missing. Something I'm forgetting.

I replay what the *kannushi* said to his daughter before she…

I lug out all of Kagura's research materials from the trunk and dedicate myself to rereading them. I still can't do much with Kazuhiko's books that Kagura hadn't translated into English, so I go through all the notes I can decipher. I tackle Hotoke's diaries, analyzing every detail and looking for anything that feels out of place.

I slog through the research I'd glanced over before our trip to Aitou—the herbal properties of belladonna, various traditions of ritualized marriages, silkworm farming, the use of bridal dolls. I look through them so many times that I'm sure I've committed the documents to memory, but I'm still at a loss, and I'm frustrated.

Auntie senses that this kind of insanity is a lot better than the anguished madness I'd been wallowing in. She says nothing about this new obsession and instead brings me meals and tea without prejudice.

I tackle Kagura's notes on *The Book of Unnatural Changes* next, and it takes me two more days to find what I've been looking for.

***

Kagura and Callie finally arrive home a few days later. A few eager reporters are still trailing behind, hoping to score an exclusive interview, and for the first time, I see Auntie transform from considerate innkeeper to protective she-wolf. Whenever one of the journalists or cameramen venture onto her property, the normally quiet old woman goes marching out, waving her broom—or in a few humorous instances, wielding a long garden hose turned on at full blast—and shrieking Japanese invectives that even the mostly foreign correspondents have no trouble interpreting. They're quick to hurry away before she can soak their perfectly coiffed hair and their equipment.

"Are you okay?" is Kagura's first question to me. Other than the sling over her arm and the faint bruises on her face, she looks the same as ever.

I force a smile. "I think I should be asking you that question."

"You should have said something, Tark," scolds Callie. Kagura must have told her everything in the hospital, because Callie is clearly sidestepping around the Okiku issue when she would normally be asking me for details. "It's okay. I'll survive. Auntie's got a feast laid out for all of us. She's really excited that you're home, Kagura. She's been cooking all day, and she even talked me into helping out."

Both women look mystified by my change in attitude, but they're wise enough not to comment on it for the moment. I make a show of ushering them to the dining table, where Auntie is waiting. For once, Auntie has forgone the traditional meals. Instead of the typical *kaiseki* fare, she's cooked up a storm of Japanese street food—fried *takoyaki* dough balls with bits of octopus, *yakisoba* noodles literally made from scratch and hand-pulled, and grilled chicken and beef skewers with sweet, green bell peppers and spring onions in her specially made sweet sauce, as well as plump green-tea mochi cakes. She's also prepared an assortment of sushi with flying-fish roe and slices of fatty tuna and finished it off with bowls of steaming rice topped with grilled eel—a favorite among Japanese schoolchildren but also Kagura's, Auntie explains, as the *miko* reddens.

The mood is equally festive. With Auntie around, we don't talk about what happened in Aitou. Kagura fends off most of Auntie's questions, leaving out mention of the village completely. Instead, she talks about wandering around the woods for days after being separated from the rest of the group, relying on her survival skills to forage for food and ration the provisions she had the foresight to bring. She found me, and then Riley, shortly before the search party located us. It's enough to mollify Auntie, and I'm relieved we don't have to explain further.

Callie is not as trusting. Once the table has been cleared and Kagura and Auntie have retired to their rooms, she pounces. "Kagura told me everything." My cousin is becoming teary-eyed again. "Oh, Tark, I'm so sorry."

I force a smile. "You've always been after me to de-possess myself, Callie. Now that I have, it sounds like you're actually wishing I hadn't."

"Don't take that tone with me, Tark. I wanted it to be amicable for the two of you—not like this." Callie sniffles. "What's going to happen next? Where did she go?"

My voice catches in my throat, and I can't speak right away. I think about the fireflies and the bridal ghosts in the meadow, happy and free. But Okiku was different. She hadn't rejoiced at achieving the peace she deserved. *I do not want to*, she said. *But I must.*

Was I biased? Am I trying to convince myself that Okiku didn't want to pass on so I can justify what I am going to do? The thought haunts me, half convincing me that I'm putting my selfishness over her happiness.

But I remember the sorrowful look on her face and the lingering way her lips pressed against me. I can believe that she would accept her fate, but I know with sudden certainty that she hadn't wanted it to end like this. Not like this.

"I'm sorry, Callie, but I need to see Kagura. It might be important."

I find Kagura in her room, looking over her father's research as she carefully packs the notebooks and parchments back into the large trunk. Her eyes are sad.

I stand by the doorway, not sure if it is right for me to enter and break the moment. But Kagura speaks.

"I saw him too," she says. "I saw my father for a brief moment. For all that happened in Aitou, at least it was closure."

"Sometimes, you try to forget about the pain in your past," I say, sinking to the floor beside her, "and you run as fast as you can, thinking you can leave it behind if you run far enough. But it has a way of sneaking back when you least expect it. Sometimes, the only way you can escape is to turn around and confront it."

Kagura smiles wanly. "It sounds like you're talking about more than just my father." She holds up the photo of a younger Kagura with Kazuhiko. She sets the picture aside; the rest she adds into the trunk. "But I think you're right. At least now I understand why his work filled up his life, so that at times, there didn't seem to be any space for me or my mother. I hope he's at peace now."

I remember the last time I saw Kagura's father, in that quiet meadow with Hotoke and the other spirits. "He is."

"Are you sure you're okay, Tark? I know you might not want to talk about it, but…"

"Actually, that's what I came here for."

The *miko* looks up at me, startled, and I pull *The Book of Unnatural Changes* from the trunk, placing it before her. I open the heavy volume and turn it to the page containing the ritual I had in mind. "I wanted to talk to you about this."

Kagura's eyes widen. "Tarquin. Are you…?"

Immediately, she is on her knees, her hand touching my forehead while her eyes look into mine, trying to sense what I already know. The darkness inside me responds to that touch, heat erupting from my forehead, and she jerks her hand back as if she's been electrocuted.

"*Kami-sama*," she gasps, falling back. "I knew there was something odd, but I never thought…"

"I'm sorry, Kagura." I can feel the energy swirling inside me—energy I took into myself when I closed the hell's gate, the power the *kannushi* so desperately wanted. "But I think you're going to have to teach me everything you know about the Hundred Days ritual."

CHAPTER TWENTY

MOURNING

I've got ninety-three more days to go.

Callie and I are back in the United States—her in Boston, and me in DC. We only spent a week in Japan, but it feels like a lifetime has passed. Leaving was hard, but I know the hardest is still to come.

Everyone's still talking about McNeil after spring break is over and school starts. As selfish as it sounds, I don't think I've spared a thought for him since leaving for Japan, and all I really want to do now that I'm back is hole up in my room and let the days pass. Dad doesn't sense anything wrong, mainly because I keep up my usual flippant attitude whenever he's around. I don't want him to worry any more than he ought to.

A lot of students give me the evil eye during class and when they pass me in hallways. They'll always blame me for Keren McNeil's death, but I'm beyond caring at this point. I walk past a place in school where some of his teammates had erected a small altar in memory of the football jock, strung with flowers and handwritten notes. Someone had placed his jersey beside a large photo of him. I resist the urge to give in

we are power

to my baser nature and remind everyone just what kind of guy their hero was. I turn away instead. He's dead, and despite everything he did, it no longer feels like he should matter to me.

I used to worry that being with Okiku brought out my darker, more depraved instincts. Now I realize it wasn't her. The darkness was in me all along, and maybe that was what drew her to me in the first place.

True to her word, Kagura taught me everything I needed to know before we left. "I've never done this before, Tarquin," she warned me. She was reluctant all throughout our lessons, but she knew that I had no choice. "I cannot guarantee that any of this is going to work."

"It's still better than nothing," I pointed out.

Hanging on to hope is the only thing keeping me from going crazy, and I don't want to think about what might happen if nothing comes out of the ritual I'm about to do.

But I *know* it will succeed. Because I am sure of the malevolence residing inside me, I know that the ritual is real. Whether or not I'm strong enough to perform it is a different matter.

Some days, the malice lies heavy inside me—restless, demanding to break free. On occasion, it takes every ounce of my self-control not to let it out. Some days, it's almost as if it's not there. Those are the days I worry I've lost my hold on it and it's found someone else to hibernate in.

Because if it's gone, I'll never be able to bring her back.

So instead of brooding on it, I force myself into a conventional pattern: go to class, go home, do my homework, meditate, go to sleep. Go to class, go home, do my homework, meditate, go to sleep. Some days, I can't help myself; when the loneliness is at its worst, I wait for her to come to me, though I know it's useless to hope.

Some days, I still wake up expecting to feel the weight of her hair on me.

"I wish you'd tell me what's bothering you," Kendele says when I have fifty-four more days to go. She's the only one I make room for nowadays, because I feel that I owe her that. Despite my reputation, she continues to be a good friend, dismissing what other people say about me. I wonder if, despite her popularity, she ever gets shunned because of me. If she does, she doesn't admit it.

"Nothing's wrong really," I say. We don't just frequent food trucks anymore. Sometimes, I bring her to an actual restaurant or take her to a movie we both want to see. I'm not exactly sure what the status of our relationship is. We haven't promised mutual exclusivity. I know that she goes on other dates but isn't serious with anyone else and that she wouldn't mind if I did the same, if I wanted to. She's not pressuring me to put a label on us. And for what it's worth, I do like Kendele, and I appreciate her sensitivity.

We caught a movie earlier, and we're having dessert at an Italian café just around the corner from the theater.

She pokes a spoon at her toffee-nut gelato. "If you don't want to talk about it, that's okay. But, you know, on the off chance that you do want to get what's bothering you off your chest instead of being such a growly, brooding alpha male about i…"

"You've been reading way too many romance novels," I tease. Miles apart from everyone else who knows about it—Kagura, Callie, Auntie, Saya—I don't have anyone to talk to about what happened over spring break. "Remember the girl I told you about? The one who…ah…"

"The one you punched McNeil for," she supplies, smiling. "I do."

"She's gone."

"What do you mean 'gone'?" Kendele looks startled. "She didn't die, did she? You look so grim all of a sudden."

That's difficult to explain. In many ways, Okiku had—and yet… The dark inside me pulses, sensing where my thoughts are heading.

"Not exactly. She had to go away, and I don't know if she'll ever be back."

"Oh." Kendele places her hand on mine. "I'm so sorry to hear that, Tark. How are you feeling?"

"A little out of sorts."

"Do you love her?" The question comes out more tentative than her usual assertiveness. "And don't give me that crap about not wanting to hurt my feelings. I want you to be honest with me."

I couldn't firmly answer her when she had first posed that question, months ago when Okiku was safely part of me. Now the answer comes naturally. "Yeah, I do." I can't classify the feeling as romantic, because it is and it isn't. It's *everything*, and the irony is that I can't really explain my love for Okiku without sounding crazy. I'm floundering without her. I don't know what to do without her in my life. She's the most important person in the world to me, and now I might never see her again.

Kendele bites her lip and looks down. "She must be amazing for you to care for her that much."

I force my dark thoughts away, not wanting to ruin the evening for her. "To tell you the truth, I wasn't sure that I should say anything, knowing how you feel. But I promised you I'd be honest." *As much as I'm able to anyway*, I add silently.

"Thank you for that. I wasn't—" Her head snaps up. "Wait. What do you mean by 'knowing how you feel'?"

"Knowing that you're desperately attracted to me, of course." I grin smugly at her, then inch away when she pretends to dump her ice cream on me.

"You are the most insufferable, arrogant, and completely obnoxious—"

I silence her by leaning over and capturing her lips with mine. She gives in almost immediately.

Dense, my ass.

"What does this mean for us though?" she asks softly a little later. She's shoved her chair next to mine so she can burrow under my arm, our gelato all gone. It's getting late and I ought to take her home soon, but for now, I'm content to have her here, snuggled at my side.

"What are you thinking?" I ask her.

"We're not going to be in the same place for long, are we? We're going to graduate in a month. You'll be going to Brown, and I'll be going to Stanford."

"Ah, yes. Stanford. Good to see that all that tutoring I gave you—which you didn't need—paid off."

She socks me lightly in the ribs. "I'm serious. We haven't exactly talked about this, but I didn't think you'd be interested or invested in a long-distance relationship. That's why I didn't ask for something more from you." Her voice softens. "I would say that I'm willing to make this work, but…I think it will be a lot more difficult than we both want it to be."

I know she's right. We'll be living in different states on different sides of the country starting this fall and haven't been officially dating to begin with.

"I think we should just let things happen as they come. No promises to make, no promises to keep. Let's just enjoy each other's company for as long as we're able to." I take a deep breath, and the cold night air fills my lungs. "Because if I've learned anything these last couple of years, it's to spend every moment you can with the people you want to be with."

***

When I've got twenty-seven more days to go, graduation arrives. There's nothing to differentiate it from other ceremonies that have gone before, and I'm sure it'll be no different from those that'll come after it. The only thing it marks for us is freedom from Pembrooke High, and that couldn't come soon enough.

Afterward, Kendele seeks me out and plants a happy kiss on my mouth, oblivious to Dad's and Callie's grins. She'll be leaving in a couple of weeks to head to Stanford early, and we promised to spend the rest of the time she's here together. Dad takes us all out for celebratory burgers and milk shakes. I think he's secretly relieved that I managed to graduate, given all the bumps and false starts we've had over the years.

"So," Callie whispers to me after Dad engages Kendele in conversation about the Washington Wizards, which both are avid fans of. "Are you guys going to do the long-distance thing?"

"I don't think so." I keep my voice low. "I really like her, and I know she likes me"—Callie rolls her eyes at this—"but I don't think we've got it in us to make it last with thousands of miles between us. She's not built for that kind of relationship, and I'm not sure I am either."

"Aw, that's too bad. I like her."

"I knew you would. But we've talked it over, and I think we've both accepted that this is just for now." I pause. "And as much as I think she's great, I sometimes feel like I'm only using her as a substitute. Like I'm using her to forget."

"About Okiku?"

"Yeah. It isn't fair to her."

Callie inhales deeply, the way she does when she's going to ask something she's afraid might anger me. "Are *you* okay? Is…is *it* still with you?"

I don't really know what to call what's housed inside my body, but the inflection in Callie's voice seems to sum it up perfectly. "I'm fine. I'm used to being occupied by incorporeal spirits, remember? At least this one doesn't talk back to me."

"Are you still going through with the ritual?" Callie sounds genuinely frightened. "I'm not going to stand in your way, but I don't think you should do it alone. I can extend my stay, so I can be here when you—"

"No." I'm firm about this. Whatever happens, whether the ritual succeeds or not, I have to do this on my own. "Thanks, Callie, but this was intended to be a private ritual. It's the only way."

***

Fourteen more days to go—and I see him.

From across the street, I watch him waiting at the bus stop. He's got a scar across his cheek and bloodshot blue eyes. He's wearing a red baseball cap. I don't know who he is, and if I had squelched the urge to wander the city tonight like I've been doing most nights, I never would have known he existed.

But he does exist—and so do the three young specters, frightened and despairing, clinging to his hips. I watch the smallest of those boys tug fitfully at the man's hair, but he pays no attention to the ghosts on his back. The man only scowls at his watch and taps a foot impatiently on the concrete.

I turn away. I can see these ghosts even without Okiku by my side, and there's no better proof that this was what I've been meant to do all along, with or without her.

***

Twelve more days to go, and I feel like I've got all the time in the world.

Kendele and her parents are leaving for California to get her settled at Stanford. I tag along to the airport to see them off, and as emotional as the moment is, I never expected her to actually cry. In full view of her parents, she throws her arms around me and plants a wet kiss on my lips, much to my embarrassment. I'd met her folks a couple of times, but I don't think they were eager for front-row seats to a tongue-wrestling match between me and their daughter, though they're more amused than angry.

"We'll always have Pho Junkies," she whispers when we finally break apart and she's no longer bothering to hide her tears.

After they go through security, I decide to walk for a little while to clear my head.

I used to hate change. Change meant never being able to stay anywhere for long. I always felt as if I was being pulled up like a weed before I ever had the chance to put down roots. Dad and I would move from state to state, so I never had anything constant to fall back on. Even the fixtures in my life, Dad and Callie, weren't always there when I needed them, even when they wanted to be.

Okiku was the first person in my life who was completely mine, in the same way that I was the only person that had ever been completely hers. She taught me to face my inner demons, that their presence did not mean I was broken. She loved my darkness, and I loved her light.

I don't know how long I walk, but by the time I snap out of my thoughts, night has fallen and the first stars wink down at me from the sky. My chest throbs painfully. The sudden pressure catches me off guard, and I stagger slightly before bracing myself against a nearby tree.

It's getting harder to fend off the energy swirling in my body. It's getting more difficult to fight off the urge to…destroy. To test the limits of what I can do.

I could level this town, I think. I could lay this city to waste. I could do what the *kannushi*, Hiroshi Mikage, aspired to do: to bend Japan under his power. I could do the same to this country. I look down at my fingers and I can practically see the energy gathering, waiting for me to give the word and unleash it on the unsuspecting populace.

I could rule over any city—over anything really—that I choose. And nothing would ever need to change again.

But I don't. I control the pain. I have years of practice. I keep these black desires under lock and key.

Even mindless, terrifying things, those that creep in the dark without any hope for light; even the malice that festers inside me, impatient at my idleness and desirous of a victim—even they want to be free.

Twelve more days.

***

One more day to go and Kagura contacts me through Skype—
which is a surprise because she's never done that before. I know
what she wants to talk about long before her face flashes on the
screen. She looks worried, just like Callie when we'd talked online
only an hour or so ago.

"How's Riley?" I ask, heading off her first question.

After the media circus died down, Stephen Riley chose to stay
in Japan indefinitely, both to recuperate and to continue the search
for his friends. We know some people, like Garrick Adams and Alan
George, are a lost cause, but he's still holding out hope for the others.

I was right in my initial assessment of him though. Much to
the *miko*'s discomfort, the man has taken a shine to her, visiting
Kagura every couple of days at the Kamameshi Ryokan. He's done
everything short of actually asking her out on a date. If his feelings
are obvious enough for Kagura to catch on, they would be obvious
to anyone else. I'm sure he'll work up the nerve one day.

The *miko* blushes. "That is not important, Tark!"

"I'm pretty sure Callie's said everything you're about to, Kagura-
chan," I tell her, laughing. "Yes, I'll be okay. Yes, I've gone over
your notes a hundred billion times, and I know what to do. Yes,
I'm prepared to accept whatever happens, even if it doesn't work.
I'll promise not to sulk—"

"Tark." Kagura is smiling. "I was not going to tell you all that. I
just wanted to talk to you again before tomorrow."

"I'm absolutely flattered, Kagura-chan. I really am."

"You still have your sense of humor, so I am taking that as a good sign."

"I always have a sense of humor. What were you expecting me to do, rampage through Washington, DC, and make Godzilla look like a hamster?"

"Are you?"

Kagura never looks like she's joking, so I watch her for a moment to make sure she's serious.

"Was that what you were afraid of? That I was going to give in to the temptation and use…this?" I gesture at myself. "Now I'm sad you don't trust me. Maybe I'll go climb a tower and swat at a few airplanes."

"But it's difficult, isn't it?" Kagura's eyes probe at me through the screen. "It was a very powerful hell's gate, Tark, and you sapped most of its power. It wants to escape, and it could still convince you not to wait out the hundred days."

"I'm keeping it in check. It's been ninety-nine days. I'm sure I can make it one more day."

"You didn't answer my question."

I close my eyes briefly. "I'd be lying if I said no. It puts ideas into my head that I'm not altogether repulsed by. But I'm stronger than it, Kagura. Let's just say that I have a more compelling motivation than to become some criminal mastermind."

"You really love her, don't you?" There is no derision or fear in the *miko*'s voice when she asks me that. No judgment or disgust.

She's dealt with a lot of ghosts as a *miko*. I suppose out of everyone, she understands my relationship with Okiku best.

"Yes. I do. In every sense of the word." I pause. "You know what's ironic? Before Okiku…left, she said she felt guilty. As if she was responsible that I didn't have a normal life. I wish I'd been able to tell her that she was wrong. She's a powerful spirit in her own right, you know? She could have been anything, Kagura. She could have ripped the moon out of the sky if she wanted to, could have been a goddess in her own right. But she chose me—to be with me, to protect me." I pause. "I know it sounds weird…"

Kagura smiles. "No, it does not. If there is one thing I am sure about, it's what the two of you have. Just promise me, Tark—promise me you'll be all right after this, whatever happens. If any part of you doubts, do not go through with the ritual tomorrow. Any lingering doubts you feel will weaken the rites, and the malice knows it. I trust you, but I cannot lie and say I am not afraid for you. It is a decision you must make on your own."

"I can't lie and say that I'm not frightened. But I love her more than I'm afraid."

After Kagura signs off, I go back to the piles of notes surrounding my laptop. I've been reviewing the necessary hymns and the *miko*'s research for the greater part of the night, remembering all I need for the ritual tomorrow.

I reread the ritual for the Hundred Days of Mourning for what feels like the eight hundredth time. I feel nervous and hopeful and scared. But doubt is the last thing I feel, because I know I want to see the ritual through, whatever happens.

***

This isn't the first time I've snuck into Rock Creek Park, and I sincerely doubt it's going to be the last. Dad was quick to let me be tonight, figuring I was still bummed about Kendele leaving and wanting to be by myself for a while when I told him I was going to take a drive.

In a way, he's right. I miss Kendele a lot, despite the numerous emails and calls since she arrived in California. But this evening, I have something important to do, and every nerve in my body is fired up. Even the energy curling inside me is eager, expectant. The anger feels diminished, more distant and controlled.

I make it to Okiku's and my favorite spot and wait for the night to settle in. I keep an eye out for any park rangers and personnel, just in case, and then wait an hour or so more before I make my move.

It's not a very difficult ritual to perform—easier than others I've done over the last few months, in fact. The problem with the Hundred Days of Mourning ritual is that the book says you never know what's going to happen, no matter how well you prepare. It's a personal ceremony. No one else may be in attendance, making it impossible for *onmyōji* to verify the success of those who claim to have performed the ritual. It seems fitting that one must give up the greatest power in private without the benefit of an audience. It proves that you are giving it up willingly in exchange for something infinitely more important.

I can't use recorded incantations or hymns for this ritual. I studied the words and committed them to memory. I know by heart every gesture needed. Kagura coached me until I was pitch-perfect—and then insisted on constant practice until there was no doubt in either of our minds that if anything went wrong during the ceremony, it was not going to be my fault.

There is no need for candles or for protective markings on the ground. When the witching hour begins, I only need to close my eyes and let the chants do their work, allowing the wind to carry my words high into the heavens so my plea can be heard.

The magic inside me shrieks, angry that it is to be used for creation rather than for destruction. But the beauty of the mourning ritual is that love can transform even the vilest, most twisted energy into a thing of redemption.

I say the incantations and lose myself in the words, and everything around me responds.

When I open my eyes, I am surrounded by pillars of light that extend so far that my eyes can't see how high they go. And then I feel the whispers, feathery touches on my cheeks and forehead, tingling where they leave their marks. Spirits surround me, some I recognize from my past. I see Hotoke Oimikado again, her face shining, and I see even Obaasan and Amaya from the Chinsei shrine, the *mikos* who traded their lives for my own a year ago.

Tears blur my vision. They roll down my cheeks without shame when I see my mother's spirit standing in front of me. The love in her gaze warms me. My chants waver, but I know my purpose and resume them with renewed vigor.

I should have been strong enough to move on without Okiku, to accept that she's gone. People lose loved ones every day, and they learn to move on. But I'm no hero. I'm just a seventeen-year-old boy who wants her back.

And in my memory, I hear her: *Remember me sometimes.* She said it as if she had resigned herself to her fate—but her tone said anything but.

The fireflies hover around me, and I feel the swirling black malice leave my body. I hear it shriek in my mind one last time—*we are power*—and then it's gone, absorbed into the bright lights. My mother reaches over and touches my cheek. *I am so proud of you, my Tarquin* is what I hear in my head before the bright lights fade and my mother and the other spirits disappear, leaving me in the darkness.

But I am not alone.

I hear someone move behind me. I am exhausted, drained of the energy that sustained me the last few months and robbed of the strength that kept the malice at bay. The presence feels so good, so familiar, that I close my eyes and tilt my face to the sky.

"Thank you," I whisper to everyone and no one all at once. I turn. And I smile.

"What took you so long?"

CHAPTER TWENTY-ONE

PEACE

For someone who's spent almost his whole life stalking his victims before he kidnaps and kills them, Steven Blair is woefully incompetent when it comes to knowing when he's being stalked himself.

To everyone around him, he seems to be a cheerful enough guy, a hard drinker who likes to hang out at pubs and tell tall tales over pints of Guinness and spicy chicken wings. He's still wearing that red baseball cap, and the scar is white against his cheek, which is flushed from the booze. At the end of one outrageous story—I'm not close enough to hear the gist of it, though his listeners' incredulous laughter confirms it—he basks in the limelight, preening his metaphorical feathers, and I sit back and let him take in the adoration. It's going to be his last performance, so I suppose I can accord him some magnanimity.

Waiters glance suspiciously at me. I could probably have a fake ID made somewhere, but I still look a little too young to make it believable. As long as I keep ordering orange juice and not hard liquor, they aren't inclined to kick me out, leaving me in peace while I wait for my target to leave.

It's about ten minutes to midnight before he finally does just that, waving to his barroom friends one last time before stumbling out into the now-empty street. I gulp down the rest of my juice, toss enough bills on the table to pay what I owe, and then sidle out after him, keeping my cap low in case there are security cameras in the vicinity. There usually are, and my dark cap and dark sweater won't give away any of my features.

I know for a fact that the alley Steven Blair just stumbled into doesn't have any cameras, which is what I was hoping for. I've watched him for a week to figure out his habits. He's at the pub most nights, and he always takes the back door. Steven stops wobbling and gets sick behind one of the Dumpsters. By the time he straightens up, I'm blocking the exit out to the street. He squints at me and scowls. I'm a little too old for his tastes, if the three five-year-olds on his back are of any note.

"Go 'way, boy." He makes a swipe at me. Because he's still about ten feet away, he misses and nearly falls on his face again.

"I'm pretty sure that's not what you told the little boys you killed," I say, my voice unexpectedly loud in the otherwise quiet.

His face pales, a touch of sobriety creeping in. "Wh-what the hell are you talking about?"

"You'll know in about five seconds." There's barely any light in the narrow alley, but there's still enough to see shadows playing on the grimy brick walls on either side. I watch as another figure detaches itself from my own, lengthening until it is of a size and shape that could not possibly be human.

I turn and stride away.

The man only screams once. His gurgles are silenced quickly. I step out into the street, hitch my coat closer around me, and check for signs of anyone who might have been attracted to the noise. No one is, not at this time of night.

I sit down on the curb and take in a deep breath, liking the chill in the air. I'm no longer haunted by these midnight excursions. If I've learned anything these last few months, it's that everyone can choose their own purpose. This is mine.

It doesn't take long before I feel her standing beside me. I can feel the warmth of the souls she carries in her arms, the peace and relief that comes with each successful rescue. Technically, I no longer need her to fend off other supernatural entities—something in the hell's gate energy cured me of that lapse when it left my body. But habits are hard to break, and while I could be miles away, back at my house asleep in bed, I find that my need to be here with her is just as great as her need to be with me.

She sits, still holding the ten-year-olds close to her chest. The changes in Okiku are extraordinary. In her darker moments, she still adopts the guise of the drowned undead, but more often than not, she chooses to appear as her human self. The hundred days she spent in the afterlife gave her the ability to retain a greater semblance of who she was when she was alive. The frightening, malevolent voices no longer speak to her. The ritual took away her malice, like it took the power I'd acquired from that silkworm tree. She is no longer driven to hunt killers because of the voices in her head.

But we hunt them all the same. For the first time in our lives, we have a choice.

It was an easy one to make, now that I think about it. It's odd how some decisions we make when we feel we have no other choice are the same ones we make when we do.

I take Okiku's hand in my own and feel the little fluttering souls dancing in my palm. As one, we release them. They glide away from us, circling us briefly the way moths are drawn to flame before they remember themselves and fly up into the night.

"Don't you have any regrets?" I ask, as we watch the spirits wink out. "You could be up there with them, you know."

"No." She squeezes my hand. "I am content."

We don't say much after that—happy enough to keep watching the sky, even when there are no other stars in sight. Just a boy and his ghost. Maybe this was a selfish choice. Someone nobler than me might have given Okiku the final peace she deserves. Someone with less baggage than she has would have let him.

But flawed as we are, we are perfect together.

After all, I'm no hero.

ACKNOWLEDGMENTS

This book could not have been possible without the encouragement and support of many, including:

my agent, Rebecca Podos, whose enthusiasm for the strange things I write shines through in every edit, email, and letter;

my editor, Annette Pollert-Morgan, whose invaluable advice I take very much to heart, even from half a world away;

my production editor, Elizabeth Boyer, and her team of superheroes, all of whom have done wonders for my book; and also to my book publicist, Kathryn Lynch, for keeping me up to speed and in the loop at every turn;

my parents, who brag about me to their friends and cause the sort of embarrassment every daughter ought to feel at least once in her lifetime;

and my husband, who took one look at my book's cover and went, "Nope. Nope. A whole bunch of nope."

About the Author

Rin Chupeco wrote obscure manuals for complicated computer programs, talked people out of their money at event shows, and did many other terrible things. She now writes about ghosts and fairy tales, but is still sometimes mistaken for a revenant. Find her at rinchupeco.com.